NORTH
to the Caliphate

Mitchell R. Stevens

Genius
Book Publishing

Milwaukee Wisconsin USA

North to the Caliphate
Copyright © 2023 Mitchell R. Stevens

This is a work of fiction. Any resemblance to actual places, events, or persons living or dead is either coincidental or is used fictitiously.

Published by
Genius Book Publishing
PO Box 250380
Milwaukee Wisconsin 53225 USA
GeniusBookPublishing.com

ISBN: 978-1-958727-09-6

230507 Trade

NORTH
to the Caliphate

DEFINITION OF CALIPHATE

The first caliphate, often considered the ruler of the Muslim worldwide community, was Abu Bakr following the death of the Prophet Muhammed in 632 A.D. The caliphate was abolished in 1924, and for a time, it was of no interest to many Islamic groups. However, in 2014 the Islamic State in Iraq and the Levant (ISIL) declared the establishment of a caliphate with leader Abu Bakr al-Baghdadi as caliph. This claim was widely rejected by the world. Since then, caliphate has been loosely referred to varying leaders of terrorist sects and the places in the world from where they rule and reside.

PROLOGUE

The factory felt like a refrigerator. There were no windows to allow daylight in, given the secrecy of the mission. Even though the temperature outside was hovering near 100 degrees, Randall found it necessary to wear a sweater.

As company commander, he was ultimately responsible for the success of any military operation. As an employee of Blackstone, sixty-two-year-old Randall Covington had more latitude in managing the operation, but not much. Uncle Sam demanded protocol when it was paying the bill. Eric King, his boss and CEO of Blackstone, did not divulge which branch of the government was pulling the strings. All he was told was that it was as top secret a mission as it gets, and under no conditions was anyone part of the mission to discuss what went on here. Whoever was behind it was anxious to deploy, given that Eric was calling him every other day, busting his nuts for a status report. He wasn't a miracle worker.

As he walked through the 100,000-square-foot factory, he still found himself amazed. On his left were a bank of ten lab pods, each manned by an engineer, scientist, and programmer, and held the particular section of the robot they were assigned. Each pod was outfitted with the latest robotics hardware and software and electronics as well as all of the components to build a robot from sensors and computer boards to interface adapters and microprocessors. Their job was to take their respective section through each of the scenarios as a stand-alone part to ensure performance.

Another team in a pod further down the assembly line would then run simulations on a completed robot through testing numerous scenarios looking for disconnects between the synchronization of sections. At the end of the assembly line was an infantry troop of forty robots, still requiring final scenario programming. These robots would be used in the next battlefield simulation.

They looked like mannequins when powered down. The high-strength, light metal composite that served as the outer shell was dark gray, almost black on purpose to help disguise them during nighttime assaults. At six-foot-six, they were intimidating, especially when the sensors in their eye sockets lit up. They reminded the commander of Iron Man, but they couldn't fly—not yet, anyway.

The programmers had developed and programmed for 1,325 possible scenarios. They couldn't afford any more disasters like the one that took the life of several of their team members during a recent battlefield simulation. They had lost control of the robots and in a few short minutes the robots had dismembered three men. Covington had to scramble to cleanse the scene. Several IEDs, which could have been planted by one of many local terrorist groups, destroyed any forensic evidence while the bodies and their severed parts were removed and properly disposed of.

The XO approached the commander with a clipboard in hand. "Lab team seven successfully debugged scenario number ninety-six."

"So we are down to one hundred and twenty-four."

"Yes, sir. Based upon the programming schedule thus far, we can expect to achieve deployment status within the next ten days."

"Excellent. Which team figured it out?"

"Twelve."

"Very well. Keep everyone on ten-hour days."

"Aye, aye, Captain," the XO said absently, moving on to complete his afternoon round of inspections.

Covington headed into the enclosed glass working area at the center of the factory floor. It housed thirty programmers, each one supporting a development team. As noisy as the factory was, it was so quiet in here that the keyboard strikes reminded Covington of crickets. The programmers seemed mesmerized as they stared into their monitors; only two noticed he had entered the space.

Everyone who was part of the operation—from the Blackstone ex-military employees to the civilian scientists, engineers, and programmers—were coached to tell friends and loved ones that they were working on a classified mission dealing with satellite communications in the Middle East. He had initially resisted the directive to monitor everyone's telephone calls and e-mails, but as he fingered the JumpDrive containing a breach, he realized it had been a good idea. The drive contained the recording of a telephone conversation between an engineer and his father two hours ago. The error in judgment was most likely the yearning for a father's approval as the engineer excitedly explained the true nature of the operation.

The commander now had to follow orders and move swiftly. He did not know the engineer, only that he had been heavily recruited away from Northrup Grumman, following fifteen years working primarily with the NSA. Now thirty-eight years old, married with two children, Nathan was considered an expert in his field. A damn shame, but orders were orders.

He had reviewed Nathan's work schedule, based upon video surveillance, and he knew that Nathan would return to his room and either rest his eyes or Skype his wife during the thirty-minute lunch break. Each employee had what amounted to a small hotel room in a barracks complex connected to the factory.

The commander walked to Nathan's room with the requisite key card five minutes before Nathan's next break. He stood quietly to the right of the door, so when it opened, he would be hidden. His years of military training instinctively took over. He slowed his breathing as he felt the adrenaline enter his bloodstream.

The syringe felt heavy in his hand. The three-inch needle was as deadly as a high caliber round of ammunition. The three ounces of yellow liquid were captured firmly between the plunger and the needle. The latex gloves he wore would not only protect his identity at the crime scene, but ensure none of the deadly liquid touched his skin.

As the door closed, Covington launched a swift kick to Nathan's left knee, unbalancing him. That was followed quickly by a hand around the mouth to capture any sound. The needle of the syringe in his left hand immediately plunged into Nathan's carotid artery. Covington pinned the target's left arm behind his back and restrained him for twenty seconds until the drug took effect.

The contents of the syringe worked to first paralyze Nathan's muscles and then his lungs. He began convulsing and Covington lowered him to the floor. Nathan's eyes were wide with fear as he stared up at Covington, unable to speak. Spittle formed at the corners of his mouth. He asphyxiated within two minutes, convulsing violently on the floor until he drew his last breath.

The commander quietly took his leave. The rest would take care of itself as Nathan would not report back to work and would ultimately be found dead in his room. The cause of death would be a massive heart attack—so unexpected for someone so young and in relatively good health, but that was what a diet of red meat could do.

Grimly, the commander pocketed the syringe and removed the latex gloves. Some days he really hated serving his country.

CHAPTER 1

Jack Landis inherited his insomnia from his father. That's about all he inherited. He wasn't close to his father, who had never been able to keep a job, which didn't seem to bother him. As a result, his mother had been forced to work two jobs; most days she put in fourteen hours. When she died at forty-five and Jack was fifteen, the doctor said she simply wore out and her heart stopped. Jack blamed his father, who had since squandered away the life-insurance money and remarried another one stupid enough to support him. He hadn't seen or spoke to his father in twelve years and had no intention of doing so.

Tonight, as with most nights, he wrestled out from beneath the sheets. A quick look at the digital clock with the angry red numbers told him it was 2:13 a.m.; it was always taunting him with some number between 2 and 3 a.m. He sat on the edge of the bed, head in hands, elbows on knees, staring at his feet and attempting to decide which exercises to complete. He discovered that igniting some endorphins could help him relax, at least temporarily, so he could get back to sleep—maybe half the time. He decided on 100 push-ups, 100 sit-ups, and 25 burpees, then slowly eased himself to the floor to begin.

At thirty-nine years old, he was a man's man and a preferred ladies' man. At six-foot-two, 195 pounds, with brown wavy hair, indigo blue eyes, 8-percent body fat, a jaw chiseled in the image of a Greek god, and a relentless smile, Jack easily stood out.

The side benefit to the restless nights was that he was as in as good a shape as when he was a SEAL. He quickly finished the exercises without much exertion, stood, and looked at the clock, which was now provoking him with 2:35. *Screw it*, he said to himself. He left the disheveled bed and clock by themselves and headed to the Keurig machine. Armed with a cup of coffee, he pulled out his laptop and checked his e-mail inbox for new mail. He found several, most dealing with potential new assignments for him to consider. One contained the interrogation report of the young Muslim he had detained in the alley several days before.

He was hoping the teen had provided names and locations that would allow him to continue working in Kirkuk to rid it of as many ISIS recruiters and recruits as possible. The beginning of the report contained mostly what he had expected. The teen had put up an initial tough front, but quickly became cooperative when interrogation techniques were explained with the help of videos. However, as Jack read on, he found the exchange between the young recruit and the recruiter had nothing to do with potential new recruits.

The teen had been approximately forty-five miles southwest of Mosul near Makhmur the week before, visiting relatives. He and his teenage cousin had taken the family's Jeep for a joyride to a deserted farm five miles off the main highway south of Makhmur; they went there to smoke opium. Teens are teens, thought Jack, regardless of nationality. After getting high, they left the Jeep at an abandoned barn and walked and talked. The teen was fairly certain they headed south. They had walked for half an hour or so and began to notice a number of large birds circling the area. They estimated they saw up to ten in the sky at one time. Upon showing the teen pictures of different birds, he pointed out a short-toed eagle as the ones that they had seen. He was adamant the birds were not vultures. *So why am I reading about birds?* wondered Jack.

The teen then described entering a meadow littered with animal carcasses; he estimated up to twenty-five. He said there were dogs, pigs, rabbits, hedgehogs, shrews, sheep, and goats. He believed the animals had been shot with a high-powered machine gun based upon how the bodies were ripped apart. They walked the perimeter of the meadow but found no signs of anyone. They did note that much of the grass in the meadow had been trampled and the dead animals did not appear to have been there very long. When their high started to wear off, they realized they could be in danger and ran back to the barn and into the Jeep to head back home. They had not shared any of the story with their family for fear of them finding out they had gotten high.

Jack set his coffee down and reread this section. Based upon the teen's claim of use, hallucinations were deemed highly improbable, but not impossible. The fact the teen claimed he and his cousin saw the same thing all but discounted the sightings as hallucinations. The report concluded with Jack's next assignment, which was detaining the teen's cousin to confirm what the teenagers claimed to have seen.

It took all of Jack's willpower not to throw the coffee cup against the wall. *ISIS is growing stronger by the minute and I'm chasing teenage fantasies and looking for carnage created by some sicko in the middle of nowhere?* he stewed. Jack was all but certain these new ISIS recruits had gotten stoned and practiced their shooting skills on anything that moved. And why throw in the birds? Vultures would not have accumulated that quickly after the kills. Jack shook his head in frustration. *Why the hell am I even trying to figure this out?*

Fully awake, he decided there was no time like the present. After a steaming hot shower, two more cups of coffee, and an apple, he was met outside his apartment by Abir, his local contact. Abir sat patiently in the rented fifteen-year-old, off-brand Nissan as Jack climbed in.

"Morning, Mr. Landis," Abir said.

"Hey Abir, how's the family?" Jack asked.

"Wife is never happy and the kids talk back too much; same old stuff."

"Another road trip?" Jack asked rhetorically as he shot his military liaison a text that he was en route and would need the cousin's address ASAP, as he would be arriving in Makhmur within the hour.

The drive was uneventful, given the early-morning hour. The pair had to stop every fifteen minutes to clear the carbon monoxide from their lungs. The battered, small sedan was muffler-less and, in spite of having all of the windows open, a steady stream of the noxious gas filled their nostrils. The annoyance was necessary to blend into the surroundings and avoid attention. Jack had his Islamic garb resting in the backseat.

The sun began to rise as he parked the car several blocks from the cousin's apartment. There was no intelligence other than the address. Jack did not know if this kid was an only child living with his parents or the address housed a gang of gun-toting ISIS radicals. His 9-millimeter was housed safely in his shoulder holster while the KABAR knife, the same one he was given upon graduation as a SEAL, was strapped to his calf. He took pride in the fact he had babied the leather handle such that it looked and felt like new, while he maintained the narrow tang due to its lighter weight. He had only used the knife once in battle and it had saved his life. He was never able to get the bloodstains totally out of the leather, and it didn't bother him one bit.

Now dressed as a Muslim, Jack cautiously walked up the residential street toward the address he had been given, with Abir two steps behind. Chickens outnumbered people at this early hour. He strolled by the apartment complex twice, observing all he could before entering the main, common entrance. The four-story complex appeared to house sixteen apartments with eight facing the street and eight the rear. He assumed his target's apartment was on the second floor, given the address began with a two.

There was no security on the main entrance, allowing Jack to enter unnoticed. He was able to discern that the apartments on the first floor did in fact begin with a one. He quickly climbed the metal staircase to the second-floor landing and found the cousin's apartment. There were peepholes in the doors, so Jack squatted down below eye level and put his ear to the door in an attempt to hear any movement from within.

Hearing nothing, Jack instructed Abir to join him at the door as he gently knocked. The door was opened seconds later by a relatively small boy with sharp features and large, black eyes, which looked back and forth from Jack to Abir.

Jack nodded ever so slightly, which was Abir's cue to question the boy.

"Are you one of the boys who saw the dead animals in the meadow?" Abir asked him.

The boy tried to shut the door, but Jack held his hand out.

"We are not going to hurt you," Abir continued. "We simply want to know what you saw."

The boy shared what he and his cousin had seen in the field, which Abir relayed to Jack.

"Now, listen," Jack began. "First, we are going to determine if this hooligan saw what his cousin saw. If so, then he is going to lead us to where they claim to have seen what they saw. On the way, you are going to get him to admit that he and his drug-addled cousin shot up the animal kingdom and made up the story about an eagle squadron."

"I'll try," responded Abir.

"We need to end this charade and get the hell out of here."

Three minutes later, Abir explained that the kid was sticking to the script.

"Tell him I am going to beat the living shit out of him unless he tells the truth," Jack retorted.

"I more or less conveyed that. He is adamant he saw what his cousin saw."

With that, Jack put his face inches from the boy's and stared him down. The boy stared back and Jack decided he was telling the truth.

"Fine. Tell him he is going to take us to the farm," Jack ordered.

The drive to the abandoned barn was done in silence, other than the teen asking to relieve himself and the periodic stops to get some fresh air. They arrived shortly before noon and promptly began to trace the walk the two teens had taken the week before. The teen talked incessantly, often repeating himself relative to what he and his cousin had ventured upon. Jack had ditched the Islamic garb for shorts, a T-shirt, and hiking boots, given the temperature was anticipated to hit 100 degrees. The shoulder holster and knife were now visible and intimidating.

Thirty minutes into the walk, the teen became animated, pointing to the sky and yelling what Jack assumed was "birds." There was no doubt in Jack's mind that the fifteen or so birds circling above were eagles. He guessed they were hovering over a three-square-mile area. But why? Well, one part of their story had proven true. They continued on as the eagles circled above.

They came upon a large, open meadow and the boy stopped, pointed, and began talking very fast.

"This is where they found the dead animals," Abir said.

"Stay here and I will check it out," Jack responded.

Jack felt a chill run up his spine and instinctively pulled his revolver out and held it in front of him as he entered the meadow. He stole a glance behind him several times to be sure the boy and Abir were still there. They seemed mesmerized, watching his every movement. He looked up and the eagles were still circling, oblivious to his movements below. *What the hell are they doing?* he wondered. His instincts told him something wasn't right.

And then he spotted it: a large pool of blood, but no body. Something had most definitely died here, based upon the amount of blood, which had not completely congealed yet. He took out one of the plastic Ziploc bags he had brought and, using his fingers, pushed some of the blood into the bag to be tested later. He wiped his bloody fingers on the grass and cautiously moved forward. Twenty yards later, another spattering of blood, but much smaller. He again captured what he could for testing. Jack ultimately encountered ten areas containing a significant amount of blood, indicating death or a major injury—an injury someone or something could not get up and walk away from. What the hell was this place and where did the injured bodies go? For the first time in a long time, Jack felt afraid.

He began walking the perimeter of the field, making mental notes and taking pictures with his smartphone. If the ground had been trampled by a person or persons, he could not find any evidence. But, given the killings could have taken place up to several days before, the vegetation could have rebounded. He was certain he would find one particular piece of evidence, but after scouring most of the meadow, he had yet to find it. If the animals were in fact killed by gunfire, there had to be shell casings. Whoever cleansed the scene surely would have missed one casing, but they didn't. And where the hell were the tire tracks from whatever vehicle took the carcasses away?

He finally gave up his search and rejoined the pair waiting for him at the edge of the meadow.

"Ask him if he heard any noises, such as an automobile or people talking," Jack instructed Abir.

After a brief exchange with the boy, Abir simply shook his head *no*.

"Ask him if he and his cousin dumped the blood."

Again, an exchange and an animated shake of the head by the teen.

Jack realized he was not getting any more from the boy. He was obviously frightened and wanted to get away from this place. They returned to the car and drove back in silence as Jack went over the scene again in his mind. The first thing to do was have the blood sampled to determine exactly what died in that field. The second thing was to get some eyes in the sky to find out what the eagles were doing.

CHAPTER 2

Sara Fahridi considered her first assignment as part of Deeprose to be exciting. She found the temporary office she was assigned at Langley not so much. At Homeland Security she had a closed-door office with a contemporary wood desk and enough room for two leather guest chairs. She had ordained her walls with high-end reproductions of Kandinsky paintings. She had fallen in love with Cubist art after visiting the Guggenheim Museum in both Abu Dhabi and New York.

As she sat uncomfortably in her used task chair from Office Depot, resting her elbows on the old metal desk and staring at the blank walls, she committed to spending as much time out of the office as possible. As the primary liaison for the operatives in the field, she would be communicating directives and receiving and reporting updates from the operatives, or moles. Since joining Homeland Security several years before, she had wanted to be involved in covert operations. This was the perfect assignment.

She checked her Cartier watch and realized she had three minutes to get to a nearby conference room for a meeting with Richard North, the CIA's deputy director, and Abdul, one of Deeprose's moles. This would be Abdul's final briefing before he was redeployed to the Middle East. She was relieved to find she was the first one to arrive; she hated being late and hated those who arrived late. Abdul and North walked in together two minutes later.

"Let's make this quick," North ordered as he adjusted his cuff-linked shirt sleeves. "I have to meet with the DNI and our retiring director; as you know, this is his last week."

Sara began. "Abdul, can you please update us on the progress made on your recent trip to Afghanistan?"

"Yes, ma'am. I successfully met a jihadi recruiter named Asaryi twice. I positioned myself as a U.S.–born sympathizer, creating a parallel with Asaryi's background and route into ISIS. Asaryi told me I had to prove my allegiance through an act praising the Prophet Muhammad to gain entry as a trusted operative," Abdul explained.

"What exactly does that mean?" Sara asked.

"It means he has to kill somebody," North jumped in.

"Is that right, Abdul?" Sara asked.

"It could very well be, or some similar act of terrorism."

"How do we handle that?" Sara asked.

Now frustrated, North responded, "We'll deal with it if and when it happens. Is there anything else we need to cover?"

Sara looked to Abdul and he simply said, "I'm ready to go back."

With that, North stood and headed toward the door just as the DNI—the director of national intelligence—walked in with a man he didn't recognize.

"I'm sorry for interrupting your meeting," began the DNI.

"Your timing is perfect; we just finished," North said.

"Good." He looked toward Sara and Abdul and said, "Could you give us the room for a moment?"

"Yes, sir," Abdul and Sara responded in unison and closed the door behind them as they left.

The DNI began. "Richard, I had wanted to handle this differently, but the president's availability, or lack thereof, and a couple of minor crises forced us to accelerate our schedule."

"What schedule is that?"

"Richard, I would like you to meet Louis Pendleton, the president's nominee to be the new director."

North felt as if he had been sucker-punched in the gut. Blood rushed to his face and he found he was clenching his jaw so tight he might break teeth. He was the one who had worked his ass off at the agency for thirty years and deserved to be director. Everyone expected it; even the press had speculated he would be nominated. This wasn't happening.

There was an awkward moment as Pendleton extended his hand to shake, while it took North several seconds to offer his in return.

"Nice to meet you," Pendleton said, recognizing the bewildered look on North's face as someone who had expected to be given the position as a long-tenured employee.

"Ah, yes, you too," was all North could muster. "If you gentlemen will excuse me, I have an urgent matter to address." And with that, North quickly exited the room, balling his hands into fists as he quickly strode down the hallway with no destination in mind. He simply had to get out of that room before he exploded.

He wanted to drive his fist through Clapper's face, pushing his nose to the back of his brain. *How could that DNI bastard do this to me?* Who the hell was Pendleton and where did he come from? North swore to himself he would make things right and those that cheated him out of the position would pay—and pay dearly.

CHAPTER 3

Jack closed the e-mails containing the toxicology and drone surveillance reports, which he had received within thirty minutes of one another. He had been anxious for both, given it had been five days since he had been to the bloody meadow. Being cooped up in the small hotel room in Kirkuk only served to test his patience.

One report was a surprise; the other one not so much. The tox report did confirm it was animal blood. *Better than human blood*, Jack thought. The surveillance report was very intriguing and lent insight as to the eagles' presence. The first two surveillance attempts were sabotaged as the eagles attacked and destroyed the drone, capturing it in their talons and crashing it into the ground as they swooped low. Were the eagles sentries guarding the airspace above? But what were they guarding out in the middle of nowhere? Who or what organization in Iraq would have the wherewithal to train eagles to attack drones?

The report went on to explain the third surveillance attempt was comprised of ten drones. Eight were again destroyed by the eagles, but two were able to fly over the targeted space, take both video and photos, and return unscathed. Jack spent the next two hours poring over the aerial views and found nothing. If there had not been eagles, Jack would have written this off to a psychopath killing innocent animals. In frustration, he slammed his laptop shut and called Abir.

"Abir, it's Jack."

"Get the blood sample results?" Abir asked.

"Yup. Appears our little friends were telling the truth, at least about animals being dead. I'm still thinking they had something to do with it," Jack said, then paused, as though he was checking his notes. "We found no blood or other related evidence in their Jeep, so we know they did not bring them or take them away."

"What do you think about the boy's claims that he had told no one other than the ISIS recruiter for fear of someone finding out they had gotten high?"

"What would you do?" Jack challenged.

"Probably the same thing. Do you think the animals were removed because the teens were spotted?"

"Possibly. But how were the animals removed? There were no tire tracks."

"No idea. And the eagles are more of a mystery. Maybe they had been trained to attack drones elsewhere and decided to take up residence in the middle of nowhere," Abir offered.

"Sorry Abir, this puzzle has too many pieces for me to solve."

Jack ended the call and began to wonder if ISIS was somehow behind it. He went back to his laptop and began internet searches for drone attacks by birds. He quickly learned that there were several governmental and military agencies throughout the world training large birds of prey to disarm drones. He found the closest possible source for trained eagles to be out of the Netherlands. The U.S. seemed to be leading the initiative, given it more or less owned the technology, but it would be hard to fathom the U.S. military deploying birds to destroy its own drones. At this point, the source of the birds was secondary to determining if there was in fact something the birds were guarding or if they were simply nesting in the area.

Given the drone aerials provided no help, he decided to review the pictures he had taken with his camera just in case he had missed something. He was hopeful the camera caught the glint of the sun off a spent shell casing and provided some evidence as to how the animals were slaughtered. He had snapped fifty pictures. He slowly and methodically expanded the size of each picture on his smartphone and moved it such that he could view the picture in its entirety.

He had worked through fifteen pictures when his cell phone buzzed.

"Landis," he answered.

"Jack, it's Burt."

"Hey, Burt. How is my favorite DoD matchmaker? I'm getting lonely and restless out here."

"It's your lucky day. I have a new assignment for you."

"Thank God. In what part of the world am I chasing the bad guys this time?"

"D.C."

"Seriously? How the hell am I going to derail the fanatics from there?"

"You'll be briefed when you get here, as I am not allowed to discuss it over the phone, regardless of how secure we assume this line to be."

"Wow, sounds interesting. I'll be on the first flight."

"How goes the demise of the animal kingdom?"

Jack went onto explain what the recent reports contained and that he had more questions than answers.

"There is something not right here, Burt."

"Well, you are in a land full of crazies, so you have to expect to find crazy things."

"I guess. I'll call you upon my arrival."

"Roger, out."

Jack discontinued the call and decided to finish looking through his pictures before he booked a flight. He found he had renewed energy, given he was being assigned to an operation that evidently had relatively more punch to it. Plus, it would be nice to eat some normal food for a change and sleep on a real mattress.

Something in the twenty-first picture caught his eye. Was it a bug that had flown in front of the lens? No, it was a black spot of some sort on the ground near a pool of blood. Jack zoomed the spot in and out in an attempt to identify it. It appeared to be a burn spot in the grass, as if someone had held a small propane torch to it. The spot was circular in shape and he guessed it was about two inches in diameter. Had the two kids stopped there to smoke and dropped a match, which caused a small fire?

He went back through the first twenty pictures looking for an identical burn mark.

Ten of the pictures had some amount of blood; in three of those he found a similar burn mark. Over the next hour he completed looking at the balance of the pictures. In eighteen of them, he found the burn marks, all about the same size and approximately four feet from the pools of blood, but all the pools were relatively small ones. Jack did not find the burn marks near the larger pools of blood.

He needed a forensic fire expert to determine what had caused the burns. Given the distinctive size and pattern, Jack was confident they were man-made. What he couldn't determine on his own was if they were created by a chemical, an incendiary device, a flame, electricity, or radiation of some sort. He dialed Burt.

"Burt, Jack again. Would you be able to have a forensic expert look at some burn marks?"

"I guess. But why and for what?"

"I discovered some consistent burn patterns in the tall grass of the meadow where the animals were allegedly killed."

"Do you have samples?"

"No, just pictures, but hopefully someone could reduce the possibilities to a few."

"I know you are anxious to contribute, Jack. Isn't this a bit of a stretch?"

"Probably, but it shouldn't take much time."

"Send them over."

"Roger, out."

Jack e-mailed the pictures to himself, created a folder, and forwarded it to Burt.

Burt was probably right. He was looking for something that wasn't there out of sheer boredom. However, his instincts, which had never failed him, told him something very strange and out of the ordinary had happened in that meadow and someone was trying to keep it quiet.

CHAPTER 4

It took Sara five minutes to get from her office to North's; his assistant had called requesting she beeline it. He was standing impatiently as she entered, always looking as he had just finished a photo shoot for a high-end men's clothing line.

"Ms. Fahridi, do you really believe this mole strategy will result in any intelligence within our lifetimes?"

Sara, who had been moving toward a side chair to sit down, abruptly stopped, realizing North was not going to offer her a seat.

"Given this is my first operation of this nature, I have to rely on the experience and knowledge of others."

"So, my experience and knowledge are not material?"

"Oh no, that's not what I meant. I meant, I am simply following orders. I haven't earned the right to render an opinion."

"I just asked you for your opinion."

"All right," Sara said as she straightened her shoulders and did her best to look North in the eye. "During my tenure with Homeland Security, the majority of my work was dedicated to identifying or uncovering Middle Easterners who had woven themselves into the fabric of the U.S. that had access to intelligence. Ninety-nine percent of those who we tracked proved to be who they said they were. However, the one percent that we uncovered could have proven to be very destructive."

"And how long did it take this so-called one percent to embed themselves in order to gain access to intel?" North asked as he leered at Sara's legs.

Sara, somewhat unnerved by his unwavering gaze, began to walk around the office as she spoke. "It varied, but on average I would say it took at least a year."

"We don't have a year! ISIS has grown tenfold in the past six months and yet we have done nothing to stop them. And I don't consider periodic air strikes a military campaign. We had better get our military shit together sooner than later and I am sick and tired of inexperienced leaders and rookies getting in the way of what needs to be done. That's all, Ms. Fahridi." And with that, Sara promptly and eagerly left his office, thinking to herself North was probably still upset he was not the president's choice for director. North all but slammed the office door behind her and sat down at his desk. His office was appointed similarly to those of his peers who also had long, decorated careers. As many offices within the CIA headquarters, his had wood-veneer paneling, a higher-grade Berber carpet, and a ten-foot ceiling. The south wall behind the massive freestanding paldao-wood desk was adorned with photos of presidents and foreign dignitaries, as well as political and military leaders. Any visitor could not help but notice the pictures and establish a perception of the importance of the man behind the desk, which of course was his intent.

North had grown up in a modest home in Arlington, Virginia that was governed by strict rules enforced by blue-collar parents, whose lives revolved around their only child. After completing twelve years of a traditional Catholic education with a 4.0 GPA and valedictorian on his résumé, his scholarship-funded collegiate career took him to South Carolina and The Citadel.

Following The Citadel, North spent a brief stint with the Army as a second lieutenant before being recruited at the age of twenty-eight by the CIA to work in the National Clandestine Service. Over the next thirty-three years, he spent time in several areas of the agency, working his way up the food chain. Five years ago, he was named the CIA's deputy director and had his sights on the position of director, a position he coveted shortly after he had joined the CIA.

The president and Pendleton had ruined everything. He was sixty-one years old and realized that Pendleton, at the age of fifty-eight, would most likely hold the position for at least five years, which all but eliminated North's chances of being named director. As North sat, trying to put reason to his misfortunate, he began to formulate a plan on how to gain vengeance. *People will pay for what they have done*, he thought to himself.

His cell phone buzzed with an appointment reminder. He straightened his tie, combed his hair, quickly buffed his shoes with the electronic buffer hidden beneath his desk, and headed to the car pool. It would take him no more than ten minutes to get to the rendezvous location.

North's Blackstone contact, Eric King, was always prompt, professional, and direct. As a former platoon leader in Desert Storm and strategic planner for operations in Iraq, Eric was versed in both field tactics and military operations. His skills as a salesman far outweighed any other of his talents. At forty-four, he was relatively young to be CEO of the United States' number-one go-to military organization for tactical operations in the field. Blackstone had access to the most technologically advanced weaponry, communication equipment, and vehicles as sanctioned, endorsed, and many times subsidized by the United States Department of Defense. North was waiting at the quiet Alexandria bar as Eric entered.

"Richard, how can we contribute to the cause?" asked Eric as he slid into the well-worn booth in the bustling coffee shop, the aroma of fresh-brewed coffee overwhelming.

North smiled ruefully and explained, "Just another relatively simple exercise for which you will be paid handsomely."

Eric smiled disingenuously. North knew Eric despised him, but had no choice but to deal with him; North was Eric's connection to the White House and the lucrative contracts his company had enjoyed for the past five years that had made him a multimillionaire.

Eric jumped right in. "What part of the world are we going to protect the U.S. from on this adventure?"

North slid a JumpDrive across the old wooden table engraved with lovers' names of the past. "We have reason to believe that a Middle Eastern member of a current operation sanctioned by the highest levels within our government has been sharing top-secret information with an individual either sympathetic to or working directly with ISIS. Obviously, the security breach potential is high and must be dealt with immediately."

"And what leads you to the conclusion that he is a spy?"

"Not a he, a she. I won't bother you with the details, but be assured that we need to ferret out this issue as any leak of intelligence in this regard could have dire consequences on our efforts to squelch ISIS and like organizations. Can I count on you, Eric?"

"Have I ever let you down, Richard?"

"I suggest your organization subdues our target, who is believed to be receiving intel from our spy. Present yourselves as an ISIS operatives claiming the target has betrayed their confidence and let's see how things play out. If the target denies association, we will use him as a pawn to bait our spy, whom we will call *Stealth* for purposes of your mission. If our suspicions are right, Stealth will share covert operations intelligence upon a threat of terminating the target, claiming any earlier intelligence information shared was incorrect or a fabrication."

"But why would..." Eric hesitated while the waitress brought their coffees, then resumed after she left. "Why would Stealth care enough to expose themselves for a random target?"

"We have learned that sympathizers have a difficult time finding a communication vehicle they can trust due to heightened security by the NATO nations. Once they find one that supports their efforts, they do not want to lose them. We believe Stealth will readily offer up information that can be corroborated."

"And what do we do with this information and with Stealth?"

"You let me worry about that. When the time comes and we have our confirmation, we will decide what the best course of action is."

Eric took the JumpDrive, one sip of his coffee, and his leave—now armed with a new assignment and anticipation of yet another large payday, thanks to Uncle Sam.

As North exited the rear of the building and walked to his car several blocks away, he smiled to himself, thinking how easy it was to play people and situations. Little did Eric know that the target was Sara Fahridi's brother, who was an engineer in Pakistan and had nothing to do with ISIS. Once Sara received the video of her brother making a plea for intelligence information that would be helpful to ISIS, North was confident she would leak some intelligence relative to Deeprose, thereby compromising her role on the team, and more importantly, making Mr. Pendleton look inept.

CHAPTER 5

The Muslim prisoner fought the restraints with every fiber of his 150-pound being, but it was no use. Being shackled at the wrists and ankles, he was unable to put up much of a fight. The straps that held him to the specially designed gurney had held men twice his size. A hood was then placed over his head, further intensifying his fear and anxiety. Upon hearing the lock mechanism release and feeling the end of the gurney upon which he lay begin to tilt down, the intensity of his struggle increased as he began to scream *na*, which was Farsi for *no*.

Frank Conover's mind wandered back to his first assignment in his job as an interrogator as an employee of the Human Intelligence Collections Operations. His superiors were beyond ecstatic over the capture of one of the self-described masterminds of 9/11. While the press and administration were self-indulgent in their praise of the removal of highly targeted terrorists and transparent with the information surrounding the capture and whereabouts of the captives, he and his now longtime partner Jim were entrusted to maintain the confidentiality of one of the most controversial interrogation techniques employed since the Spanish-American War. He didn't care; he was paid extremely well for pulling the truth out of terrorists.

The waterboarding interrogation room—or *the tank*, as referred to by those in the intelligence community—had very few, but essential features. Plumbing providing both hot and cold water was located three feet off the floor for ease of access. Hoses were available if spraying the prisoner down was part of the session. The walls, ceiling, and floor were concrete, painted a cement gray, while the floor was slightly graded so all water would flow to the drain located in the center. The room measured twenty-five feet by thirty feet with a supply and return air vent. The thermostat was located just left of the only access door, which was forty-eight inches wide to allow ample gurney access. Two supply cabinets housed plastic Solo brand cups, duct tape, facial chamois clothes and hoods, latex gloves, eye goggles, and disinfecting-related cleaning supplies. The only piece of furniture—a specially designed gurney— occupied the middle of the room. A single fluorescent fixture hung from the ceiling by chains. Frank had spent over 200 sessions in the tank, the room becoming more and more depressing with each visit.

"Are you ready?" Frank looked to Jim.

"Yup. How long with this one, you think?"

"You never know. After he pissed himself the first time, I thought we'd be done. Maybe the second time is a charm."

"Are you using hot or cold water this time?"

"We'll try cold, since we used hot the first time."

"Okay. We have to be in a briefing in an hour, so let's break this little prick."

Frank turned on the hose and began to pour water over the nose and mouth area of the man believed to be an arms dealer supplying ISIS, as Jim timed the interrogation. Frank moved the hose as the man moved his head back and forth, ensuring a steady stream of water prohibited his ability to breathe in an unencumbered breath of air. Frank and Jim had practiced the technique on one another, knowing the prisoner felt as if he were drowning. They also knew at what point to stop to ensure the prisoner was able to recover and ideally provide them the intelligence they sought. After approximately forty seconds, Jim gave Frank a thumbs-up and Frank turned the water off.

The result of each interrogation session was captured in a report typically prepared by the interrogator who was the team lead. Frank worked only twenty to twenty-five hours per week, and that included the detailed reporting requirements, as he was the team leader. Protocol dictated that Jim review Frank's reports in detail before signing off concurrence; however, after having worked together for nearly a decade, Jim had come to trust and highly respect Frank's report-writing skills and for the past two years had simply signed off without reviewing the reports. Regardless of a previous day of binge drinking, Frank always meticulously, accurately, and professionally completed the post-interrogation report. Jim had administered interrogation techniques for the CIA for three years prior to Frank's arrival. Jim's prior partner finally succumbed to mental health issues as a result of fifteen years of interrogating war criminals.

Frank moved the gurney's tilt mechanism again, allowing the prisoner's feet to tilt downward, providing the man a better opportunity to cough the water from his lungs and regain his breath. After several minutes of coughing and sputtering, Frank moved to remove the hood. He knew from experience that the prisoner's eyes would be all-telling regarding whether they were ready to talk or were prepared to endure more waterboarding. Frank removed the hood. The man's eyes appeared to be bulging from their sockets; he was ready to talk.

After Frank and Jim finished with the prisoner, they headed to the designated conference room for the briefing the DNI had scheduled earlier in the day. Attempting to avoid eye contact so no one would see his bloodshot eyes from the previous night's drinking, Frank slithered into a chair at the end of the table. His wrinkled shirt and unkempt mop of gray hair served as good distractions. He couldn't care less what people thought. He didn't give a shit about his appearance—why should he care if others did?

Frank had worked with—or rather worked *on*—several alleged jihadi operatives before. However, based upon the energy in the briefing room, this was not just any jihadi operative to be discussed. He knew something extraordinary was in play when, in addition to the normal contingent of staffers, some high ranks sat at the table. Most notable was the DNI, General James R. Clapper. Frank picked a bad day for a raging hangover.

Those in attendance included the relatively recently appointed CIA director, Louis Pendleton, and his deputy director, Richard North, as well as the director of Homeland Security.

"Gentlemen," the DNI began, "I am pleased to report that we have successfully captured whom we believe to be one of ISIS's top leaders. He is currently being detained at Guantanamo, but will be brought to Langley during the next forty-eight hours. Frank and Jim, he will become your top priority. We need him talking and as quickly as possible. This may prove to be our best opportunity to get ahead of ISIS and serve a decisive blow."

CHAPTER 6

The flight to D.C. had been uneventful and so was his briefing, for that matter. Jack was given little information other than he would be working with the CIA as a member of a small, covert team. What piqued his interest was that a former colleague and friend was now running the CIA and therefore would ultimately be calling the shots. He looked forward to working with Lou; he respected and trusted him.

He had stayed behind at the café after the briefing to have another cup of coffee and read the fire forensic report that he had received that morning. He found the obligatory disclaimers and provisos annoying, but no one wanted to lose their job for missing the call on a burn spot from a picture instead of a sample. The one conclusion the report was confident about was that the burn marks were consistent in size. Based upon that, chemicals, fire, and explosions were ruled out. Light amplification by stimulated emission of radiation was believed to be the cause. *Lasers*, thought Jack, *on a deserted farm in Iraq?*

The report went on to talk about spatial coherence and near–Gaussian beams, which Jack interpreted to mean that the beam could be kept consistently narrow over a long distance. The irradiance, or intensity, of the beam could not be determined from the pictures, but if the assumption was made that the beam killed the animals, then the radiant flux, or power, was relatively high and lethal. The other assumption that the report made was that burn marks were found near the smaller areas of blood due to the trajectory of the laser beam. And based upon the distance of the marks from the blood, the lasers were fired from a height of approximately three and one-half feet. Jack could reach the next assumption on his own: The lasers were fired from the height from which one would fire a gun.

Jack was aware the Army had contracted first Boeing, then Lockheed Martin, to develop lasers, or what the military occasionally referred to as *directed energy weapons*. The Navy had been testing laser weapons systems (LaWS) in the Gulf, while the Air Force intended on outfitting planes with lasers within five years. However, as far as Jack knew, these were laser developments on a large scale with large beams, certainly much larger than the ones that left the burn marks in the meadow. Would one of the military branches be running smaller weapon simulations in the Middle East? Would they slaughter animals? Or, possibly, one of the businesses developing the technology had set up simulations in a region of the world they thought was uninhabited. All except for the unfortunate animals.

Jack began to search the internet for any recent developments on smaller, possibly handheld, laser weaponry. He discovered the DoD intended to spend $371 million this year on laser technology. There were also many YouTube videos depicting handheld laser weapons, but none were sophisticated or powerful enough to inflict the damage he was investigating. There were many articles dealing with burst vs. pulse beams; much of the technology was over his head. The forensics report believed the burn marks were most likely from pulse beams, as the intended target could be tracked longer while the laser's capacitor would still have the energy to fire another beam without having to recharge as with a burst.

After an hour of searching, Jack didn't find any information that could explain what had happened in the meadow. Based upon the carnage, he estimated there had to be multiple shooters, which would seem to increase the risk of eye damage. Jack needed to talk to a laser expert, which meant another call to Burt.

"Burt, Jack here," he began.

"Did the briefing not happen?"

"It did. I need another favor."

"Not the animal kingdom again. Did you get the forensics report I requested?"

"Yup, and it begs for more answers."

"Whattaya need?"

"I need to talk with a laser-weaponry expert."

"A what?"

"Did you read the forensic report?"

"No, I didn't read the report. It's not my job to follow every piece of intel that goes back and forth. Think of me as an HR specialist who recruits for and places those civilians that possess special skills to support a governmental operation. In addition, I am to provide you the resources you need, within reason, to get the job done. Why do you need to speak to a laser expert, assuming there is one?"

"Oh, I trust there is one, given that every branch of the military is competing with one another to come up with the most effective weapon. And I would like to speak with them as soon as possible; today would be terrific."

"Oh, of course. But first, I have to raise a few people from the dead and walk on water before I can get to it."

"Sarcasm works for you, Burt, because you are so good at what you do."

"Ah, and now the patronizing bullshit."

"I guarantee if you send the forensic report with the request for a quick chat, you will get an immediate response."

"All right. I'm not sure where to start."

"I would think the DoD would have some type of governing body, given all branches are in play."

"Makes sense. Wish me luck."

"*Luck* is not a business or military word, Burt."

"Whatever. Roger, out."

Forty-five minutes later, Jack's phone rang. The number was listed as a private

caller.

"Jack Landis," he answered on the first ring.

"Mr. Landis, my name is Dr. Lee Chang. I am responding to your request to speak with someone with laser weaponry knowledge."

"Thank you for calling, Dr. Chang. Who do you work for?"

"Indirectly for DARPA."

"And what does that mean?"

"My paycheck comes from a company, who chooses to remain anonymous, which develops state of the art laser weaponry. Myself and others from my company are working hand in hand with DARPA. The director of national intelligence has ultimate oversight."

"I see. Had you seen the report before Burt forwarded it? I would assume that given the nature and sensitivity of your work and the report's content, you would have eyes on it."

"Unfortunately not. You would like to think that the report's author would recognize the potential importance and attempt to share. But, at the end of the day, we are all one big bureaucracy with a gazillion spokes that may never intersect. Nonetheless, thank you for sharing the report; we found it both intriguing and unsettling."

"How so?"

"Mr. Landis."

"Jack…"

"Yes, Jack, the information I am about to share is extremely confidential. There are only twelve people—you will be the thirteenth—who are aware of the current developments in laser weaponry."

"Who are the others?"

"The president, DNI, secretary of defense, director of Homeland Security, chairman of the Joint Chief, and the seven of us on the development team."

"I consider myself honored to be part of such a select team."

"I would have called you a half hour ago upon receiving the request, but it took an additional thirty minutes to get clearance to provide you with the information. Evidently, you have some friends in high places."

"I don't. I think my military career earned me a ticket to the dance."

"What would you like to know?"

"The report led me to conclude that smaller lasers, possibly handheld, were used to kill the animals. Has the technology advanced such that the weapons are now available?"

"Yes and no. Within the past six months, we have made significant advances in wavelength tuning, achieved pulse methodology using shorter dispersive elements, and created a newer, hybrid photoluminescence process."

"Doc, English, please."

"The short answer is *yes*, we have developed the technology such that a sidearm or rifle-sized weapon can deliver a lethal laser beam."

"Are they in production?"

"No, and the reason is that we have yet to develop the appropriate level of eye protection. If a human were to fire this gun now, even with the most sophisticated eye protection available, they would suffer temporary blindness at a minimum, but most likely permanent blindness."

"So how are we able to watch beams from larger lasers?"

"Primarily due to the size and intensity of the beam. Larger beams, less intensity and lower risk to the eyes. That's not to say there haven't been some accidents where a few soldiers have lost their vision. But all in all, if proper precautions are taken with the larger lasers, the risk is minimal."

"So what do you make of the report?"

"I don't know what to make of it. First of all, how did this technology end up in Iraq? Second, how was anyone able to shoot the lasers without blinding themselves? The most troubling conclusion is that someone else, meaning some other country, has developed both the technology and the necessary eye protection."

"What would be the odds of that?"

"Based upon what we know of other countries' efforts, I would say a million to one."

"May I contact you if I have more questions?"

"Of course," Chang said, and he shared his contact information.

With the call ended, Jack drained the last of his coffee, turned off his laptop, and took leave of the café. Armed with this new information, he allowed himself to think back to the meadow and attempted to reconstruct what had happened: Animals are eating, walking, and possibly sleeping in the meadow as they do every day. It's hot, the sun is out, and there may be a slight breeze. Wouldn't the animals smell or hear someone approaching? Okay, let's assume the wind is blowing toward the assailants so the animals cannot pick up their scent and they are far enough away when they fire the lasers so that the animals don't hear them. But how far would that be? Those who fired would have to be very good shots. Some of the smaller animals certainly could not be seen from a longer distance. Did the shooters have some additional tracking capabilities to lock on the target? But how would they do that with a handheld weapon?

Jack pressed on with this mental recreation even though there were already too many holes in it. Okay, the shooters are some distance away and begin shooting the animals. They continue to shoot even though they should be blinded. Why aren't these people blinded? What if humans weren't doing the shooting? What could be shooting a handheld weapon that could be accurate from a long distance, not have a scent, and not be heard? "Oh shit," Jack said to no one but himself.

CHAPTER 7

The balance of the briefing centered on Operation Deeprose.

Lou turned to North. "Richard, as you have been the one involved in every Deeprose briefing, as well as present when the president and Joint Chiefs approved the strategy, can you please give us a full summary?"

"As you wish," responded North as he calmly adjusted his diamond-studded cuff links. He had the floor and wanted all in attendance to know it. North had served his country and the CIA well for three decades and believed he deserved to be running the show. He turned to the assembled group. "Deeprose is a joint covert operation between the CIA and Homeland Security, approved by the president, governed by the Joint Chiefs, and led by the director of national intelligence. The primary objective is to destroy and/or significantly cripple ISIS and/or related terrorist organizations. Tactically, we have placed two experienced intelligence officers into play. Their objective is to penetrate ISIS by becoming trusted operatives and get themselves as close to the leadership as possible. Having done such, their job would then be to gain and share as much intelligence as possible in order for our military forces to undermine ISIS's efforts. With the advent and success of cyber-jihad at educating and recruiting via the internet, the sooner we can dismantle the proverbial nerve center, the better.

"Deeprose should be considered a relatively passive strategy with any impact being long-term. Given the recent acceleration of ISIS's recruiting and successful movement throughout the Middle East, it is time that we seriously consider and recommend aggressive military strikes."

"Richard, I understand that more aggressive actions were proposed, but the decision, which was supported by the Joint Chiefs, was to continue to support the Iraqi efforts," Lou interjected.

"With all due respect, Lou, these fanatics seem to have a mantra and following that is more appealing than any terrorist group before them. We are going to be caught asleep at the wheel while their numbers and reach grow to a level that will be formidable. We have access to advanced technologies that could eradicate terrorism with minimal casualties. Now is the time to act!"

"Deeprose was sanctioned a little over a month ago and there is no additional intelligence that indicates we should alter our course at this time."

The rebuff from Lou was registered by all and served to further heighten the molten anger burning inside of North. He could feel his face turn flush red, but he continued as he turned to Frank and Jim, "You two are obviously being briefed as you will be conducting the interrogations of the ISIS leader and we felt it important you had full disclosure in the event the information helped your interrogation strategies."

After a quick review of the operatives' significant contacts and results, the meeting was promptly adjourned. North immediately left the conference room to avoid a confrontation with his new boss. He straightened his $200 Armani tie and ensured every hair of his head was in its appropriate place as he strode down the hall. He swore to himself he would right the wrong, no matter what. He would show these imbeciles his was the right way.

❦

Lou was getting accustomed to his new role and routine after three days on the job. He found his large office to be over the top. It was a colossal waste of space, and government had obviously spent too much money to furnish it. He had to admit he liked the plush carpeting, as he typically removed his shoes when working at his desk. He rarely wore a suit and whatever sport coat he had worn that day could be found thrown over the back of the couch in his office. He was trying to start a trend of no ties, but old habits die hard.

In his opinion, ISIS was relatively well organized and sophisticated. The IT expertise it had developed since 9/11 would rival any *Fortune* 500 company on Wall Street. It regularly employed proxy servers and specialized software that removed original IP addresses. It created fake jihadi sites to throw off Western intelligence agencies, hacked into benign websites to create folders in order to share intelligence, and created short-lived e-mail addresses. Therefore, having only two moles was not enough to counter the number of potential ways the operative could be found out and neutralized. Be that as it may, Deeprose was now his pet project and he would follow orders and manage it accordingly.

As he opened up yet another e-mail, he heard a knock at his door.

"Mr. Director," Jack bellowed into the office.

"Jack?" said Pendleton. "How the hell did you get in here?"

"Now, is that any way to talk to a new member of your team?"

"You're the new operative?"

"In the flesh."

"I'll be damned," Lou said as he and Jack met in the middle of his office and vigorously shook hands. "I knew that we were adding a retired military guy, now working as an independent contractor, with specific experience with jihadi recruiting. I had no idea that it was you or that you had begun to work for the government."

"Yeah. After I retired, I found I had this burning need to get even."

"It wasn't your fault, what happened in Iraq."

"That's debatable, but let's not get into that. Congratulations on your appointment. The agency could not have picked a better man for the job. I already feel more secure walking the streets."

"Hardy-har-har," barked Lou.

"So when do I jump into your operation?"

"It's called Deeprose. I can't do it now, as I have to put together some information for my boss. Let's hook up tomorrow and I can fill you in. I wish there were two of you."

"Why's that?"

"Ironically, I really need someone in the Middle East, where you just came back from."

"For what?"

"An insurance policy of sorts. Deeprose is certainly a viable strategy, but I think we need more feet on the street."

"I know a guy."

"Yeah?"

"Abir. He's a subcontractor of sorts I use when I can't do ops solo. He is very dependable, tough, speaks the language, and knows how to keep a low profile."

"Is he available?"

"For the right price, I'm sure he is."

"Excellent. Let's discuss it when we review Deeprose."

"Aye, aye captain."

CHAPTER 8

The ropes he used were of the highest quality, and after having both her wrists and ankles bound for nearly an hour, he knew she would be grateful they would leave few—if any—marks or bruises. The expensive satin sheets and array of vanilla-scented candles were his choice. Expense was no concern for the client base; the service catered to every detail, and it was first-class, including any accompanying sexual toys and props.
He was meticulous, almost obsessive, as he carried out his fantasy.

There was certainly risk in paying for sex, but North viewed it as a perk due to his importance. The executive escort service was considered the best of the best, primarily due to the quality of its servicing staff and its reputation for confidentiality. The target clientele were primarily government employees, such as himself, in relatively high ranking influential positions, and with special needs.

The escort service owner, Ms. Toni, provided atypical sexual encounters that fulfilled assorted perverse addictions. North respected the fact that Ms. Toni was first and foremost a business owner and ran her company with the organized precision of a Wall Street CEO. She had built a lucrative niche business and her income rivaled most Csuites on Wall Street. He suspected that over the past ten years she had amassed millions of dollars and her worst-case scenario was five years in jail, which was unlikely due to the high-profile attorneys, government employees, and federal decision makers comprising her clientele list.

The executive service required not only beauty but brains, which was equated to the ability to maintain confidentiality and understand the dynamics of the engagement. Most had postgraduate degrees from private schools. Like her peers, Shay—born Francine Fulbright—was twenty-six years old, exquisitely beautiful, and extremely bright, having earned her master's in economics at Brown. North had found her bio above average when compared to the others in the portfolio. He deserved above average.

North was penetrating her anally as he began to think about retribution over the director role. He became too rough and Shay pulled away, complaining. He quickly apologized, explaining that he had been drinking and that he was upset and distracted for being passed over for a big promotion that he had earned and deserved.

On his way home, North realized he had lost his control and said too much. This was very much out of character, an aberration he blamed on the administration and its recent personnel decision that all but ended his lifelong aspiration to run the CIA. He had never felt such anger and contempt. He would have his revenge and, like any intelligence operation to accomplish such, he had to evaluate his options, resources, and probable outcomes.

But now he had an immediate issue: How much of a risk had he just created with Shay by sharing the missed promotion? She was bright. Would she put two and two together? He pondered this question as he drove his high-end German-engineered automobile to his multimillion-dollar estate in McLean, Virginia, where his pathetically devoted, brutally handsome wife of thirty years slept in her wing of their shared existence, oblivious to his engagements or the vengeful vile building within him.

❧

Covington, having just finished his morning walk-through of the factory, settled behind his desk to complete his brief report, which would indicate that things were progressing well. Only fifteen bugs remained and morale was good. Halfway through his report, he received a call from Eric.

"Randall, Eric here."

"Yes, sir."

"How goes it?"

"I was just completing this morning's update. Everything is progressing well. Based upon the performance rate, I anticipate all programming glitches to be worked out within thirty days."

"Excellent. Are you able to continue production regardless of the programming issues?"

"Yes, the bugs are all software-based and can be updated as they are fixed. We have produced three hundred and twelve as of this morning."

"I need you to ship several to ARobotics in the States. We need three from the civilian assembly lines—two men and one woman. We also need one military robot sent to a different address."

"Before the bugs are worked out?"

"Are there any remaining that could create an issue?"

"Not really. Most are minor timing and recognition issues with the artificial intelligence. But the laser capability will not be added to the military robots until we are ready to deploy."

"Understood."

"I guess the brass wants to see the real thing."

"Indeed."

And with that, Eric provided Covington the alternate shipping address to ARobotics. As they hung up, Covington wondered where the hell he was going to get the crates and a military transport to the factory undetected.

CHAPTER 9

Frank began the second round of waterboarding as Jim ensured the straps pressing the body to the gurney were buckled tightly. Even though the interrogations had become routine, even somewhat depressing, Frank found he was enjoying interrogating one of the heads of ISIS. The man stared defiantly at Frank as he slipped the hood over the man's head. The smell of fear, a unique odor that Frank had come to recognize, betrayed the man's bravado. The first time they interrogated him, he shat himself, requiring a delay and sterilization of the tank; he had been on a liquid diet since.

"Give us information and we stop," Frank repeated. The captive unsuccessfully attempted to shake his head free from Frank's grip to avoid the stream of water pouring into his nose and throat. After forty seconds, Frank stopped, providing the opportunity to choke water from his lungs.

The water had drenched the man's short-cropped beard and dripped onto the floor, eventually running into the floor drain.

After the fourth round, he started talking. *These so-called tough guys usually break sooner than later*, thought Frank.

Collectively, Frank and Jim were fluent in Arabic, Farsi, Azerbaijani, Kurdish, Turkish, and Hebrew to effectively conduct the interrogations.

At first the man choked out words as his lungs allowed. "Organized," followed by coughing and wheezing. "East coast..." more coughing; "silent killer." As the man slowly regained his composure, he went into great detail. His demeanor changed as he did so; he became angry, almost incensed, as he outlined players, timing, and locations.

Frank and Jim shared a triumphant glimpse between themselves.

"The guy is a true fanatic," Jim said as the man finished his diatribe.

"He scares the hell out of me. Where do they find these nut-wings?"

Dressed in a T-shirt and sweatpants, the captive looked like any other Middle Easterner. Frank couldn't get his head around the fact that this guy had been involved in the murder of many innocent people, and before his capture, had been in the process of planning the murder of thousands more. Sixty minutes later, the prisoner, now deflated and defeated, was back in his cell while Frank and Jim retreated to Jim's office.

"Do you believe it?" Jim asked.

"I guess it doesn't matter what we believe. Whether this information is true or not, people smarter than us will deal with it. Considering the potential significance, I want this report to be nothing less than perfect," Frank responded.

"I agree. Considering it is late on Saturday and you don't have to submit it until Monday morning, why don't you invest an extra twenty-four hours or so in the report before you submit it?"

"Sounds like a plan. This new intelligence should prove to be a bombshell!"

With his craving for alcohol raging, Frank headed to one of his favorite watering holes not far from Langley. The bartender saw him enter and had his drink ready for him by the time he got to the bar.

"How's Mr. Frank today?" the bartender began.

"Living the dream."

"So what brings you in this early in the afternoon?"

"Oh, got a lot done at work and figured I don't want to overachieve—they may begin to expect it."

The bartender laughed and returned to stocking the coolers with bottled beer.

Interrogating had begun to take its toll on Frank as it had done his predecessor. Frank's drinking had evolved from a stress reliever to a full blown addiction. Frank had added a gambling addiction two years ago. Ironically, he was now a prisoner to the bottle and his debtors. The torture from both usually occurred most mornings when he awoke with a hangover and a mounting debt load. It was a useless routine he went through every day.

Frank had multiple accounts at online casinos, no money in the bank, and nearly $100,000 in credit card debt. It had finally come to the point where he could not meet his normal, monthly living expenses plus the minimum payments on the credit card accounts. Even though he averaged $275,000 in income per year, Frank was all but bankrupt.

He needed a miracle. What he chose instead was to borrow money from a local loan shark named Vinny. He had borrowed $50,000 to pay down the credit card debt to provide him some breathing room. A repayment plan was negotiated with the remaining debtors.

Frank ordered his third drink as he headed to the restroom. There was something about getting a buzz on when the sun was shining brightly that just felt right. He was using one of the two urinals when he heard another guy walk in and begin washing his hands. Frank shuffled over to one of the two sinks to wash his hands when the large man swung Frank around and pinned his face to the wall with his forearm, while also pinning one of his arms behind his back.

"What the hell?" Frank managed to say.

"This is a friendly payment reminder from Vinny. Pay on time, no trouble. You don't pay, I'll be back, but I won't be this nice next time."

And with that, the man pushed Frank away and quickly exited the bathroom and the bar. Frank rubbed the back of his neck and decided the best and only thing he could do was go back to the bar, finish his drink, and consider his options. Who was he kidding? He didn't have any options. As he left the restroom, he was glad the mirror was cracked so he couldn't look at his reflection; he would be disgusted.

***

The mandatory, very sporadic surveillance reports of the Deeprose members were completed and forwarded to North for review. North found the reports contained nothing unusual. He was finishing reading Conover's report and ready to close it and move to the next when Conover's home address caught his attention. His residence was in a relatively modest area of Fairfax, Virginia, which was inconsistent with his income level. Frank probably had multiple homes or kept his money in more liquid investments. However, North decided it was worth a second look.

He went online to the agency's secure database, pulled up Conover's file, and drilled into his financial information, including his tax returns for the past several years.

Things did not add up. Frank's average annual compensation was approximately $275,000. He was divorced with no kids and no alimony payment, yet there was no interest, dividend, or capital gain or loss reported. Even given D.C. was a very expensive place to live, Frank should have been able to afford a larger residence, having ample disposable income for investments. What was he spending all of his money on? Expensive cars and extravagant trips first came to mind; however, a quick check of motor vehicles and Conover's travel history removed these as possibilities. Was he paying high dollar for an escort service?

North went back through the surveillance file and again reviewed the notation of an exchange between Conover and someone in another vehicle. The file noted a brief conversation interpreted to be one asking the other for directions. North ran the plate on the other vehicle. His reward for persistence jumped onto his monitor screen.

Vince DeSalvio, aka Vinny, was a well-known and respected loan shark working the greater D.C. market. Conover's financial condition and Vinny D's discussion with Conover was no coincidence. Conover was most likely into Vinny for some significant change. North immediately ordered the surveillance on Conover be intensified, including a tap on his home computer.

The next morning, North had what he needed. Conover had spent the previous evening gambling online, losing close to $8,000. He decided to discontinue the sporadic surveillance, as he had what he needed, while it was a time for a call to Blackstone to put his second pawn into play.

CHAPTER 10

Louis Pendleton's career aspirations had always been one of leadership within the intelligence community. However, he had never specifically targeted the role of CIA director. He was genuinely surprised when, six months before the incumbent's anticipated retirement date, he was contacted by the White House to request he agree to the vetting associated with the pre-nomination process. Pendleton's nomination from the president was considered by those among the inner circles as a quid pro quo for an influential and significant campaign contributor. His decorated career included over thirty years in the Navy, beginning as a petty officer 2nd class and moving up to captain, vice admiral, and most recently admiral chief of naval operations. He left the navy for the FBI, where he had led several intelligence operations over the past three years. It wasn't but one day after he had received the initial call from the

White House that Pendleton figured out how the proverbial winds had changed months before.

Shortly after a celebratory dinner of sorts with his wife of thirty-five years, he received a call from a college buddy from the Naval Academy whom he had not seen or spoken with in over five years. "Lou, this is Hank Morely. How the hell are you?"

"Hank," answered Pendleton, "what a surprise. I think the last time I saw you was at our thirtieth college reunion when my head was spinning, catching up on all of your global interests and activities. Are you in town?"

"No, I wish I was, so we could catch up over a beer or two. You know I'll never tire of buying you a beer and recalling that night long ago when you became my hero. But my call tonight is simply to congratulate you on your impending nomination as the new director of the CIA, arguably the second most important position behind the director of national intelligence."

"How—what... where in the hell do you get your information, Hank? I received the call only yesterday; Kate just found out during our dinner together tonight."

"Well, I have to admit I was fishing just a tad, but you confirmed my hope. You will make a terrific director and you will always have my support in whatever endeavor you choose."

"Well, Hank, I'm not sure I am the best choice, but I'll give it my all. Your access to information is unbelievable, and I admit, somewhat alarming. However, given your status within the elite, I am not surprised you have a friend or two at the big house."

"Indeed, my good friend, indeed. Give my best to Kate and let's grab that beer next time I'm in D.C."

Upon hanging up the phone with Hank, Pendleton immediately called to request a report of the largest contributors to the president's reelection campaign, either corporately, individually, or as part of a super PAC. If his suspicions were correct, Mr. Hank Morely was again repaying a debt of their college days, when Lou had safely extricated him from a bar brawl that saved most of Hank's front teeth and his place at the academy. Had the academy learned of the fight, Hank would have been expelled. A 1960 Dodge Dart had proven to be both their alibi and escape route—and Hank still owned it.

This time, Lou suspected Hank's gratitude was via a significant political contribution with an inference for more if Louis Pendleton was seriously considered for the role of the next CIA director. Two hours later, Pendleton's smartphone chimed with the e-mail containing the list of contributors. Hank Morely was the fifteenth-largest individual contributor to the current administration, the majority of which had been contributed within the past two months. The coincidence was too great to ignore.

❧

The surveillance team leader was accustomed to North's guidelines and expectations and was prepared for another routine assignment. The National Art Museum was convenient and relatively quiet on this Sunday afternoon. The visitors reminded North of zombies as they shuffled, seemingly aimlessly and silently, from one display to the next. He imagined he could herd them all up and toss them in the dump and nobody would miss them.

"This may be one of your easiest jobs ever, Sam." North was matter-of-fact as usual. "We have members of our intelligence community that, from time to time, participate in activities deemed not necessarily typical of a normal lifestyle and that may present a security risk. This is not uncommon and we simply need to keep our eyes and ears open, which is where you come in. This assignment involves surveillance of an executive escort service known to cater to high-ranking political and military officials. More specifically, you are to focus the majority of your time on several escort service employees."

He passed Sam a manila envelope.

"This file contains the names of CIA employees believed to be clients, although some maybe aliases. I need a record of all encounters for the next thirty days."

North concluded his orders with a handshake and walked off. What he didn't tell Sam was that several of the client names were erroneous; North had included names of those he did not necessarily like or agree with within the higher echelons of the intelligence community. As he left the museum, he thought it ironic how even the prostitution business had been whored out. What was this country coming to?

As he walked up Fourth Street past Jefferson to his awaiting BMW, he was relieved to know that very soon a dangling participle known in the escort circles as Shay would soon be terminated for illegally obtaining and selling top-secret U.S. government information.

North then proceeded to telephone Eric to take care of another issue.

"Eric, I have another relatively urgent assignment for Blackstone. It seems that we may have more than just one sympathizer in our ranks. Our strategy to lure this rat into a trap will be with the age-old seduction of money. We need Blackstone to approach a gentleman by the name of Frank Conover.

"Conover is intimately involved with obtaining, interpreting, and reporting on intelligence gained from jihadi captives. We need to determine if Conover is corrupt and a spy for terrorism, or if he has been mistakenly identified as a potential spy. As he plays a very important and strategic role in antiterrorism, we have to be absolutely sure of his allegiance."

"Do you really think an offer of money will persuade this Conover to admit he is a spy? Won't he be able to corroborate our claim with his terrorist contacts if he is in fact aligned with them?"

North had to acknowledge Eric had a formidable intellect, but he was certainly not capable of outsmarting him. "These are good questions and we anticipated these scenarios," North began. "If Conover reaches out to his contacts to confirm and they deny any knowledge of your offer, then he will not show up to receive the cash. If Conover is not aligned with them, he will immediately inform his supervisors and we will then be able to remove him from the suspect list.

"If Conover does show up, we have uncovered a weak link in the chain before it can do harm to the United States. We will then be cleaning up our house and, of course, justifying your handsome fee."

"What do we do with him if he shows up?"

"Nothing. Simply give him the cash and let us take it from there. I will need all of the related audio and video recordings."

"Oh, and before I forget, what are we paying Frankie boy to do?"

"That's fairly simple. Tell him he is to share no information with you and to simply listen. In fact, tell him he may not speak; otherwise, he will be harmed. He is to bury, lose, or destroy any significant intelligence information he obtains by whatever means."

"When do we need to begin?"

"Now."

North then provided Eric information on Conover to support the operation. He realized he was probably relying on Blackstone too much, but to use staffers was too risky. He had to maintain as much of an arm's-length distance as possible. If push came to shove, he would deny everything, and no one would ever doubt his word.

CHAPTER 11

Frank was nursing a relatively healthy Sunday morning hangover as he stumbled from the bathroom after downing four aspirin and two eight-ounce glasses of water. He was somewhat giddy regardless, as last night he had recovered his gambling losses of the past week with a strong blackjack streak. And for a change, he quit while he was ahead. He now had to conjure the willpower to not bet the winnings in his account and request a withdrawal be wired into his checking account. However, even with his $1,000 net winnings for the week, he would still owe Vinny $61,500.

Frank needed a distraction, so he headed out the front door of his modest 1400-square-foot ranch to grab the Sunday paper. He was able to make three short steps out onto the entryway before he felt three sharp jabs to his kidneys, followed by a hood placed over his head and a strong, beefy hand covering his mouth. He was promptly dragged back inside and the door was quietly closed.

There were two men, very strong men, who tossed him around like a rag doll. His head made a loud *thud* on the wooden floor as they forced him down. Frank attempted to get to one knee, but a karate chop to his back knocked the air from his lungs and sent him reeling back to the floor. As he attempted to regain his breath, one of the men wrapped duct tape around the hood where Frank's mouth was, further increasing his anxiety. The other man pinned him down, using both knees in the middle of his back, extenuating the breathing difficulty. Next, his arms were held behind his back by the elbows, exerting great strain on his shoulders and causing numbness in his hands.

Having been the one delivering interrogation techniques most of his career, Frank found himself incredibly calm throughout the attack, although the nerves near his kidneys and shoulders were sending excruciating, painful signals to his dehydrated brain.

As he began to assess his situation, his first thought was that Vinny and/or his buddies were making a simple courtesy call to again remind him of the importance of repayment. It seemed a little over the top, considering he took possession of the cash just a week ago, but he was a new client and maybe needed a thorough understanding of how business was done.

As he attempted to process this, one finally began to talk. "Mr. Conover, my client is interested in conducting business with you. We apologize for the circumstances of our inaugural meeting, but these were our instructions. The services you're to provide can be simply stated: Any intelligence that you obtain from any individual associated with terrorist organizations—beginning immediately and until further notice—is to be lost, misinterpreted, misreported, or simply not obtained. In other words, in your role as a government employee, you will be unsuccessful in gleaning any significant information. In return, my client will pay you two-hundred-thousand dollars in untraceable cash. You will have twenty-four hours to consider this offer. Details of the next meeting will arrive in your mailbox tomorrow. The meeting will occur within the next three days. Shake your head if you understand."

Conover slowly shook his head up and down several times. The one kneeling on his back promptly duct-taped his wrists together, but rather loosely. He then got off him and Frank could hear them both walk to the back door, open it, and leave.

It took Frank three minutes to wrestle the duct tape from his wrists and pull the taped hood from his head. He was acutely aware of the silence in his home. The early-morning sun was filtering through his front windows, creating beams dancing with the small dust particles that the violent encounter had created. The bells from a nearby church began announcing the start of Mass. He did his best to quiet his breathing and slow the beat of his heart. Frank was certain the intruders were long gone, but he couldn't bring himself to move quite yet. As his adrenaline began to subside, the pain between his shoulder blades, and in his kidneys, shoulders, and head, increased. The pain motivated him to slowly proceed to the bathroom for more aspirin, four of which he swallowed in one gulp. He caught his reflection in the mirror and wondered how the hell his life had gone so wrong. His face was puffy, with noticeable bags under his eyes due to the fifth of scotch he had drunk the night before.

His plan for the day had been simple: complete some paperwork, have a light workout at the gym, take a nap, and rent a movie with possibly a glass of wine or three. Now he had to clear his head and digest what had just happened. To do so would require a brisk walk at the least. Moving slowly due to his injuries, Frank donned an old gray sweatsuit and sneakers and headed out into his quiet Sunday neighborhood, turning south to a nearby park. He found himself stealing glances behind him more than a few times on his way, while his heart and head were in competition as to which could pound the hardest and loudest. Should he take the cash? Should he tell his superiors? Should he get the hell out of town and hide? He had to make a decision within the next twenty-four hours.

The infantry of ten moved effortlessly, almost naturally, as they progressed toward and surrounded the enemy. The enemy changed directions several times. The infantry reacted immediately and changed course, sensing, recognizing, and leveraging the natural cover that existed in the rough terrain. The infantry traded head and hand signals to communicate their next move. They were assimilating information instantaneously and altering their movements and actions accordingly. North believed the Turing test was finally achieved; his robotic infantry was perceived as real. The simulation was complete when the infantry destroyed the three enemy combatants with laser fire.

The first simulated battle six months ago had been a disaster. North closed his eyes as he replayed the scene in his mind. The infantry moved slowly, cautiously, toward the designated battlefield. Three engineers and two former military leaders were supervising the simulation from the right flank, seventy-five yards away. One of the engineers had raised his binoculars to get a better look, and that caught the attention of the nearest robot. The robot hand-signaled the other nine robots, and they immediately converged on the five men, who—once they realized what was happening—turned and ran toward their vehicles, which were parked nearly fifty yards away.

One of the engineers was 100 pounds overweight and the first to be caught— rather, dismembered—by two of the robots. The first robot leapt into the air, landing his feet on the engineer's back, forcing him face down into the dirt. The robot then grabbed his head, twisted and pulled until the head came free from the neck. The second robot grabbed the right arm and tore it from its socket as if the man was a scarecrow and the arm made of straw. Blood spewed freely from both mortal wounds.

The other two engineers died similarly before they could reach the Humvees. The two ex-military, still in some semblance of shape, made it to the vehicles, agreeing each would drive one in an attempt to improve the odds of survival. Three robots were on the first Humvee as the engine started. They easily broke through the glass, entered the vehicle, and pummeled the driver's head into an indistinguishable ball of blood, skull fragments, and brain matter. The second Humvee managed to accelerate to a speed greater than thirty miles per hour, which was the robots' top running speed. He escaped, but refused to participate in any more simulations. It had taken the programmers five minutes to decommission the robots, to basically turn them off, but the damage had been done. Subsequent simulations presented programming issues, but nothing as devastating as the first one.

Opening his eyes, North watched the current combat via Skype. Several of the infantry could now be seen picking up pieces of the enemy and placing them into a large plastic container. No evidence could be left on the training battlefield. He assumed the programming glitches had been corrected, based upon the infantry's performance. He needed to witness several more successful trials before putting his covert infantry into action.

The $300-million investment in his personal war against terrorism was but a drop in the bucket relative to his net worth. Given he had oversight of billions of dollars in operations, he was easily able to skim funds from multiple budgets without anyone noticing. God, he loathed having to play the administration's game of cat and mouse relative to military strategy. Hah! *Strategy* was a stretch. The current administration had not defined or instilled a military doctrine. The United States was flying by the seat of its pants relative to the development, testing, and use of advanced technologies in military affairs. It reminded him of the 1917 battle of Cambrai, when the British tanks broke through the German lines and had no plan what to do next. The offensive died out several days later.

North would not make that mistake. Even though the current administration was opposed to integrating this new breed of fighter into military operations due to the potential loss of control, he was pushing forward with his own agenda. His army would annihilate the terrorist community without any U.S. casualties and he would be exalted as a hero. In the immediate future, all hell would break loose in the Middle East.

CHAPTER 12

Habib Fahridi enjoyed his job as a computer engineer, so much so that he often worked late, as was the case tonight. He had no wife or children waiting for him at home; not even a pet. He was completing programming for a simulation, which if successful, would put his employer in the lead in terms of developing a new chip architecture that would combine processing and memory macros on a single chip. He considered himself blessed to be working for one of the most progressive technology firms in Islamabad.

He initiated the simulation and would eagerly await its results upon his return to work in the morning. He stuffed his backpack with the dirty containers that had held that day's lunch and headed to the exit and the bicycle rack. His long hours complemented his choice of transport, as the traffic and heat were relatively less early in the morning and during the early evening. His five-mile route home was uneventful, save for the pedaling past the Marriott that had been the deadly target of a suicide bomber in 2008.

Habib was deep in thought about the simulation and hadn't noticed the other bicyclists until they were upon him. There were three, one on each side and one behind him, and all very close. All wore *ghutras* secured with *egals*. Habib realized that they had picked a quiet and secluded street before circling him and he assumed they wanted what was in his backpack.

Habib began, "Listen, my friends, there is nothing in the backpack but my dirty lunch dishes and two issues of *Spider*, which is a monthly computer magazine. I do not travel with rupees, as it is too dangerous."

"Pull your bicycle to the side of the road," the man to his right ordered.

"I tell you I have nothing."

"Do it now!"

Habib obliged. He slowly brought his bicycle to a stop and removed his backpack and handed it to the man who had spoken. The man threw it to the ground. At that moment, a car pulled up to the men, the back door closest to them opened, and the same man ordered Habib to get into the car.

"Who do you think I am? I am but a computer engineer," Habib said with an elevated pitch to his voice.

Two of the men grabbed him by the arms and stuffed him into the backseat, where another man was waiting with a rifle pointed at him. One of the men opened the trunk and put Habib's bike and backpack inside. Then the men rode off on their bicycles as the car sped off. The man with the rifle threw a blindfold in Habib's lap and nodded for him to put it on, which he did compliantly.

Habib repeatedly asked where they were going and what they wanted with him. Neither the driver of the car nor the one holding the rifle said anything during the twenty-minute ride to their destination, which was an empty flat in a deserted apartment building. Habib could hear the sounds of several parties as they drove; the expatriates were drinking and carousing as they did every night. He found himself wondering how they could live such a lifestyle and contribute at work the next day. The car braking to a hard stop brought him back to the reality of his situation.

"Out," ordered the armed man, as the driver was already out of the car and opening Habib's door.

Habib, still blindfolded, slowly exited the backseat and immediately dropped to his knees, folding his hands in front of him. "Please, I am not who you think I am. You have the wrong person. I am nobody."

"You are exactly the person we want, Mr. Fahridi."

Upon hearing his name, Habib began to sob. The two men grabbed him beneath his arms, lifted him to his feet, and pulled him forward into the building and into the first floor flat, where he was unceremoniously dumped into a wooden chair sitting in the middle of the largest room. His hands were secured in front of him with a bungee cord and the blindfold was removed. Habib looked around to find a total of four men peering at him with angry eyes. The tallest man, who was loosely holding a large machete in his right hand, spoke, "You know why you are here, infidel"—more a statement than a question.

Fighting back hysteria, Habib answered, "No. I am not an infidel. I am a Muslim like you."

"You are nothing like us. You would never be worthy to join us, ISIS."

At hearing ISIS, Habib began to sob again. The Blackstone contractors Eric had hired for the abduction were all Middle Eastern and therefore easily passed as jihadis.

The man continued, "We know you are sharing intelligence about ISIS with your sister, who works for the United States military. We should slit your throat now for being a traitor. Instead, you will now be our pawn in gaining intelligence from the infidels!"

"My sister works as a language interpreter for Homeland Security; she is not involved in intelligence operations."

"Silence!" the man roared. "No more lies or we cut out your tongue."

One of the other men set a battery-powered video camera and bright light several feet in front of Habib. He then held up a posterboard with a message written on it.

"You will look into the camera and read this message. If you do not, I will cut your head off. If you say anything other than what is written, I will cut your head off. Do you understand?"

Habib violently shook his head to the affirmative. The man with the machete stood behind Habib so he could be seen in the video. He nodded for the other man to begin recording. Once started, the man with the machete slapped Habib hard enough on the back to knock him out of the chair. Two other men picked him up and set him back in the chair as the machete was placed against his neck and he slowly began to read: "Sara, I have been captured by ISIS. If you do not provide them with top-secret U.S. military intelligence that they deem significant and actionable, I will be beheaded. You are to convey this intelligence using the following Gmail account, and your Social Security number is the password. You are to only prepare a draft e-mail containing the acceptable intelligence; do not send it. You need to create this email within the next twenty-four hours." Habib went onto provide the Gmail account and was tempted to tell his sister that he loved her and to avoid putting herself in danger, but he was too afraid of the consequences.

The video camera and light were turned off, the bungee cords removed, and Habib and the others were given plates of *kabuli palaw*, an Afghan staple comprised of rice, carrots, raisins, and lamb, along with hot tea to drink. He had no idea where the food had materialized from, but was grateful for the break in the tension. The men seemed to lose interest in him as they all sat on the floor to eat their meal.

The man who had been holding the machete spoke, "We will spend the night here. You will not be harmed if your sister provides what has been requested. We have brought mats to sleep and you will be taken to the outside toilet. Give us no trouble and you shall not be harmed."

"I have no intention of giving you trouble. I just want to go home," explained Habib as he wondered what the hell his sister was into and what the odds were of him getting out of this alive. He couldn't take his eyes off the machete as he ate his food, while his bowels screamed for a release.

CHAPTER 13

Sara thought it odd to receive a video file from an anonymous e-mail address. But the longer she worked on Deeprose, she was learning that oddity was becoming the norm. Her laptop told her the drive had been recognized and contained one file. Before she opened it, she went to the commissary for a cup of hot water for green tea, which she drank religiously at the beginning of every day. It was one—if not the only—simple pleasure she enjoyed as part of working in her dump of an office.

As she reentered her office, she closed the blinds on the windows to block out the morning sun so it would not cast a blinding glare on her computer screen. She double-clicked the icon to initiate the file, sat back, and raised the cup nestled between her hands to her lips to enjoy the first sip. As she began to swallow, the first image of her brother bound and distressed jumped onto the screen. Her shock resulted in her inhaling versus swallowing, which caused her to choke as the hot liquid traveled down her windpipe. She instinctively jumped from her chair, dropped the cup, struggling to breathe. After twenty seconds, which seemed like twenty minutes, Sara regained her breath and did her best to breathe slowly and evenly. She closed the door to her office and remained standing as she started the video from the beginning.

Sara stood stunned and immobile as the sixty-two-second-long tape of her brother ended with a hooded kidnapper slapping the back of her brother's head hard enough to knock him out of his chair. The computer screen went black and time seemed to stand still. Tears began streaming down her face as she knew from experience that her brother's odds of survival were not good.

Her first emotion was anger, quickly followed by fear, and shortly thereafter hopelessness. And, at some deep level of consciousness, there was guilt. She felt guilty for thinking about the potential negative consequences upon her and her career.

After five minutes of her emotional roller coaster, she took a deep breath and resolved herself to think through the alternatives and potential outcomes until she was satisfied that she had exhausted every possible scenario that could save her brother's life. Considering ISIS had given her twenty-four hours to provide them with what they, and only they, deemed *substantive, valuable, and actionable* information on America's efforts to derail their organization, would they consider changing the plan to behead her beloved brother?

No, she thought. Her brother would not endure what Daniel Pearl had many years before. She sat down, pulled out a clean legal pad of paper, and began to write everything that came to mind relative to her conundrum. The seed of a plan began to germinate.

CHAPTER 14

Frank was less than attentive during the morning's debrief, doing his best to figure out who was behind the attack. He suspected he had helped out his two assailants by deciding to go out and get the paper when they were most likely casing his house, attempting to determine the easiest way to break in. It was obvious someone knew what his job was within the CIA. If any of those in the know, most of whom were sitting around the table, leaked the information, why in the world would they want to squelch any intelligence? None of it made sense, at least not yet. Everyone involved had motivation for interrogations to be successful. Well, evidently someone did not.

Frank could not wait to leave the debrief and Langley. Was he paranoid, or was Lou looking at him curiously in the meeting? He was sweating; not from the heat, but from anxiety. Had anyone noticed? Could someone sitting in the meeting be behind the offer of cash? The odds were yes, but again, he couldn't answer the *why*. When he awoke that morning he was fairly certain he would take the cash, but now, sitting among the CIA power brokers, he wasn't so sure. He needed a drink.

Fifteen minutes later, he sighed with relief as the meeting ended. He headed straight to his car, turned the AC on full blast, and headed home. Earlier that morning, he had put an outgoing bill payment in the mailbox. The red flag was now in the down position, indicating the mailman had been there. Now the question was: Had someone put the note in the mailbox? He opened the box and found a few standard-sized envelopes— all bills he recognized—along with an 8.5"-x-11" manila envelope with no writing on the outside. This was the note he had been anticipating! He looked up and down his street before quickly entering the house and opening the envelope. He sat down at his splintered wooden kitchen table to read the note:

> *Mr. Conover,*
>
> *You will find payment for your services in a metal box at your back door. Although our client had originally purposed a follow-up meeting, they were confident that you would agree to the offer and that you would behave as requested. Therefore, a follow-up meeting was deemed unnecessary. However, if you have unfortunately decided not to provide your services in this matter, my client will be extremely dissatisfied, the results of which can only be imagined. My client understands you have the option to share the details of our inaugural meeting, this note, and your cash payment with your employer. However, it is anticipated your employer may have suspicions and be forced to invoke some level of caution and protocol, which may result in your being removed from your current position, at a minimum. Having considered all of the information, my client trusts an acceptable deal has been reached. It is recommended you destroy this letter and*

> *dispose of the metal box. Insofar as the cash, my client suggests*
> *you not deposit it such that it presents an abnormality in the*
> *trend of your normal depositing behavior. Be discreet, or we*
> *will be in touch.*

Frank reread the letter three times before setting it down. The threat if he did not play nice was loud and clear. But how in the hell would the so-called client have any idea if he cooperated or not? He could not wrap his head around a motive.

He guessed it really did not matter, since he had decided he would take the risk and the money. He had no choice. He was broke and in debt and this was a way out. He went to the back door to retrieve his reward. As he opened the door, the possibility struck him that this was his employer testing his resolve and loyalty. The thought quickly evaporated as he looked down. There it was: a black, metal strongbox. He bent down to pick it up then slowly looked around his backyard. He quickly stepped back inside, then shut and locked the door.

He set the box on the kitchen table next to the letter and opened it. Tightly wrapped wads of $100 bills were neatly stacked to the top of the box.

"This must be the two-hundred-thousand-dollar metal box," Frank said to no one but himself.

Considering he had already earned some of the payment, Frank decided it deserved a celebratory drink and poured himself a double neat Maker's Mark.

He justified his decision to take the money, telling himself they had been unsuccessful in getting any intelligence from the ISIS captive— until the last interrogation, anyway. No one would be expecting any significant intelligence, would they? All he knew is that he needed the cash, regardless.

Frank considered the odds of forging the intelligence report versus sending an accurate one. There were a lot of smart people working at the CIA that could figure out he falsified information. What if someone discussed the most recent interrogation with Jim? The lie would be exposed and he might be considered a traitor and incarcerated for the rest of his life. On the other hand, if he submitted an accurate report, the probability of anyone finding out except for the people on the team seemed very low. If the person behind the cash was part of the team, what was the worst they could do—beat him up again? He could handle several beatings for $200,000.

Frank, being the gambler, decided his odds were best by submitting an accurate report. To be on the safe side, he might lay low and check into a hotel for a week or so just in case the goons came back to get the money. Hell, he could afford it. Feeling relieved at making a decision, he poured himself another drink, opened his laptop, and sent an e-mail containing accurate interrogation results to all those concerned.

❧

Jack knew he needed to do some research before he discussed his suspicions regarding what had happened in the meadow. Suggesting to Lou that robots were killing animals in the farmlands of Iraq without any more intelligence than he had now would be a rookie mistake and potentially jeopardize his role. He and Lou went way back, but to dump this in Lou's lap without more information would be unprofessional, to say the least.

Jack also knew he couldn't involve Dr. Chang anymore, due to his ties with the DoD and the current directive to stand down. He needed to talk with experts outside the military or other branches of government, which left industry and academia. Based upon Chang's employer's alliance with the military, there was no way to be sure which industry or company was in bed with the military. That left academia.

Jack began to search the Web for universities and colleges that specialized in robotics and/or artificial intelligence. There were several, but the one that caught his eye was Carnegie Mellon University. More specifically, a Professor Pratt specializing in national security, military diffusion, and contemporary warfare had recently posted information on an online newsletter regarding laser development and their use in warfare.

Jack decided the professor was a good place to start.

Jack called the college and was fortunate to find Pratt in his office between classes. "Professor Pratt, my name is Jack Landis and I was hoping you had a few minutes to enlighten me on current developments relative to lasers and artificial intelligence."

"And why the interest?"

Jack had prepared a response anticipating the question. "I am conducting research for my first novel—a mystery-thriller."

"I see. Have you written anything else?"

"No, this is my first foray into writing."

"Can I find you on LinkedIn or Facebook?"

Jack hadn't anticipated that question. "Ah, no... I live in the Stone Age when it comes to social media."

"No matter. Most of what I learn I post on my blog."

"Yes, that is how I found you."

"So, maybe not so much in the Stone Age, then?"

"I stretched my limits."

"So where do you want to start?"

"The videos on laser development and technology lead one to believe that the technology is available now—are we using it?"

"*We*, as in the military?"

"Yes, by soldiers, as with a gun or rifle?"

"Lasers or directed-energy weapons have been under development in some form or another for decades. In June 2000 a laser shot down a U.S.–fired Russian Katyusha rocket traveling seven hundred miles per hour. This was probably the real tipping point relative to the belief that lasers would someday become the weapon of choice. Since then, the military has partnered with private industry and academia to further the development of both defensive and offensive capabilities. For example, drones equipped with lasers instead of rockets and forcefields comprised of plasma. I believe we are only a decade or so away from the realization of these technologies on the battlefield.

"The Center for Strategic and Budgetary Assessment, a think tank funded by the DoD, believes lasers will become a transformational game changer in military operations. As far as a handheld weapon, it would only take approximately a thousand watts of power to inflict some level of damage upon another human being. However, it is more likely that a higher level, possibly a hundred-thousand watts, would be pursued to ensure termination. To my knowledge, there is no advanced development for a handheld weapon. It may take years to develop a prototype that can control and disperse that amount of energy from a relatively smaller device."

"Are there any risks to those that fire a handheld laser?"

"I believe there is or was some concern with proper eye protection, but most likely with the higher-energy lasers. But again, most of the focus has been on larger deployment tools such as planes, drones, and battleships. You may want to consult with a Dr. Roger Lyer at Stanford University. He focuses much of his time on photonics."

"Photonics?"

"The science of light, or photon generation, detection, and manipulation through emission, transmission, modulation, signal processing, switching, amplification, and detection-sensing. Arguably, a close relative to lasers."

"I'll do that. How about artificial intelligence?"

"The advent of this technology is probably further out than lasers. Robotics has certainly advanced at an accelerated rate over the past decade, considering UAVs are currently used in the air and on the ground. However, as I trust you know, these require human involvement and control at some level. There is an active ethics and policy debate going on within the inner circles of development. In spite of the DoD's directive that all AI technology be more or less sanctioned, I suspect there is some level of ongoing research and development. The biggest concern is that we create artificial intelligence that ultimately wipes out mankind.

Can you imagine if our enemies, especially those without regard for life, were to get their hands on lasers or artificial intelligence?"

"Sobering for sure."

"Indeed. These are fascinating topics that deserve our brightest minds, and most importantly, strong and able leadership."

Jack thanked the professor and ended the call. He had gained a sense that robots could have very well roamed the meadow, but there was still doubt relative to the handheld laser technology. He had more research to do and more phone calls to make. He was tempted to call Lou and bring him into the loop of his thinking, as Lou was always a good sounding board, but it still all seemed a stretch.

How the hell would he begin? *"Oh, by the way, Lou, I know you're the director of the CIA, but somebody is running robotics operations armed with lasers in the Middle East right under your nose."* Yeah, he would have to put more meat on the bones before teeing that one up. Shit, he wished he had someone else to talk to about this. Or did he?

CHAPTER 15

The fact that her biggest client had not scheduled an engagement for several weeks hadn't necessarily concerned Shay, especially after the last time when he shared more than he should have about his job. Not that Shay cared or would ever try to find out who he was; she didn't want the lucrative paydays to end. What concerned her was spotting who she believed to be the same man three times in three different locations over the past week. It could be that he lived in the neighborhood and frequented the same places she did, but still, it felt creepy.

She began to feel better as she drove her car through the security gate at her condominium complex, scanning her card and waving to the guard. One of the reasons she chose to purchase here was the level of security. Guards were posted at the only entrance to the adjacent parking garage and at the entrance to the elevator bank 24-7. In addition, there were more security cameras than she could count.

"Morning, Leonard," Shay said to the guard near the elevators as she pushed the *up* button.

"Morning, Ms. Fulbright. Another workout?"

"Can't let those calories catch up."

"Yeah, right," said Leonard as he unconsciously held his beer-fed gut and stared at Shay's chiseled ass.

Shay's income afforded her a larger unit on the top floor with an amazing view of D.C. Upon entering, she locked and dead-bolted the door before heading to the bathroom where she turned on the shower, stripped off her sweaty clothes, and turned to examine herself in the full-length mirror. She was pleased with what she saw; her disciplined eating and workout habits were paying off.

As she finished looking herself up and down, she thought she saw a shadow to her right. Before she could turn to look, a garrote was swiftly wrapped around her neck. She stared in horror at the attacker in the mirror. He wore all black, including a black stocking mask over his face and black gloves. Then she saw the blood.

She grasped with both hands to try to pull the metal wire away from her neck but couldn't get her fingers underneath it. She kicked involuntary, occasionally connecting with her attacker's legs. She couldn't breathe, and the blood, so much blood; her blood. Her final thought, as the wire cut through her carotid artery, causing blood to gush onto the mirror, was that her john was killing her and her beautiful body.

The contracted agent removed the bloody garrote from her neck, placed it in a Ziploc bag, and inspected the crime scene to ensure he left no evidence. He then ransacked the unit to make it appear as though it had been burglarized. He had easily created a distraction on the street—two men pretending to fight—to pull the guard away from his post. Armed with the latest lock-picking tools, he had effortlessly broken into the unit and hid until she came home. The video feeds would show a masked man carrying an empty duffel bag, hoping to fill it with someone else's personal property.

As he prepared to leave the unit, he placed a call to one of his two accomplices, instructing them to stage another altercation on the street in front of the complex. He cautiously opened the door, looked up and down the hallway, and exited the unit as he adjusted the long wig, fake beard, baseball cap, and glasses he had stowed in the duffel bag. He exited the complex unnoticed as Leonard stood at the door watching the two men yell at each other in the street, unaware that Francine lay dead in her apartment for allegedly sharing top-secret military information with the Russians.

CHAPTER 16

Sara had slept only three hours, but found herself energized on her morning run. She had made her decision at 2:00 a.m. No matter what scenarios she played out in her mind, none provided as high odds of saving her bother than giving his captors what they wanted. She had allowed herself sleep after making the decision, realizing she still needed to identify information that would be perceived significant enough. And that is what occupied her mind as she raced through the streets of her Old Town neighborhood.

Deeprose was the most significant part of her job and she knew that revealing any intelligence could have severe consequences, not only upon her, but those involved with the operation. She knew if she concentrated long and hard enough, she could arrive at a solution that could both satisfy ISIS and minimize any damage to Deeprose. She was halfway through her run when the idea came to her.

Upon arriving at work, Sara walked into Pendleton's office as he was signing off on a significant budget increase.

"What is Abdul's status?" Lou asked.

Sara began, "Abdul's transmission from last night is concerning. He fully expects that he will be required to participate in a test that will result in physical harm to someone. For the first time since connecting with Asaryi, he advises that his last two correspondences have not been from Asaryi, but rather from another operative claiming to be representing Asaryi and working closely with him. This change in communication is atypical in any scenario similar to this when trust has been established. This is especially odd in lieu of the next meeting, which is deemed to be the final test for Abdul to be brought in, assuming at the lowest level of ISIS." Sara could not maintain eye contact for long, delivering this report to the team, as she knew it to be false and part of her plan to save her brother. She knew that by doing this her career could be over and she could face criminal charges.

"All right Sara, advise Abdul to proceed with caution."

She walked dejectedly back to her office, realizing her attempt to have an order for Abdul to break off discussions with ISIS had failed. She should have known that any potential collateral damage, as her peers called human sacrifice in pursuit of freedom, would not derail Abdul's orders to infiltrate ISIS. She had hoped she would have been directed to tell Abdul to stand down and discontinue communications due to the potential risk.

She had also decided that, without a directive to remove Abdul, she would autonomously issue the directive herself and follow through in giving up Asaryi. She went immediately to her office and sent the following transmission to Abdul:

> *Intelligence reveals your covers have been removed. Immediately disengage and use predetermined passage to safety and await further instructions...*

Since it was 9:00 a.m. in D.C., it would be 7:00 p.m. in Islamabad, and Abdul would be awake to receive the communication. Sara would wait until 2:30 p.m. EST to send her intelligence information to ISIS, which would give Abdul over five hours to exit the country. Would that give him enough time to get out unharmed?

CHAPTER 17

North was still picking at the lunch plate that had been delivered to his office two hours earlier. He had developed unusual eating habits at an early age. He was fixated on his looks and paid special attention to avoid those activities, environmental influences, and food products that could adversely affect him. His wife had learned to stop cooking for him before they were married and finally acquiesced to him completing his own grocery shopping two years into their marriage. When they were growing up, his children were elated if Dad decided to eat some cake and ice cream at their birthday parties

He turned his attention to the *Washington Post* lying on his desk. On this day, as was too often the case, murders in the nation's capital made the headlines. Yesterday claimed three victims, the pictures of each underneath the byline. The one female was beautiful and he recognized her immediately. The article explained that Ms. Francine Fulbright, age twenty-six, a graduate of Brown University and a model, was believed to have surprised a burglar breaking into her apartment and was killed. North smiled to himself, knowing no one would ever be the wiser.

As North finished taking one bite out of each of the cheese slices on his plate, he decided to access the Gmail account Sara had been given during the videotaping to determine if she had, in fact, communicated some intelligence. Sara had been given an innocuous Gmail user name, and the password was simply her Social Security number. Sara had been instructed to access the account, create a draft e-mail, save it, but not send it. This way the e-mail and information could never be traced since it was never sent. Little did she know that her brother would be released within twenty-four hours, regardless of her response, or lack thereof. North quickly moved to close his door and returned to his desk so he could read the draft e-mail on his secure laptop:

> *You fucking bastards. What hurts the most is that we are of the same land. We all have choices, and you have chosen the way of the coward, all in the name of a prophet who somehow in your little minds justifies the terrorism and human injustice you glorify in his name. You are puppets with no spines, morals, or values. I love my brother more than anything and therefore I will give you want you want. Your operative, Asaryi, has been secretly meeting with one of our operatives over the past month, sharing information about ISIS and your operations. Unfortunately, your timing is good in that Asaryi was going to introduce our operative to the next level within your organization so we could learn even more. Asaryi regrets turning on his homeland, the United States, and this was his attempt for retribution. I trust this is significant enough information to immediately release my brother unharmed. I expect a call from him within the hour letting me know he is safe. God help you if you do not fulfill your end of the deal.*

North laughed out loud. He had to hand it to Sara in that she used an element of truth in the email so if ISIS actually did read it, it would arouse suspicion regarding Asaryi's allegiance. The calculated risk in his plot was that Sara would not allow Abdul to be subject to any danger due to her decision to create the draft for who she thought was ISIS. She would have already advised Abdul under some pretense that he must remove himself from danger, thereby thwarting any potential of him penetrating ISIS. Deeprose's momentum would be derailed, Pendleton's armor of credibility would receive a serious chink, and she would have to admit to her indiscretion sooner rather than later.

He immediately contacted Eric to instruct him to free the prisoner, claiming all was well and the agency's suspicions had been just that: mere suspicions. What North had not planned for was Sara's ingenuity. Had he underestimated her? No matter. If she became an obstacle, she too might be discovered as a spy sharing top secret intelligence and have to be dealt with accordingly.

❧

Asaryi was very proud of himself for having recruited an American. Today was to be the final meeting at an abandoned animal shelter, wherein Abdul was to demonstrate his commitment by shooting a traitor in front of Asaryi's superiors. Asaryi had no idea Abdul would be a no-show, as he was well out of the country. Inside the shelter, Asaryi was met by his superiors and their respective guards. "Our new recruit should be here momentarily," he said.

"He had better be," one of the superiors began. "Tell us how you came upon this recruit."

"He, like many others, had posted interest on one of our websites."

"And you conducted a full background search on him?"

"Yes."

"And he is an American, like you?"

"Yes. That makes Abdul an even better recruit; to turn one of the infidels against the West."

"There was nothing in his background that made you suspicious?"

"No. He came from a broken home, had rebelled against leadership beginning at a young age, has posted many anti-government articles on social media, and is a devout Muslim."

"Well then, we are anxious to meet this new recruit. Your Abdul is late."

"I don't understand. He was prompt at all of the previous meetings and had confirmed his understanding of the time and place yesterday."

"Abdul is not coming, you fool!"

"What? How would you know that?"

"Grab him!"

Two of the guards grabbed Asaryi by the arms. One tied his hands behind his back, then tied his legs together at the knees. He was thrown to the ground and laid on his back. Sticks were then pounded into the ground between his arms and sides so that he could not roll to either side—he was immobilized. Another guard carried a backpack over to Asaryi and pulled out a large block of plastic explosives with a timer wedged into its pliable surface. Wires snaked out of the timer into the soft explosive. He set the bomb onto Asaryi's stomach, taping it securely.

Asaryi began to scream. "No, I have done nothing but what you ask of me!"

"Abdul is a spy for the infidels. What did you tell him?"

"Nothing. I asked all of the questions."

"You lie!"

"No, believe me. Have I ever failed you?"

"Set the timer for ten minutes," the superior ordered the guard.

"*Noooooo*," Asaryi screamed again, rocking his body as hard as he could to dislodge the bomb from his stomach.

"And tape his mouth, he is giving us all a headache."

Ten minutes later and a quarter mile away, the ISIS members heard the explosion that send Asaryi to be with Allah.

CHAPTER 18

Sara answered her cell phone on the first ring. "Habib?"

"Sara."

"Are you all right?"

"I think so. They let me go."

"Oh, thank God. Where are you?"

"They dropped me at a shopping center near my flat. Did you give them the information they wanted?"

"I can't talk now. I will call you back in a bit."

Sara couldn't believe her luck. She kissed her cell phone for the second time in the past twenty-four hours. The first was upon her creatively initiating the order to direct Abdul to exit the country. Asaryi had been killed by a bomb for which no one had yet taken responsibility. The fact that Abdul was already well on his way was a fact she hoped she could take to her grave. She determined Asaryi was deemed a risk as a result of her email and most likely killed by his own people.

She feverishly brushed her teeth as she thought proudly about yesterday afternoon, when she had contacted a colleague at Homeland Security who worked in the cybersecurity division to learn of any methods or tricks to sharing an e-mail or post such that jihadis would see it sooner rather than later. She really did not learn anything of value, but was able to confirm the top websites were *al-Ansar, al-Firdus, al-Faqih,* and *al-Neda.* Each had a particular core competency of information, but all were considered legitimate sites that ISIS used to run their business. In addition, unless one could scramble or disguise the IP address from which their e-mail or post was sent, it was unlikely they could pass themselves off as someone that could be trusted.

As soon as Sara hung up the phone with her colleague, she had headed to the closest hotel with a business center, the Marriott in Crystal City. But first she stopped to purchase a wig and nonprescription eyeglasses for a precautionary disguise in case of any hotel video surveillance. Upon arriving at the hotel, she was in luck and found someone working in the business center, which was accessible only with a hotel key. She politely knocked. The man inside was at first skeptical when he turned to see who was knocking; however, upon seeing a beautiful woman dressed impeccably in a business suit, he opened the door to let her in.

"I am so sorry to bother you," Sara began, "but I have already checked out and forgot to check my e-mail account."

"No problem," said the elderly businessman.

Sara had stopped at the front desk on her way to the business center to request the user ID and password to access the hotel's internet. She now had internet access with an IP address that could not be traced to her, assuming her disguise would hold up under any potential scrutiny. First, she created a fake Gmail account. Again, she was a quick study. She studiously worked through the websites that her colleague had given her and either sent an e-mail if an address was provided or posted a message if a bulletin board or blog was accessible. The message she sent or posted was similar to the one she had created as a draft e-mail earlier that day, but she went on to provide details of the meetings between Asaryi and Abdul, including dates and the names of the cafés. She accomplished this in less than thirty minutes then quickly returned to Langley, disposing of the wig and glasses in a dumpster on her way.

Now, a day later, she was taking a shower to help her wake up before she headed to CIA headquarters. She turned the water temperature up to the highest her skin could bear in an attempt to wash away the filth of the past twenty-four hours.

She had several things to figure out. First, what would she do if during Abdul's debrief—which was inevitable—it was discovered that there was no new contact. Had Asaryi always been the contact? Second, if discovered, how would she explain the approximate twenty-hour time difference between Abdul's actual departure and the directive she clandestinely created to do such? Third, what would happen when one of the U.S. intelligence agencies discovered the e-mails she posted, all written in Farsi, on the jihadi Web sites?

Sara left the building for an early lunch hour so that she could call her brother in confidence. She also planned to take a thirty-minute catnap in her car, as the last twenty-four hours had caught up with her like a ton of bricks. As she exited one of the first-floor elevators, she looked to her right and saw Lou with an extremely handsome gentleman she hadn't seen before. She was struck by the confidence and strength the stranger exuded. She realized she was staring when the stranger sensed her presence and turned and looked directly into her eyes before abruptly turning back and walking onto the elevator. Sara froze. Was she breathing? She knew she wasn't moving. What had just happened? She took a deep breath and began to put one foot in front of the other heading toward the exit.

She realized she was exhausted both physically and mentally, but suddenly she had found an energy reserve that propelled her quickly out the door and to her car. As she drove, she dialed her brother. He answered on the first ring.

"Sara, what took you so long to call?" asked her brother.

"I'm sorry, Habib, but it's been a very busy and stressful day."

"Why would ISIS have me send a message to you? What are you involved with, Sara?"

"It's complicated."

"What information could you possibly have that they would be interested in? I don't understand any of this."

"I'm not comfortable discussing any of this over the phone now. It may not be safe."

"Safe? Tell me about *safe*. Neither my employer nor my friends know where I am. I've been missing for two days now, Sara. I need to let people know that I'm okay."

"You're right. I'm sorry, I have been busy thinking through so many things I haven't had time to give that any thought. Are you due any vacation time?"

"Yes, Sara. But we're in the middle of a significant project. I can't leave now."

"I want you to come to America to visit me until things settle down and I can understand what is going on and why you were taken hostage. As good as an engineer as you are, Habib, I trust a short-term replacement can be found. We need to come up with an excuse as to why you were AWOL for the past two days and why you need to take an extended vacation for a personal emergency of some sort."

"I could lose my job."

"You could lose your life. Just do it, Habib. Call and let me know your travel plans, and please be discreet in getting out of the country. I love you."

"Sara, what have you gotten me into? All right, I'll do it. I love you too."

Sara ran into North as she returned from lunch.

"Any additional news on Asaryi?" she asked.

"Al Jazeera is reporting that a U.S. drone was the cause of the blast, which we know is not true. Our people are currently in discussion with

Al Jazeera, refuting the report. Other than that, there is no additional information to share."

They both continued their separate ways, each considering their involvement in Asaryi's death. Sara had no idea North knew exactly what she was thinking.

CHAPTER 19

Frank had spent most of the afternoon dressed in the same dirty T-shirt and jeans he had passed out in the night before, researching ways to safely deposit the cash so he could use it to pay off his remaining debt as soon as possible. Regardless of the method, it was money laundering, which was illegal. He wasn't sure why he had developed a conscience regarding laundering money, considering he had already borrowed money from a loan shark and seriously considered falsifing a governmental report in return for a payoff. At this point, he really couldn't do himself any more harm. "What a shitstorm," he said to himself.

As he considered the methods, he immediately dismissed those that involved creating fake invoices and troublesome number-fudging for a shell company or a legitimate business; it was too much work. With regard to an offshore or overseas bank account, they appeared to be relatively simple to open; however, the primary catch was coming up with an underlying, legitimate, and legal reason for the deposit. In addition, there was no FDIC to insure any deposits as in the U.S. Structuring deposits seemed to be a relatively easy method. Recognizing any deposits greater than $10,000.01 raised a red flag, Frank could open accounts at several banks and make multiple deposits less than $10,000.01 and hopefully remain under the radar.

The one method that obviously caught Frank's eye was gambling. Dirty money can be cashed in for chips anonymously and turned back in for clean money. Frank realized his challenge would be turning it back in and not losing it gambling. He went into the bathroom and washed his face. As he toweled himself dry, he looked at his reflection in the mirror. He stared at himself for several seconds, then said, "You can do this."

He decided he would open accounts at five banks, deposit $8,000 into each, and take the balance to several casinos to cash it in for clean money. Ninety minutes later, he found himself sitting at a blackjack table in Baltimore's Horseshoe Casino. He was at his favorite place in the world, armed with a large stack of cash and an unlimited amount of free drinks. He consciously acknowledged that gambling was better than anything, even sex.

He casually weaved his way through the aisles of slot machines and around the large pits of table games. He likened his anticipation to foreplay. As expected, the carpeting was a combination of brilliant, loud colors, while the slot machines were buzzing with their normal chorus of bells, music, and other obnoxious sounds. The majority of the slot players were senior citizens seemingly caught in a trance as they stared emotionlessly at the machines. One thing that was noticeably different: no more stale-smelling cloud of exhaled cigarette smoke.

He had his game plan down pat. He would move around to different table games, play a little, then cash in less than $5,000 to avoid receiving a 1099. He knew he couldn't launder the money at only one game, as the respective pit boss would be on to him. For no other reason other than proximity, he sat down at a roulette table and handed the dealer $3,000and asked for $10 chips. With it providing one of the best payoffs in the casino over several bets, Frank figured he might as well try to win a little extra while he was there. He quickly ordered a double bourbon, neat, and settled in. He felt a rush of giddiness wash over him; he couldn't help smiling to himself. The adrenaline rush was on and he was going to ride it, but just for a few more bets.

His betting companions at the table were a middle-aged woman wearing a sundress that possibly used to fit and a young black man who appeared to be wearing every piece of bling he and his extended family owned. They seemed harmless enough and not ones that would slow the pace of play.

He pulled his stack of chips close, placed his bet, and took a deep breath. Let the games begin. On the second spin, his 18 came in, on which he had bet $200: a $7,000 payout. Net his other bets, he was up $5400—he could play on the house's money for as long as he wanted! He started betting cautiously to make the winnings last. His luck continued as he hit several more numbers, providing a net payout of $2200. He cursed himself for not betting more; he was hot. He noticed his gambling companions had lost all of their chips and moved on. He had the table to himself.

Frank checked his watch. He had been at the table for nearly two hours and six drinks and was still ahead by $3000. It was time. His numbers had not hit for over half an hour; he was due. He ordered another double and increased his bet to $300 per number, on six numbers. If he hit, his payout would be $10,500, less his $1500 losses on five of the six numbers—a cool $9000 profit on one spin.

As the dealer signaled *no more bets* with the swipe of her arms across the betting surface, Frank took a big swallow from his drink, licked his lips, and watched the little white ball as it spun around the wheel. He felt like he was a kid on a roller coaster feeling the exhilaration of the ride. All those at the table cranked their necks and leaned toward the wheel so they could see the ball as it bounced toward the winning number.

"Zero!" Frank yelled angrily at the wheel. "Who the fuck plays zero?"

"Sir," said the pit boss as he leaned over the table, "we respectfully request no swearing at the tables."

"Oh, right. Sorry." And then added "fuck you" under his breath.

No problem, thought Frank, *one of my numbers has to hit*. He again bet a total of $1800 on six numbers. Again, no hit. Frank bet like an intoxicated rookie, and chased his bets until he had lost $16,000.

☙

The Old Ebbitt Grill was hosting a typical lunch crowd comprised of political insiders, business professionals, journalists, and a tourist or two. Being situated just blocks from the White House, it catered to a relatively elite clientele. The patrons could be seen periodically raising their heads and looking around like ostriches in case someone important was nearby. Lou considered Jack's history and how fortunate he was to have Jack assigned to his team.

As a Navy SEAL, Jack had excelled at the initial basic underwater demolition training and responded well physically and mentally to the rigorous training. He was already recognized as an excellent swimmer by the age of eight. Having grown up in California with easy access to the beach, he learned to surf and swam on his high school's swim team, setting state records in the 200 breaststroke and 100 fly. He knew college was not for him and was always up for a challenge, so he enlisted as a Navy SEAL.

Due to his prowess as a SEAL and his intellect, Jack was assigned to counterterrorism, where he spent the majority of his nineteen-year career. His had been a decorated career, as he was admired by superiors, peers, and subordinates for his courage, loyalty, ability to think under pressure, and operational success rate.

Jack's career had taken a fateful turn one night in Iraq. He had been in charge of sixteen men assigned to take out a small band of jihadists hiding out in a home in Fallujah. Surveillance had identified ten armed men. The Blackhawk helicopters had landed without incident a mile outside the city limits. The pilots and three SEALs remained with the choppers. The remaining eleven men converged upon the target.

The night was clear with good visibility, but regardless, the SEALs wore night vision goggles. Jack stationed five men at the rear of the home and five in front, awaiting his command to enter. Given it was 2:30 a.m., the assumption was they would find the combatants asleep. Jack climbed atop an old truck approximately twenty-five feet from the house. He stood on the cab and took out his binoculars to make sure there were no sentries posted on the roof. As soon as he brought the binoculars to his eyes, the house erupted into a ball of flame. The blast threw Jack ten feet through the air.

It had been a trap. None of his men survived the explosion. He was able to make it safely back to the helicopters, but his mission had failed, and miserably. Shortly after the incident, Jack threw himself totally into his work in an attempt to forget. He volunteered for the most dangerous missions and often, to the point that he did not take any time off for three consecutive years. He eventually crashed and crashed hard. He spent a month in a psych ward learning how to deal with grief and death. The Navy respectfully accepted his resignation and acknowledged his decorated and exemplary career and service to his country. Jack had worked through the grief, but not the anger, and that anger propelled him to continue to support the efforts against terrorism as a contractor.

As soon as the two were seated at their table, Lou's phone rang. He reluctantly pulled the phone from his coat pocket to check who was calling. "Sorry, Jack, I have to take this."

"No worries. Take your time," Jack responded as Lou left the table to find a relatively quiet alcove to take the call.

Jack's mind wandered back to his last assignment before heading to D.C. The five-inch serrated blade missed his midsection by at least a foot as the man swung it wildly, displaying his lack of fighting skills. Jack had singled him out following a brief exchange the man had had with the operation's primary target, a recruiter for ISIS. He needed him alive and talking and felt confident he would be able to subdue the smaller man without injury, but experience told him never to underestimate an adversary. Training also taught Jack to check his blind side, which he did and found no one else coming down the alley.

The man, eyes wide with fear, was now holding the knife to his own neck and yelling at Jack in what he suspected was Farsi, the preferred language of the region.

Jack's hand-to-hand combat skills were instinctive after decades of experience, but he had not encountered an adversary trying to kill themselves. This was new territory. Jack, now within three feet of the man, slowly lowered his hands and took two deliberate steps backward in an attempt to get the man to lower the blade. The man's eyes darted wildly from Jack's feet to his eyes, attempting to determine whether Jack meant him harm. Although it was barely discernable for the untrained eye, he could see the man's grip on the knife loosen ever so slightly. Jack began to take one more deliberate step backward, looking for an opening. As Jack's left foot was mid-step, the man began to slowly lower the blade, which prompted Jack to reverse his back step into a forward lunge, wherein he planted and turned his left foot and brought his right leg up for a side-thrust kick. He had estimated the distance from the man perfectly, such that his foot landed squarely in the man's face, knocking him off his feet. Although he was able to hang on to the knife, the kick had rendered the man all but unconscious, and Jack easily disarmed him.

As the man attempted to regain his bearings, Jack threw the knife to the side and placed a call to the acquisition team waiting in the immediate area, providing them his location so they could retrieve their new prisoner and sequester him for questioning. Then Jack examined the face of the man he determined could not have been more than seventeen years old. A mere boy recruited to kill for reasons he probably didn't understand or comprehend. Because of his youth, Jack hoped he would share information sooner than later and avoid interrogation.

Jack had been so immersed in his thoughts that he didn't realize Lou had returned until Lou asked him a question.

"Have you ever eaten here, Jack?"

"Uh no, can't say that I have."

"Well, it is known for its jumbo crab cakes. Better said, I'm known to be here for the crab cakes. In addition, on occasion you can bump into the who's who in politics if you're unfortunate enough."

"I wouldn't know anyone if I ran right into them. I have to admit, I have lived under a mushroom working in the Middle East for the past year or so."

"What are the odds of you chasing down jihad recruiters and my first assignment is trying to place moles with these recruiters?"

"Must be fate. So, what's my assignment?"

"I don't believe everything adds up now, but can't put a finger on it. I need you to be another set of eyes and ears; a very quiet, invisible set. Only the DNI and I know that you will be on the payroll for this assignment."

"Okay, I can handle that."

"Good. I want you to start with surveillance of some of the team members."

"Really, you have a rotten egg in the basket?"

"Not sure, but want to be."

"No problem. Who am I spying on?"

"Frank Conover and Sara Fahridi. Frank is an interrogator and has been with the agency for ten years or so. Sara is Deeprose's field liaison. This is her first intelligence mission—supposedly. As a matter of fact, Sara was at the elevator bank as we were entering earlier today."

"The Middle Eastern woman?"

"Why, yes. Did you see her?"

"As a matter of fact, I did notice her."

"I guess your skills are as sharp as ever."

"When we met the other day, you said you wished there were two of me."

"Ah, yes. I just think we need another set of dependable eyes and ears on the ground in the Middle East. You mentioned an Abir."

"I use him often when I can't go solo. He is good and dependable. Abir's journey to working with the U.S. is a tragic one, but one that has happened often since the formation of ISIS. His one and only brother had been falsely accused of helping the infidels and was butchered like a pig. Abir has committed to getting even and figured the best way was to help the U.S. and its allies defeat ISIS. And it pays better than farming."

"Excellent. We may need him."

CHAPTER 20

North generously tipped the man who had security clearance to Langley for the sole purpose of shining his shoes. The income from North alone allowed the man to pay one-third of his monthly mortgage payment. As North considered the sheen on his Allen Edmonds, he realized he needed to fabricate a relatively more substantive blow to Deeprose. Clapper's demeanor during the last few days had led North to believe that the DNI was going to give Pendleton a little more rope than he should be given. *Keep your anger in check*, thought North. He reminded himself that he had dealt with idiots and imbeciles his entire life and this was simply one more dance with the dumbasses.

He had begun thinking in terms of timing. He needed Pendleton out as soon as possible, but what was a reasonable time given the circumstances he had to work with? If Pendleton was able to keep the job for more than a few months, it would be harder and harder to displace him unless he made a colossal gaffe. North thought this unlikely based upon his assessment of Pendleton thus far; Pendleton was handling the job and himself reasonably well. Regardless, North was the best man for the job and the country needed him in that role.

What were Pendleton's weaknesses? How could he exploit them to take Pendleton off his game and get him to become careless and ineffective? Better yet, how could he tarnish his credibility, possibly raising suspicion about his allegiance to the flag? North needed to set a trap, a very elaborate one in which his boss would be blackballed and North would come out smelling like a rose. North did his best thinking in his home office. He decided to head there immediately.

"Jake, I'm going to finish the day working in my home office. Don't hesitate to contact me for any reason. I have to take my wife to dinner tonight, so be sure to interrupt me, even if it is not urgent."

"Understood, Mr. North," responded his administrative assistant.

Jake had worked for North for six years and had come to know the man well, including his narcissistic tendencies, dislike of his wife, lack of friends, and his penchant for always seeming to come out on top. Jake—a thirty-three-year-old closeted homosexual—was efficient, discreet, and loyal to a fault. He was paid well for managing North's affairs and ensuring his boss was never put in a compromising position. Jake was as effective at working the network of his peers at Langley as North was working the highest levels of the intelligence community. They made a good pair.

"What time is your dinner?" asked Jake as North headed out the door.

"Eight. Don't be late," North said with a rueful smile.

"Got it."

As North headed out of the building, he knew he could count on Jake to place a timely call to him at approximately 7:45 as the couple was heading to dinner. North would apologize profusely to his bride again for yet another CIA crisis that required his immediate attention. He would divert his BMW from its original destination to CIA headquarters. He would give his wife the keys to the BMW, begging her to invite a friend to take his place at the Capital Grille for dinner, then immediately go to the motor pool to sign out the black suburban he had reserved for the evening. The only plans he had for the evening were to think about his dilemma, and he certainly couldn't do that listening to his sedate mate chatting on about insignificant things over dinner. He acknowledged that he had not had sex with her for more than a month and he would have to oblige her within the next week; otherwise, she would begin this obnoxious pouting, which he abhorred more than sex with her.

North drove to the National Mall and parked such that he could view the Washington Monument, which he had often used for inspiration during his career. He never tired of marveling at the obelisk built in 1884, commemorating the nation's inaugural president. As he sat in his car, watching the sun slowly descend behind the Lincoln Memorial, North realized he needed to strike hard and fast.

Think, think, think.

The most tried and true reasons for someone's undoing were sex and money. Pendleton came from family money and never really needed to work, so it would be difficult to contrive a plot wherein money incented unacceptable behavior. North had come to know that Pendleton was happily married for more than thirty years. Could it be believed that Mr. Louis Pendleton, devoted husband and military career man, was having an affair?

People were having affairs all the time. Our weakening social fabric somewhat accepted extramarital affairs for those in leadership positions. However, the administration would not allow the president's handpicked director of the CIA to remain in office after such a scandal was made public.

CHAPTER 21

Jack decided to begin his snooping with Sara. He had to acknowledge that spying on her wouldn't be the worst assignment he had ever had. He had a couple of hours to work at her home before she was scheduled to end her day at Langley. With the sophistication of today's listening devices, Jack would not have to break into her house, but rather place the devices around the perimeter. In addition, he was installing two action activated video cameras. It would take him no more than thirty minutes, dressed as a cable repairman from a known D.C. cable company, to complete the installations.

He had ensured that the video feeds from each camera and microphone were working before he exited the van and headed across the street to Sara's unit. Given her Old Town brownstone was not a separate condominium, but rather one of six units housed in one building, it was easier to go unnoticed, as everyone would assume he was working on someone else's unit.

He set his ladder against the brick façade two feet to the right of her front door, climbed to the roofline, and quickly installed the battery-powered camera, which weighed less than one pound, under the gutter. He then installed the small listening device four inches from the camera. They were well hidden and could be seen only if someone was specifically looking for them. The camera would catch anyone entering or exiting the front door, while the microphone would capture any conversation within the unit. He repeated the exercise near the slider in the rear after finding and opening the latch for the gate, allowing him entrance to her private courtyard.

Upon finishing, he went to his nearby rented van to double check both the audio and video feeds. Fortunately, Sara had a clock that chimed on the half hour and hour, which confirmed the listening devices were working properly. Satisfied, he again exited the van and installed a mini shotgun microphone in an oak tree across the street to pick up any outdoor conversations. Finally, he would place a GPS tracker on her automobile later that evening after she returned from work. Conveniently, their homes were only ten miles apart.

Jack parked the van a block down from Frank's house, checked the equipment, and carried the ladder to the front of the house. He was struck by the relatively dilapidated state of the house and lawn. The house needed a coat of paint, while several shingles were missing from the roof. The bushes surrounding the house were overgrown, while the flowerbeds were overrun with weeds. If any of the neighbors noticed him, they would probably hope he was there to repair something. When he peeked into one of the windows, he found the inside as disheveled as the outside.

He installed the surveillance similarly to how he had at Sara's. He decided to drive back to Sara's place and see if she came home within the next hour or so. He parked the van around the corner and patiently waited. He wished he had eyes and ears within Langley to know when

Frank and Sara were coming and going; however, he was flying solo with the exception of Lou, and he couldn't expect him to keep tabs on them.

At approximately 6:15, Jack saw and subsequently heard Sara arriving home. He saw her approach and enter her front door. The listening device was able to pick up the slightest of sounds, including whispered conversations. The unfortunate thing was they also picked up other subtle sounds, such as someone using the bathroom, which Sara had just completed doing. Sara was walking briskly through the house, revealed by the *clickclack* of her heels on the hardwood floor, indicating she was either late for something, or was not quite ready to relax from the day's work. Jack thought he heard the refrigerator open, followed by a silverware drawer. He assumed she was preparing a meal, which would provide him the opportunity to place the GPS device under her car.

No sooner had he attached the device to the undercarriage of her car, he heard her front door open through his earpiece. He immediately pulled down the black baseball cap he was wearing to better shield his face and began walking down the sidewalk away from Sara's brownstone. She must have eaten a quick snack or brought the food with her.

After Sara pulled away from the curb where she was parked, Jack quickly double-backed to the van and turned on the GPS to learn where she was headed and if it was worth following her. It didn't take him long to learn that she was headed to the airport, which was only five miles away. If she was boarding a flight, he had better find out where she was headed, especially if this was going to be her last time in D.C. for a while. As unlikely as it was that Sara was fleeing for whatever reason, Jack had to consider all of the possible scenarios.

He quickly drove to the airport and found her car parked in front of terminal B. He parked fifteen spots away and darted into the terminal, which housed several carriers that flew international routes. This was yet another indication that Sara might be flying the coop.

Although Jack did not hear her fumble with any luggage while she was home, she could have easily packed a bag earlier and had it stowed in the trunk. But why would she bother stopping home? Unless, of course, she had forgotten something vital to her travels, such as a passport. Regardless, Jack started with the check-in counters at Delta and United for any departing international flights, which were the best odds of finding her if she was leaving the country.

After eight minutes of searching, he moved toward the gates between terminal A and B that housed American Airlines, JetBlue, and Virgin America. On his way, he spotted her purchasing bottled water at a vendor kiosk. He did not observe any luggage. She could have already checked in, but he did not notice a carry-on either. Given this, plus the bottled water, which would be confiscated by TSA at the security check-in, Jack deduced she was picking someone up. He would now make himself invisible and track her movements.

As soon as he sat down his earpiece *pinged* with Frank's arrival home.

The first thing Jack picked up was the clinking of ice in a glass while Frank whistled. The man was definitely in a good mood. He listened to Frank fumble around his house for the next several minutes, while he kept an eye on Sara. Jack heard Frank unzipping something, possibly luggage of some sort, which indicated Frankie boy was going to take a weekend trip. His two targets were definitely not homebodies.

Sara seemed annoyed as she routinely looked at the arriving flights monitor. Given the only delayed flight was an American Airlines out of New York's JFK, Jack assumed her package was on that flight. The monitor indicated she only had another ten minutes until it arrived.

If Sara was, in fact, the rotten egg Lou was concerned about, then it was possible she was meeting a collaborator of some sort. Based upon his international travel experience, Jack knew that JFK serviced Middle Eastern countries, which increased the probability Sara was picking up someone not necessarily fond of the United States.

❧

Ms. Toni picked up after three rings.

"It has been a while," North began.

"Who may I say is calling?" she asked, even though she recognized North's voice. Ms. Toni was wise enough never to admit to recognizing one of her client's voices. It could prove lethal. She was especially leery, given that this was Shay's biggest client and she had ended up dead due to an alleged burglary gone bad.

"Mr. Jonathan Doe the third," responded North.

"How are you, Mr. Doe?"

"I'm in need of a special service that will pay very handsomely."

"We aim to please and can meet most of our clients' needs. How can we help?"

"This particular service is somewhat beyond your core competency. Simply stated, I need a woman to claim to have been having an affair with a high-profile individual."

Ms. Toni did not miss a beat, regardless of her initial inclination to yell *Hell, no* into the phone. "Tell me more."

"We need someone who is in her early to mid-forties, no criminal background, has a track record of verifiable employment, is believable, and will not waver, regardless of the pressure and attention. It is likely this person may have to testify, while a polygraph is doubtful. Your fee will include a sum allocated for any legal-related costs."

"I'll need a few days to build an employment history utilizing a few of my other, relatively more legitimate businesses. But other than that, no problem."

"Excellent. When you have the personnel file complete, please e-mail it to my Gmail account, which you should have on file."

"Again, no problem, you should still have my Cayman bank account number on file, correct?"

"Indeed. You may look forward to a deposit of three-hundred-and-fifty-thousand dollars once I approve the personnel file."

"To employ the person I have in mind, it will require a minimum of five-hundred-thousand dollars."

"Done," and with that North clicked off.

☙

Jack watched Sara watching the passengers flow through the concourse exit. A Middle Eastern man wearing a turban, wire-rim glasses, wrinkled khakis, and a sport coat one size too small lit up a smile when he saw Sara. His smile was all but hidden amid the scraggly black beard his small, round face bore. Jack quickly dismissed any thought of a terrorist, based on the man's appearance. This guy had to be friend or family.

"Oh, Habib, it has been too long," Sara said as she embraced her older and only brother in a hug.

"Two years Sara; much too long."

"Let's not talk here. I'm parked just outside. Let's get out of here."

"As you wish. You were always the boss, even though I'm three years older."

"Get used to it. There is something very strange going on."

Jack followed Sara and the bespectacled man from a respectable distance. He assumed they were heading to her brownstone, but assumptions could often get one killed. He could kick himself for not placing listening devices in her car. Maybe he was a little rusty. Regardless, he had barely enough time to place the GPS on Sara's car, and he would place listening devices inside her car if the opportunity presented itself. As the little caravan headed toward Alexandria, Jack heard Frank leave his house.

As expected, Sara returned home and the duo went inside immediately. The man had brought only a small carry-on, which indicated he was not staying long. Their conversation began, or rather resumed from the car ride, immediately upon entering the house.

☙

Sara was adamant to get as much information on the table so she did not miss anything. "Habib, let's go through it again; take your time."

Habib responded, "We've already been through it. I can't remember anything else."

"I understand. Maybe a good night's sleep will help and we can revisit it again tomorrow."

"Thank you. Now, please explain to me, as best you can, what you're involved with."

"I work for Homeland Security. What I have told you about my job as a Middle Eastern expert of sorts is true. Up until my most recent assignment, the projects I have been involved with have been fairly generic and routine in terms of their impact upon U.S. security. My current assignment still leverages my skill set, but the mission is classified top secret and is singularly focused on terrorist organizations, which one would expect given my employer and skills."

"You must possess some pretty important information, given my captors asked you for it and a condition of my release was you providing it."

"It's complicated."

"Oh, really? Tell me about it, Sara. I'm plucked from my rewarding job and life, held by these gun- and machete-toting terrorists threatening to behead me if you don't give up the goods."

"I'm sorry. I'm simply trying to protect you by not sharing any more than I should. Based upon what has happened, I think the more you know, the more at risk you are."

"I'm your brother, for God's sake! How much more risk can you put me in? This is my life and I want to know what the hell you have gotten me into."

"I have not gotten you into anything. Listen, I know you're angry and I would be mad as hell too."

"Sara, I want to know everything, from the start."

"I will not divulge any information about my job or my current assignment. I love my job and my country, and I will do nothing to be disloyal. Well, almost nothing." Sara began to cry, quietly at first, but it grew to a healthy sob within a minute.

She leaned into her brother. He hugged her and quietly told her, "I know you're dedicated to your job and your country and evidently your love for me forced you to compromise your convictions. You were placed under duress, given a short time to react. I'm sorry I haven't thanked you for saving my life yet, but thank you. What you did was courageous, although knowing you I trust you believe you have done a great injustice. At the end of the day, blood is thicker than all and you and I must stick together through thick or thin. You did the right thing, Sara, whatever you did, because I'm here, alive, with you."

Through sniffles, Sara said, "Thank you for that. I have been very conflicted. I know I did the right thing, but as a result, a portion of our mission was compromised. One of the bad guys was killed, which isn't necessarily a bad thing, given Homeland Security's charter, but I'm still somewhat remorseful. But you know what, more than anything, I'm angry. Why they would blackmail me, a relative nobody, seems a stretch. I don't believe I have been angrier in my life, but I don't have a tangible target for my anger."

"How do you mean?"

Sara then told Habib the entire story, including her thought processes and daily movements from the time she opened the videotape. She could tell by the look on Habib's face that he had a whole new level of respect for her. Twenty minutes and a cheese sandwich later, Sara could hear Habib sleeping heavily in the spare bedroom.

CHAPTER 22

North's call had the intended effect upon Ms. Toni. She was afraid. The fear she experienced was more for the ongoing viability and success of her business rather than her personal safety. Supporting this type of request could prove detrimental to her ability to carry on her escort service. She knew she was trapped; she could not refuse, knowing Doe would kill her as he had most assuredly done to Shay. It didn't matter that Ms. Toni did not know North's real identity. It was enough to know of him and what he was capable of.

The woman she had in mind for the job was herself. Who else could she trust to pull off such a ruse? Having been exposed to the backstabbing and gamesmanship that went on in D.C. for the better part of her career, she had no illusions regarding the magnitude of North's request. She knew the risk associated with her profession would eventually outweigh the reward, but she had hoped to continue the escort service for a few more years.

There were basically two choices. One was to refuse the request, which was all but suicide. The second was to position herself as the mistress, pocket the $500,000, finance the purchase of her escort service for one of her senior employees, and move to the French Riviera sooner than planned. At forty-five years old, Ms. Toni would be the right age for a mistress for an older, successful man. She acknowledged that the high forehead and broad nose she inherited from her father had limited her suitors throughout her life, but she was attractive enough to make this ruse work. And what man didn't like an extra twenty pounds to love?

As with most effective leaders, Ms. Toni was logical and action-oriented. Upon reaching the decision to act the role of mistress within an hour of speaking with North, she immediately began making a list of people and other resources she would need to help create the life and career history her role would require. This would cost her up to $50,000, mostly to those she knew who would lie to their mother, but the payoffs and relative safety of this choice necessitated it.

Within two days, she would create the identity of a single, never-before married, forty-something who was blessed with a large inheritance and had spent the majority of her working career volunteering, mostly for disadvantaged-women's organizations. Her neighbors, if asked, would honestly convey she was a recluse and was rarely seen. She would not have had a routine schedule or related commitments for the past decade, providing ample opportunity to manipulate her whereabouts to complement whatever free times her alleged married lover had in his calendar. The net impact was that anyone researching her background would find very little, while what they *did* find would be mundane and barely newsworthy if this charade got a lot of attention.

❦

When Frank eventually lost all $16,000 and became belligerent, he was asked to leave the casino. Thereafter, he checked into a local hotel.

Frank woke up at the hotel on Saturday morning with what he called the double-sicks: He had a raging hangover and had lost a shitload of money. How in the hell could his luck have been so bad for so long? Casinos were so good at what they did. They sucked you dry and gave you some paltry incentive to get you back to lose whatever other assets they hadn't gotten their greedy hands on. And the addicted gambler always fell for it. It was 11:00 in the morning as Frank sat on his hotel bed, staring at the casino voucher, knowing exactly what he and his remaining $4,000 were going to do.

Four aspirins, sixteen ounces of water, two bananas, and a shower later, Mr. Frank Conover would be back on the adrenaline ride. Hell, he still had a fortune at home and was due for a good run. Lingering in the back of his mind were the potential repercussions of his filing an accurate interrogation report. Another day of drinking and gambling would help numb his anxiety.

By two in the afternoon, Frank was broke and drunk. As he drove home in a depressed stupor, he had to admit the saving grace was that he had not brought all of the cash with him; otherwise, it might all be gone. In a little less than two hours, he would be home safe in his bed, sleeping off the binge of the past twenty-four hours.

❧

Having just spoken with Ms. Toni, North thought back on his engagements with Shay and how much he enjoyed them. He should have kept his mouth shut, but it wasn't his fault. They had picked someone else to be director. Now Shay was gone and he had to manage his marriage.

North rolled off of his wife, attempting to calculate how many times he had had to make love to her during their thirty-year marriage. He had never been passionately in love with her. Her family wealth and connections in D.C. were what he wanted. He used both to support his rise in power and influence during his celebrated career.

He had to continue on with the marital ruse until her mother, age eighty-four, finally passed away and the inheritance was complete. Her father had passed five years prior and North was hopeful that his mother-in-law would soon follow so he could ensure he shared in the windfall inheritance before he divorced.

As his wife rambled on about how much she loved being with him and how they needed a quiet getaway, North was anxious to get to his e-mail and read Conover's most recent report. The report should be another disappointment for Deeprose and Pendleton's reign as director. The president would find it unacceptable that the U.S. had a coveted ISIS terrorist captive and the CIA's interrogation couldn't get any intelligence out of him—how perfect!

An hour later, Pat heard a crash in her husband's home office and hurried from the kitchen to find out what had happened. She found the door slightly ajar and heard her husband first as she approached.

"Goddamn sorry son of a bitch. How dare he double-cross me?"

"Dear, what's the matter?" Pat said as she opened the door all the way. North watched her as she looked at him and then the taxidermy from his big game hunting excursions that adorned the walls. He knew she hated them.

North quickly composed himself. "Oh, sorry honey, just having a little problem with my financial planner. He told me he was going to sell some shares before the market closed last week and I just learned he did not."

"It must have been a big trade, seeing you threw one of your favorite drinking tumblers against the wall, apparently just missing your prized lion head. You don't miss too often," Pat added in an attempt to lighten the situation.

"Now I'm embarrassed. I guess I need a little break from work. These weekend emergencies are beginning to take their toll on this old man. I'm sorry I startled you. I'll finish up here shortly."

"Sounds like a good time for you and I to take that getaway."

Oh good God, North thought. "Possibly when things slow down a bit, dear. There is no way I could break away now. Hopefully, over the July Fourth holiday in a month or so we will have some extra time."

"Love you, Richard."

"Ah, love you too."

As soon as Pat left, North went back to his computer monitor and once again read the interrogation report from Frank.

Un-fucking-believable! What was he thinking?

He was either overly patriotic or extremely foolish, or both. Did Frank truly think that $200,000 would fall into his lap if the payer did not have the ability to verify that he kept his end of the bargain?

***

The Deeprose team assembled in Pendleton's office as soon as possible after reading the interrogation report. Louis began, "If, in fact, the developing network and alliances are real and they are considering biological weapons, we need to be on Homeland Security's advisory system's severe or red alert immediately with a major reallocation of resources to protect our nation!"

The veins in North's neck were about to explode. He could have killed Conover right then and there. Had Conover kept to the agreement, North would have been able to annihilate any jihadi insurgency before it became known and lethal. Now Pendleton would be taking the lead—his lead—in escalating the war against terrorism.

"It is absolutely frightening," added Sara.

"Let's talk this scenario through to get a feel for the ramifications," Lou continued.

Talk through the scenario? We've done enough talking. God, these people are all idiots. If we had initiated an aggressive military campaign as the center strategy of Deeprose, we would not find ourselves and our country in this position, North thought to himself.

Lou continued, "Okay, let's begin with the organizations supposedly part of this newly formed superpower. Hezbollah, based in Lebanon, is backed by Syria and Iran and is a major foe of Israel. Their leader,

Hassan Nasrallah, has been consistent in the use of violence and support of fanatical leadership in the Muslim world. Their close alliance with Iran and Iran's continued pursuit of the development of nuclear weapons has been on our radar screen for some time.

"Mullah Omar and the Taliban are no surprise, as he and bin Laden had been tied at the hip for some time. Since Hezbollah has thrown in, it only makes sense that Hamas has joined in, as this group is arguably a division of Hezbollah. Khaled Meshaall is their current leader.

"Jamaat Ansar al-Sunna, grounded in Iraq, should be considered the wild card of the bunch. If, in fact, they have been managing the indoctrination and military training of all of the recruits that have flooded to Iraq for the past several years, their numbers could have grown to two-hundred-thousand, as the interrogation report indicates. ISIS fighters alone total approximately a hundred-thousand.

"Given the history of these organizations' inability to play nice together, even though one of their common objectives is to rid us infidels from their soil, why would they decide to form a common union now?" North asked, trying to slow Pendleton's momentum.

"If you recall, shortly before bin Laden was killed, he referred to himself as the stable force among the brotherhood of Muslim leaders and that we would be sorry if his voice was ever quieted. The formation of ISIS and this allegiance could be the very thing he warned us about. If these groups are now joined at the hip, we can assume that they have forged an alliance, most likely a newly formed, universal fatwa, or manifesto, which includes targeting the U.S. beyond Middle Eastern borders. Removing the infidels, or Westerners, from their respective countries has been the only common objective among them."

Sara interjected, "The success of our remaining Deeprose mole is critical in the short term."

"Give me a break!" yelled North, finding an outlet for his anger. "We don't have time to fiddle-fuck around with any more cloak-and-dagger spy games. We need to identify their nerve centers and blow them to kingdom come, or to Allah, wherever these wingnuts go."

"Easy, Richard. We appreciate your position and understand your inclination to go in with guns blazing, but let's take a minute to digest the information."

"Digest the information? This is ridiculous. The fanatics are working together to use biological weapons and what are we doing? Waiting until they use them and kill thousands of Americans? I want no part of a weak and ineffective initiative." And with that, North stormed out of the room, slamming the door behind him.

Pendleton turned to Sara and shrugged his shoulders. "He'll be okay—everybody needs to blow off a little steam now and then. Sara, I appreciate the thought and there is no harm in us continuing with Deeprose. I'm going to call the DNI and suggest an immediate briefing with the president, which if it happens will most likely result in an emergency meeting of the Joint Chiefs."

"This is getting scary," Sara exclaimed.

"I think we're past scary."

CHAPTER 23

At six o'clock, Jack found himself primping in front of the mirror, trying to decide what to wear. His options were limited, so he went with the slacks from his new suit and a cashmere sweater that accentuated his muscular frame. He certainly wasn't disappointed when Lou asked him to meet with Sara under the pretense of getting her perspective on a new Homeland Security initiative and to give Lou his assessment on whether she was a spy or not. He wondered if she would recognize him from their quick eye-to-eye exchange at Langley. If so, he had an alibi prepared.

Twenty minutes later he was at the restaurant, securing a table in the back. Five minutes later, Sara walked in, dressed in a tight-fitting yellow sundress that fit her like a glove. She immediately spotted him and headed over to the table, doing her best to keep the smile she felt from spreading across her face. "Hello, there. Are you my six-thirty?"

"I am indeed, Ms. Fahridi. My name is Jack from Homeland Security."

"I've seen you before, at Langley, just a few days ago."

"Yes, I believe you're right. I was providing Mr. Pendleton a report. Very standard stuff."

"And you come all the way to Langley to provide a face-to-face report on so-called standard stuff?"

"Well, Lou and I have become friends over the years and decided to meet over lunch."

"How interesting. How long have you been with Homeland Security? I don't recall ever seeing you. Which department do you work for?"

Jack thought it would be less risky to weave in some truth. "I was in the Navy most of my career and that is where Lou and I met and worked together for many years. I have been with Homeland Security for only three months; I work in border security."

"I see. Well then, since you brought me out on a Saturday night, are you going to buy me a latte?"

"With pleasure."

"Where should we start, Jack? May I call you Jack? I guess I have to, since you haven't given me your last name or your business card," she said.

"I apologize, but I was given instructions to provide my first name only. I trust you understand?"

"The more I work at Langley, the more I understand."

"Is this your first assignment at Langley?"

"And what assignment would that be?"

"I don't know. I was simply making conversation. I do know, based upon our employer's records, that you have worked at Homeland Security for some time, have an extremely high IQ, have been successful in every project you have been involved with, are fluent in both Middle Eastern cultures and languages, and that you have a strong work ethic."

What Jack wanted to add was that she was extremely gorgeous and that she had his undivided attention.

"Well, I think you may have exaggerated what is in my personnel file, but one's self-esteem can never have enough stroking. And yes, this is my first assignment with the CIA. And yes, I do admit I'm a novice of sorts. We all have to start somewhere and sometime."

Although Jack had not been on a date for some time, he was pretty sure Sara was flirting. Or was she? Jack was never a real believer in chemistry, but he was beginning to be.

He took the bait without hesitation. "I agree, and I'd like to help."

At this, Sara blushed and lowered her head, not sure what the next move would be, but Jack smoothly handled that.

"I have a proposal. How about we complete the discussion about the Homeland Security operation as quickly as we can, then take advantage of a beautiful spring evening in D.C. with dinner and conversation?"

"Deal."

As after-dinner coffee was served, Jack realized he had lost all track of time and forgot to report in to Lou. When he excused himself from the table to use the restroom and check his cell phone, he had three texts from Lou, each containing an increasing sense of urgency regarding a response. He felt like a kid caught out too late on prom night.

❧

At first Frank thought he was dreaming, but when pain from the jab to his stomach brought him fully awake, he quickly looked around his bedroom. It was dusk, but there was just enough of the day's remaining sunlight to illuminate the two goons with ski masks hovering over him in his bed. As he was hunched over, trying to catch his breath, one of the goons pulled his arms behind him and clamped on a pair of handcuffs. With this complete, he was shoved face down onto his bed while they bound his legs in duct tape from knees to ankles. He was then turned over and tossed on the floor. Each goon grabbed one foot and dragged him into the bathroom.

"We are going to ask you several questions and we want the truth," said the man who had taped his legs.

"I understand," Frank choked out between ragged breaths.

The other man brought in a chair from the kitchen and they hoisted him onto it. Frank realized with certainty that whoever had given him the cash was pretty high up the food chain and had somehow found out that he had not held up his end of the bargain. It was also obvious his chances of surviving this were pretty slim.

Frank's torso was duct-taped to the back of the chair and his already taped legs were taped to the front two legs of the chair such that he couldn't move. He and the chair were then positioned perpendicular to the bathtub with the back legs two inches from the tub. Frank knew what was coming next. He and Jim had used a variation of this technique. The combination of the immobility and the rocking back of the chair on its two back legs accelerated the anxiety felt by the captive and would often result in obtaining the desired information sooner, rather than later.

"There is no need to do this!" screamed Frank in a high-pitched voice. "I'll tell you whatever you want. I have nothing to hide."

"Where's the fun in that?" said the man holding the chair. "Although me and Johnny here would just as soon get what we came for as soon as possible and leave, our instructions are to make this as uncomfortable and painful as possible."

"Please, I know very well how this works and that I'll eventually provide you all the information you want, so let's save ourselves some time."

The chair was tilted on its back two legs such that Frank's head was hanging over the tub. Frank and Jim had practiced waterboarding on one another as part of their training to understand its effect, so they could refine their techniques to push the captive to the brink without harming them. He now leaned on that experience to prepare himself for what was next.

The one called Johnny brought a water pitcher from the kitchen, which he filled with cold water from the tub faucet. Frank forced himself to relax and not fight it; he had to last forty seconds, assuming these goons knew what they were doing.

The other guy pulled a towel tight over Frank's face as Johnny slowly poured the water onto the towel in a small, continuous circle where

Frank's nose and mouth were. Frank anticipated the flow and moved his head up and down and side to side to divert as much of the water as possible in order to take quick bursts of air through his mouth, such that he could blow it out his nose in an attempt to minimize the water that entered his throat and lungs. He told himself he could last through the pitcher of water, which he did, relatively successfully.

When the water stopped and the chair was brought upright, Frank exaggerated the coughing and sputtering to make it appear that he was suffering more than he was.

"Where's the money?" Johnny asked.

"It's—it's in several places," choked Frank. "Forty thousand dollars is in five separate banks, eight thousand in each. The bank information and related receipts are in the top drawer of my desk. I paid off a sixty-two-thousand, five-hundred-dollar debt to a loan shark last week. There is seventy-seven-thousand, five-hundred dollars in the box underneath my bed. I lost the remaining twenty-thousand at the casino over the past few days."

Johnny brought a second water pitcher from the kitchen into the bathroom.

"You really expect us to believe you lost twenty-thousand dollars at a casino? You got balls to lie, pal," the other guy said.

"I'm not lying. Listen, please. I think I still have the receipt for my hotel in the car. And there's a water bottle in the car with the logo from the casino on it."

"Big fucking deal. I think you won money at the casino and are trying to hide that along with the twenty thousand."

With that, the chair was tipped back and the waterboarding began again. But this time, two pitchers were used, one right after the other, and Frank could not keep the water from entering his throat and lungs. He began to struggle against the duct tape with every fiber of his being. The water had flowed for longer than forty seconds. He was going to drown. Just when he thought his heart was going to explode and he was going to black out, the water stopped. It took what seemed like an eternity to get the smallest breath of air into his lungs as it fought for space with the water he had ingested. He coughed, sputtered, wheezed, and choked for several minutes.

"Where's the rest of the money?" Johnny asked again.

"Gone. I really lost it at the casino. You have to believe me."

"Who else knows about this?"

"No one, I swear."

"C'mon now, out with the truth."

"Why would I be stupid enough to tell anyone?"

"Why would you be stupid enough to get yourself in this position? Because you're fucking stupid."

Two more pitchers and a near-drowning later, Frank found himself fighting for his breath again.

"Who else did you tell?" Again, Johnny asked.

"*No one!*" Frank screamed.

The other guy then pulled a syringe out of his pocket and emptied its contents between the big toe and index toe on Frank's left foot. The drug cocktail, primarily composed of GHB, would begin to take effect in less than one minute. The general anesthetic would render Frank unconscious, during which time they would remove Frank's pajamas, place him in a tub full of warm water, slit his wrists, return the chair and water pitchers to their rightful places, clean up their mess, take the cash, metal box, and bank information, and quietly leave Frank to bleed out. The razor-blade cuts on Frank's arms and wrists would camouflage any potential bruising from the handcuffs.

Armed with the bank information, a falsified death certificate, and power of attorney, the two brothers would have the five bank accounts cleaned out and closed by 9:30 on Monday morning, thereby completing their assignment and payment for their services, as they were told to keep all the cash they confiscated. The last thing to do was to send a confirmation e-mail to their boss and copy an anonymous e-mail address they were given. It read:

Target compromised following interrogation resulting in recovery of $117,500; $82,500 lost to untraceable sources. 95 percent odds no one else made aware of transaction. One note, surveillance equipment not found upon first engagement six days ago. However, upon sweep of premises this engagement found sophisticated surveillance equipment around the perimeter, which was removed prior to entry. Out.

CHAPTER 24

Human Resources delivered the files, hard copy, to Jake by 11:00 a.m. on Monday, and they were on North's freshly polished desk by 11:02. North poured over Pendleton's appointment calendar, searching for pockets of unaccountable time and/or routines, wherein a secret rendezvous would be difficult to deny. He had discovered that Pendleton ran thirty minutes almost every day with a longer run on either Saturday or Sunday each week, which required at least two hours to complete. There were also a number of trips requiring air travel and overnight stays that would be helpful. Other than that, this man was either on the job or with family. Regardless, there was plenty to work with. He would put together a report of the dates, times, and cities and forward it to Ms. Toni via one of his secure e-mail accounts. She would be given one week to grease the palms she needed to grease, establish a record of a relationship, and prepare her script. *Then all hell would break lose for our dear CIA director.*

With the tenuous review-exercise complete, North's thoughts returned to the email from the Blackstone operative regarding Conover. They had found surveillance! He knew the Mob was getting more and more sophisticated every day, but for Vinny to employ high-tech equipment to find more of Frank's cash was hard to imagine. What was easier to imagine was for a couple of broken noses to beat the hell out of Frank until he gave up the goods. No, this was the work of experts.

But who?

It brought North to only one conclusion: Frank had, in fact, told someone of the cash—like his employer—and they were keeping tabs on him in an attempt to learn something. With Frank dead, the cash trail erased, and several possible reasons for suicide—including job stress— North had nothing to worry about. Without a doubt, Pendleton had to have ordered the surveillance. This new angle made the impending demise of Mr. Louis Pendleton, CIA director, that much more intriguing. God, wouldn't Pendleton just shit if he knew the second-in-command was totally screwing with his life and career? The proverbial noose was about to get tighter.

Having finished with his weekly haircut, ensuring that he was always photo ready, North placed a call to Ms. Toni.

"Did you receive the dates, times, and locations?" North asked.

"I did and began to work on it immediately," she responded.

"Can you build the network of deceit in a week?"

"A week? If everything goes smoothly, I was thinking two weeks would be an aggressive schedule. I know you realize I have to either persuade people who are in these places now, plant my own people while having to establish a false track record of their existence, or have people removed who are more righteous than greedy."

"I need it done in a week. If you can do it, there is a hundred-thousand-dollar bonus for you."

"As much as I would like the money, I simply don't think it is feasible. The good news is there are a few relatively consistent openings in Pendleton's routine that I can create a scenario around. Having the experience that I do, I have many good contacts at several hotels in town. The easiest place to start and where most of the quote-unquote evidence will come from is a couple of hotels that our lovers frequented most weekends over the past two years. The travel dates that are within a reasonable driving distance from D.C. are fair game, but will take a bit longer."

"All right, do what you can and let me know when you're ready. By the way, where did you find our mistress?"

"Yours truly, Mr. Doe. Once this adultery charade is over, I'm retiring."

"I'm feeling better and better about this. Knowing that you're involved gives me the utmost confidence that I can trust all will be executed professionally."

"I'm most professional and discreet."

"Indeed. When this is over, can you please forward the contact information of the new Ms. Toni?"

"Of course," Ms. Toni replied.

"Excellent. Please think about how we will leak the sordid affair and give me some ideas." And with that, North clicked off.

He could not have been more pleased with himself. Deeprose's primary mole had been compromised thanks to Sara, Conover had been successfully erased, and now Pendleton would be exposed as an adulterer. He would be calling the shots at the CIA very soon.

಄

Lou and Kate had just gotten into bed, each wearing conservative pajamas, when Lou's cell phone buzzed, which resulted in a raised eyebrow from Kate. "I'm sorry, honey, but it's Jack. If he is calling this late, it must be important."

"As always, my dear, I understand," said Kate as she rolled her eyes.

Lou answered on the fourth ring.

"Sorry to bother you so late."

"What is it, Jack?"

"Conover's place went silent at around seven p.m. tonight."

"What do you mean, *silent?*"

"The listening device simply stopped. So I immediately went over to Conover's, which is where I'm calling you from. The surveillance equipment has all been removed."

"By whom?"

"Your guess is as good as mine."

"Is Conover home?"

"Hard to tell. All the lights are off. The last I heard was him snoring the day away."

"Is his car there?"

"I never had a chance to place the GPS on his car. I can't tell without breaking into the garage—no windows."

"I guess it is possible that Frank found the equipment, threw it in the trash, and went back to bed. What do you think?"

"Anything is possible. How about I hang out for another hour or so to see if there is any activity?"

"I appreciate that. Maybe you should attempt to break into his home tomorrow after he has left for work. I know that he has an aggressive interrogation schedule. I trust he will be into Langley no later than eight a.m."

"Okay, I'll be back here at seven tomorrow morning in hopes of catching him leave for work. If he leaves before then, can you simply text me if you find out when he arrives, assuming you will be at Langley tomorrow."

"I will. Be careful, Jack."

"Roger. Night."

CHAPTER 25

"Morning, Lou," began Jack as he sat in the van down the street from Frank's house.

"Hold on, let me see if he has checked into work yet this morning."

Two minutes later Lou was back on the line. "Frank's not here. I'll give him a quick call to find out where he is and call you back."

Five more minutes and Lou and Jack were back on the phone.

"He didn't answer," Lou said.

"I also tried his cell phone and threw rocks at the windows. So he is either still sound asleep or left with someone else and either forgot his cell phone or is refusing to answer."

"We need him here doing his job as soon as possible. I already received a call from the DNI asking for the results of this morning's interrogation."

"Does Frank have a girlfriend, or boyfriend?"

"Not that anyone is aware of. As far as we know, he is pretty much a loner and tends to imbibe a bit more than the average bear."

"Want me to try to get into the house?"

"I would say no, assuming Frank will eventually call with a plausible personal emergency of some sort, but given the surveillance equipment is missing, see if you can get inside without alerting the neighbors or making a big mess."

"I've already checked out the windows; should be a piece of cake and relatively inexpensive for Frank to replace."

"Okay, let me know if you find anything worthwhile."

"I'll call you back in a few."

Six minutes later Lou and Jack were back on the phone.

"We have a problem, Lou."

"What's that?"

"Frank's dead."

"What! How?"

"It appears he killed himself. He slit his wrists and arms while sitting in the bathtub. Based upon the fact his body is cold and stiff, puts death between eight and thirty-six hours ago. Since I heard him snoring away mid-afternoon yesterday, he did it sometime between approximately seven p.m. when the listening devices went quiet and midnight."

"Do you think there is a correlation between the listening devices and his death? I mean, really—who the hell wakes up from a nap and offs themselves? Is there a note?"

"If there is a note, it wasn't left out in plain sight. It's pretty gory. The bathwater is dark crimson, almost black, while he looks like an albino. I wonder... hold on a minute."

"What's the matter?"

"Someone is knocking—rather, pounding—on the front door, yelling Frank's name."

"Can you get a look at who it is?"

"Hang on... yes, there is a peephole. Some guy, about five-ten, short-cropped blond hair; looks like he spends most of his free time at the gym."

"That would be Jim, his partner."

"What do you want me to do?"

"Nothing. I don't want Jim finding you there. I'll call him and order him back to Langley, and then you get the hell out of there. Take some pictures with your phone before you leave."

"Will do; talk later."

As Jim was heading around to the back of the house where Jack had broken a window to get in, his cell phone rang and his optimism rose for a moment, but then just as quickly diminished when he realized it was Louis Pendleton calling, not Frank.

"Jim, where the hell are you, and where the fuck is your partner?"

"Ah... well, I'm at Frank's house. Frank didn't show up to work today and I couldn't reach him on his phone, so I came over here to check on him."

"Okay, I understand. But I need you to turn around and get back here immediately, do you understand?"

"Yes, sir."

"I have the DNI sniffing up my ass for your interrogation results this morning."

"I can't do it alone."

"I understand, and given our bad guy, we need to discuss how to handle that. Now move!"

"Yes, sir; running to my car now."

Lou sat and stared at his phone for a long moment. *Yet another shit bomb*, he thought.

He had better call Clapper and give him the news. But first he would have his AA contact Human Resources and let them handle contacting the police regarding Frank having gone AWOL. Due to the broken window, the police would most likely consider homicide a possibility and conduct an investigation, which would be a nuisance he and the CIA did not need right now, but since he had another mystery on his hands, an investigation might be a good thing.

The dots would connect for Lou if the police found the surveillance equipment somewhere in the house or garage with Frank's prints on it.

Otherwise, Frank was into heavy shit with some relatively sophisticated bad guys. Oh, how the DNI would be overjoyed with the latest development.

❧

After snapping pictures of Frank's corpse and random shots of the bathroom, bedroom, and living room, Jack quickly left the same way he entered, leaving no trace he had been there. He blended into the fabric of the quiet morning of the neighborhood as he walked slowly back to his van parked several blocks away. Although his gait was slow and deliberate, his mind raced wildly. Jack's training served him well now. His senses were all operating at peak level, while his strategic skill set propelled his mind to run through scenario after scenario.

Upon arriving at his apartment, he sent Lou a short text letting him know he had gotten out undetected. He then went back to listen again to the audiotapes and check the videotapes from Frank's place to determine if he had missed anything and to confirm the exact time the equipment was removed. The video equipment did not activate, indicating no movement, and remained dormant, so the assumption was it was detected and removed before it activated. All he heard from the audio recording was intermittent snoring right before the recording went dead at 7:16 p.m., which all but confirmed that Conover was not the one who disabled the equipment and that his death was more likely a homicide.

He called Lou with this intelligence and was told his next assignment would be Jim's new interrogation partner and to get his ass to Langley immediately.

CHAPTER 26

Given the new interrogation intelligence regarding terrorists intending to use weapons of mass destruction, specifically anthrax, Jack knew he was most likely less informed than the rest of the team relative to potential delivery methods. He figured there was no time like the present to try to get up to speed. Plus, he didn't like relying on other people for information, especially suits.

He found a cybercafé two minutes from his apartment. He arrived shortly after seven and the place was bustling with millennials. All of the men resembled one another, to some extent. All were rather small in stature, with scraggly facial hair and glasses. Appearance was not a priority for the women, and many were wearing ball caps, baggy sweatpants, and no makeup. All were engrossed—rather, tethered—to whatever electronic device they had brought to share their morning coffee and oblivious to others around them. The smell of fresh-brewed coffee was heavenly and pulled him immediately to the counter to order a large cup, black.

Jack attempted to make himself fit in. He had worn his most tattered jeans, a ratty T-shirt, and black Converse sneakers. He had purchased a tablet the day before, receiving a ten-minute tutorial from the retail clerk. As he opened and closed what few applications on the tablet he pretended to be working on, he looked around the café, searching for his target. After fifteen minutes, he had made his selection and made his move.

Jack eased into the seat across from the twentysomething who did not notice him until Jack cleared his throat. The geek slowly took his eyes off his laptop screen and peered over the top of his monitor at Jack through his horn-rimmed glasses. He blinked a few times as if he didn't recognize another human being. Jack swiftly offered a handshake and introduced himself as a newcomer to the area. The younger man had yet to utter a word and Jack started to wonder if he was mute.

"Listen," Jack began, "I'm sorry to bother you, but being new to the area, I don't know the hot spots to pick up the newest technology."

"What are you looking for?"

"Drones."

"You mean UAVs?"

"Ah, yeah," he responded, vaguely recalling an acronym for the official name for a drone. Maybe he had not prepared himself well enough for this conversation.

"Steph," responded the young man, pointing his finger across to a short-cropped blonde sitting on the other side of the café. "Steph is an expert on unmanned aerial vehicles—UAVs. She knows everything there is to know, and she sells the small ones at a retail outlet."

Jack thanked the young man for his time and made a beeline for Steph.

CHAPTER 27

Today's simulation, being the first of its kind, had drawn the interest of all of the employees such that Covington stopped production and invited everyone to watch the spectacle on three large monitors that hung in the employee lounge area. Many had likened it to fight night.

Part of the programming and preparation dealt with the anticipation of encountering an enemy robot, as remote as the possibility seemed. A quarter-mile from the factory, two robots had been programmed to remain within a thirty-foot square area and destroy the other; the unknown was if the artificial intelligence would drive similar movements in each robot.

Controllers within the factory were prepared to decommission them immediately if things went awry, while military personnel were placed on the perimeter with bazookas just in case. Two video cameras were prepared to capture the live action. Covington remained with the controllers to ensure his directions were understood clearly and timely.

"All right boys, turn our little monsters on."

The sensors in the sockets came to life as each robot fixated on the other, each on opposite sides of the invisible boxing ring. They moved in unison as each took a few steps to their right, then to their left, bobbing their torsos as they did so. Then they raised their arms, not out in front like a boxer, but rather tight to their midsections with their large claw hands set tightly near their waistlines. You could hear a pin drop in the factory as everyone watched with anticipation as to what would come next.

And what happened next scared the living shit out of Covington. The two robots walked slowly toward one another, looked each other up and down, very slowly, then turned and put their backs to one another and began looking left and right, as if looking for an enemy attacker. Their artificial intelligence had overridden the programming. They somehow determined they were equals and not enemies, and had joined forces to protect one another.

"Shut 'em down," Covington ordered and marched back to his office to share the disturbing news with Eric.

***

The D.C. police found Frank's body later that morning; the broken window provided probable cause for entry into the home. Anticipating the call from the police, Lou had assembled the Deeprose team, which now included Jack.

Sara realized her face lit up upon entering Lou's office and seeing Jack sitting next to North, and she quickly attempted to disguise her joy. "Well, Mr. Jack, you do make the rounds."

"Hello, Ms. Fahridi. It is good to see you again; however, I wish it were under different circumstances."

"What's happened?"

Lou broke in, "Frank's dead, Sara. He was found in his bathtub with his wrists cut."

"He killed himself?"

"Well, it appears that way, but for some reason the police are conducting a full investigation due to a broken window at the back of his house."

With that comment, North's head snapped a little too quickly in Pendleton's direction. "What do they think happened?"

"Everything associated with this operation has been odd for the past week or so. I trust it is standard operating procedure; however, we may be asked to give them statements, so I ask that you keep a low profile and if you happen to receive an inquiry, which I doubt, refer it to me."

"Oh my God, that is horrible," Sara said.

"Yes, Frank was a good man and was very good at what he did. He will be missed," Lou said.

"Are you taking Frank's spot on the team, Jack?" Sara asked.

"For the time being I am. Based upon my most recent assignment tracking jihadi recruits, Lou believed it made sense for me to join Deeprose. The fact I have conducted a few field interrogations more or less sealed the deal."

"And do you have a last name yet?"

"Landis. Jack Landis. Lou and I have worked together many times over the years."

"I see. Well, welcome, I guess."

"I hope to make a contribution."

Given the bombshell that Conover's termination might not be tagged as a suicide, North had to deal with that before responding to Ms. Toni. North's attention returned just in time to hear Pendleton direct everyone to keep themselves available. He took this as his cue to head to his office and try to contact Eric.

As the others left his office, Lou said, "Jack, please stay for a minute to review the interrogation schedule,"

"Of course."

"Please close the door."

"Well, here we are again, boss. Another shitstorm, but I believe this one beats them all."

"I want to see the pictures you took at Conover's place."

"Are you sure? It's pretty gruesome. I saw no signs of foul play, if that is what you're looking for."

"I believe I'm obligated to at least take a peek."

"Here you go."

"Aw, Jesus. He looks like a ghost sitting in a tub of red wine. So how did they get him in the tub and cut him without a struggle?"

"Must have drugged him. If the police run an autopsy, they'll most likely find it."

"Do we want them to find it?"

"Good question. Listen, I need to remove the surveillance from Sara's place tonight."

"Agreed."

"I did a little drone research last night and had a very interesting conversation early this morning."

"And?"

"I can't believe we have to wait for a real threat before we take action. It feels reactive. Why aren't we leveraging our drone advantage more? The jihads could be getting their hands on it as we speak."

"Jack, we have over three hundred operatives working on the drone initiative. They track—with the use of drones, ironically enough—the manufacture, distribution, use, and research of other countries, as well as the known players in the United States. Hell, we have executives from the two major manufacturers working with us on several strategic committees. The Defense Advanced Research Projects Agency maintains drone research, development, and deployment as one of its top priorities. We are continually, secretly constructing airstrips to launch drones. Today there are undisclosed airstrips in Turkey, Afghanistan, Qatar, Philippines, United Arab Emirates, Yemen, Ethiopia, Djibouti, and Seychelles with plans to build more. In other words, there are a whole lot of people smarter than you and me watching over this technology."

"Are they watching over it, or pushing its limits to reach full-blown artificial intelligence?"

"I suspect both. So what did you learn this morning that compels you to think that the terrorists are a blink away from acquiring drone technology?"

"I received a crash course on the history of drones, including the ground-based PackBot, Talon, and SWORDS operating in wars of today, and their total is estimated to be upwards of twenty-thousand. The real concern, of course, are the UAVs or airborne drones. The Predator is about the size of a Cessna. How many times do we hear about a small plane entering prohibited airspace? Are our radar systems truly sophisticated enough to not only detect, but deter, within our borders? And then there is the Shadow, which is just over twelve feet long. It takes off and lands just like a seven-twenty-seven. Granted, its flight distance is limited to seventy miles; however, can you imagine an orchestrated attack with multiple drones?"

"Where did you get this information?"

"From a twenty-three-year-old computer engineer named Steph who follows drones as a hobby. She is considered the best pilot in her drone club. She started playing remote-controlled video games when she was four years old, which she attributes to her prowess in the drone obstacle course her club created. Hell, she was telling me about the advancement of lasers, evidently referred to as the Holy Grail of weaponry. Supposedly, we currently have the capability to fire a laser to bounce off a mirror on a drone and then hit a target. And she said the advances in artificial intelligence may all but eliminate human war casualties in the next decade. If all this is true, I find it hard to believe that the bad guys cannot get their hands on simple drone technology."

"Jack, trust me, this issue is front and center with the secretary of defense."

"Lou, drones are everywhere now. Retail chains have explored using them for smaller home deliveries. You can buy toy ones off the shelf. At this point, based upon the fact the technology seems to be ubiquitous, I would be more concerned about how our enemies will use it rather than obtaining it. I would assume they already have the technology."

"I doubt it. And for them to find it truly valuable, it would have to have the capability of flying thousands of miles to get from the Middle East to the U.S."

"Hmm. What if they believed the technology could travel that far?"

"What do you mean?"

"Could we lure them out using it as bait?"

"I doubt they would engage with any Americans."

"What about the Russians? What if we approached the Russians, requesting their help in expanding our intelligence reach into the Middle East?"

"As I recall, you speak Russian, or at least you did at one time."

"Yes, it was my focus language at the Naval Academy. I was able to use it on several assignments, the most recent one being approximately eight years ago. I'm definitely rusty."

"The most difficult part of your idea is getting Putin in our boat," said Pendleton. "What's in it for him?"

"Putin's a smart guy. He would use any opportunity to negotiate for something, most likely economic in nature."

"Would your buddy Abir be up for participating?"

"Without a doubt. I'll give him a heads-up."

"All right, I'll review it with Clapper and see if we can put a plan together."

☙

Situated in the Oval Office, the president, secretary of defense, and Lou were discussing the latest intelligence gathered from participating NATO nations on developments in the Middle East, relative to the growing threat of terrorism.

Lou began, "Mr. President, the growing number of ISIS members in Iraq has been corroborated to a great extent by allied intelligence agencies. Although they do not identify themselves as ISIS, but rather as the Islamic State of Iraq, we're all but certain they have committed themselves to the newest fatwa, or objectives of this so-called allegiance of terrorists."

"How real is the threat of this new allegiance forging an organized attack against the U.S. and how would they accomplish it?" asked the president.

"Biologicals. During the recent interrogation of a head of ISIS, we learned that there is a coordinated effort underway to deploy anthrax."

"And what about the ability to obtain anthrax? To inflict the mass destruction you are referring to, it would seem to require a significant amount."

"More than likely, they will produce it themselves, given the probability they have access to chemists with the knowledge. To produce it, basically they induce endospore formation, dry the spores, and combine them with chemical stabilizers to help the spores remain airborne longer."

"I have been assured that our biodefense laboratories have the freeze-dried spores under lock and key."

"Sir, there are several countries that are believed to have the spores and the knowhow. North Korea and China top the list and we believe they both have Ames and Vollum, the two most contagious strains. And as far as deployment, they don't necessarily need to disperse it into the air, although that would be the most effective and devastating."

"Can anthrax survive in water?"

"The Air Force Research Laboratory advises that the spores can attach themselves to the pipes, especially if they are iron, and survive water treatments to kill the spores. So yes, there is the possibility it can reach consumers' drinking water."

"We have no choice but to accelerate our effort to destroy and degrade ISIS and whatever partners it has recently aligned with."

"Agreed, sir."

"I trust you have come prepared with recommendations."

"Yes, sir. The core of any offensive against ISIS, or other terrorist organizations, has to be the annihilation of the Caliphate, or successor to the Prophet Muhammad. As you know, violence is called out in over 100 verses in the Quran. The true believers consider killing and sexual slavery of non-Muslims their duty in the eyes of Allah. The Caliphate is how Muslims have attempted to organize themselves for centuries following the death of Muhammad. One could compare the Caliphate to Hitler and Nazi Germany: Equal rights for all must come to an end and all nonbelievers must be executed.

"ISIS is the most extreme organization we have witnessed to date. Not because of its brutal behaviors, but because it implemented the Caliphate. Literally defined, the Caliphate is an area containing an Islamic steward, or caliph, who is considered the successor to Muhammad. Adl Aziz al-Batal, the head of ISIS, has claimed the mantle as the new prophet, with Syria and Iraq currently comprising the area from which he controls the Muslim nation.

"Now that the caliph stake has been put into the ground, it will be more difficult to defeat what we define to be terrorism. If we eradicate ISIS, another extremist organization will take their place. The war against terrorism will only be won when we have destroyed the supremacist faith in the Caliphate. ISIS is a relatively easy target to eliminate, as they occupy relatively uncivilized areas of the world. The Muslim Brotherhood, a relatively moderate promoter of the Caliphate, uses modern political methods to conquer non-Muslims in civilized countries, such as the U.S. But if they are indeed Muslims, they believe they are the super race and will ultimately follow the Prophet.

"Consider the scenario, as apocalyptic as it may sound, wherein all of the Muslims around the world—approximately one-point-seven billion, twenty-three percent of the world's population, were to unite and attack non-Muslims. Given there is now a self-proclaimed prophet, it is a possibility, although remote, that they could all disperse anthrax or some other biological weapon and kill an unprecedented number of people."

"You're beginning to sound like Richard North."

"Well, I believe North's concerns are valid, but his military doctrine may be extreme."

"What's your recommendation?"

"Our air-strike campaigns have had minimal success. We need someone on the inside getting real-time intelligence so we can increase the success of our strikes."

"Says easy, does hard. How do you propose we do that?"

Lou went onto explain Jack's idea of selling the bogus long range drone technology.

"Russia? I believe our latest intel indicates they are behind in the drone race," said the president.

"That is true. Israel and China have developed the most advanced technology to date, while Russia and Iran have developed them at some level, but any progress is doubtful, due to a lack of industrial and innovative capacity. China has leapfrogged the U.S. recently in terms of investments and advancements, while Israel is believed to be selling drones with intelligence-gathering technology to friendly nations supporting their position in the Gaza Strip. Russia would be the most believable with regard to selling what they have to the highest bidder."

"All right, give me the plan."

It took Lou an additional ten minutes to review the details before he was given the green light. Operation Deeprose just got a boost.

❦

Sequestered away in his office, North phoned Eric. "What the hell kind of ship are you running, Eric?" he screamed into the phone.

"What's the problem?"

"The problem is that your goon squad left a mess at the target's home and now the police are treating it as a potential homicide."

"Impossible. Why would they do that?"

"Because your boys broke a window to get in and did not clean up their mess."

"The team had a key. They made impressions of all of Conover's keys during their last visit and used the key to quietly enter and exit the back door."

After a long pause, North resumed. "I guess it is simply bad luck the dumb bastard had a broken window that he didn't fix."

"The forensic experts may be able to determine when the glass was broken. If it was broken for several days, they may indeed save the taxpayers' money and not run an autopsy. Besides, there is nothing to point it toward you or us."

"Loose ends are always a problem, and you know that."

"Relax, Richard. It isn't like you to be paranoid. Also, I received a call from Covington a few minutes ago."

"And?"

Eric shared the results of the robot fight.

"Unbelievable," responded North.

"Unbelievable and unacceptable. Can you imagine if these things banded together and decided their makers were the enemy?"

"Relax, Eric. Have Covington work on the programming so it doesn't happen again."

The call ended. North considered the worst-case scenario relative to the artificial intelligence and figured it was worth the risk to blow ISIS off the map.

CHAPTER 28

In a remote and desolate area of Kashmir province, sixty-five miles northeast of Islamabad, two men sat at a makeshift table made of empty oil barrels and a wooden plank from a long-ago demolished rooftop and sipped tea as their translators stood behind them and their security details stood outside the bombed-out schoolhouse keeping watch. They were representatives of their respective interests sent to negotiate the terms and conditions of a verbal contract, the successful execution of which would create a global military threat administered by a regime unlike any other in the history of warfare.

As the midday temperature reached ninety-five degrees, the two sat dressed in the Islamic garb of their environs, which made the smaller, clean-shaven Asian man look like a child from an Ali Baba production. This was the third meeting of the men, with locations alternating between Pyongyang and somewhere in Pakistan. The purchase price was not the concern of the Afghan representing ISIS. The buyer wanted confirmation that the seller had successfully developed the ability to manufacture the substance in high quantities. The Asian promptly set his tablet on the table and opened a video, which showed a large manufacturing facility and related test labs, as well as a stockpile of the deadly powder spores.

"What guarantees do we have of the purity and potency?"

A second video was opened as the Asian explained the two men shown were criminals sentenced to death. Four men entered the scene wearing Hazmat suits and forced the two criminals to inhale the powder spores. The infected men were taped the next day and had signs of the flu, both exhibiting the chills. Both men were dead the second day.

The Asian explained, "Inhalation anthrax takes two days, while the initial symptoms resemble a bad cold or flu, thereby disguising the threat until it is too late. The victim will experience bloody fluid in their chest cavity and around their lungs, and infections in the brain and spinal cord, while eventually succumbing to respiratory failure."

"And if not inhaled?"

"It can be ingested or come in contact with skin. Ingestion is typically from eating contaminated meat. If in contact with the skin, it is most effective if the spores come in contact with a cut in the skin."

"But we also have the advantage of the infidels contaminating one another."

"No, this cannot be passed from person to person. However, if there are spores on the infected clothing, it can be passed to others."

"What is the mortality rate when there is skin contact?"

"There will be a black ulcer on the surface of the skin within five days, most will seek medical treatment and be given a vaccine and antibiotics. Of those that receive treatment, over fifty percent will recover."

"But their medical facilities will be overwhelmed with those in need; many will not receive the needed medicine in time."

"Most likely."

"Very well. How much time do you need?"

"Can we arrange our next meeting in one month?"

"I look forward to it. Ideally, we will conclude our negotiations then and begin to execute the fulfillment of our transaction. I will see you in Pyongyang."

"And how will you arrange transport from Algeria to your targets in the west?"

"We are working on finding a delivery method now."

"We will make history, my friend."

"The infidels will pay for their disrespect of our culture and all the suffering they have inflicted."

❧

Sara decided to seek Richard's advice relative to Abir's new role as a drone expert, since he had been opposed to Deeprose thus far. Dressed impeccably in her most conservative business suit, she took the elevator up a floor to his office and found both he and his assistant away from their desks. She decided she would wait in North's office for a few minutes in case he returned. As she had never been in his office, she took the opportunity to look at all of the pictures and awards that hung from the walls. At the same time, North had just completed a brief discussion with the DNI and was headed back to his office.

As Sara strode behind his desk, the letterhead of one of the envelopes caught her eye. ARobotics was the name listed as the sender of the correspondence with a post office box address. Given the recent discussion with Jack regarding the meadow, the name piqued her interest. She quickly stole a glance toward the door before deciding to look inside the envelope. North had just turned down the hall that housed his office twenty feet away.

Sara had already opened the envelope, prepared to pull out the letter, when North walked into his office. Sara froze as he stopped in his tracks, the look on his face conveying his surprise and anger.

"Can I help you, Ms. Fahridi?"

"Oh, hi, Richard. I... uhm... came to ask your opinion about Deeprose and was admiring your pictures and found this envelope on the floor and was putting it back on your desk," she lied as she placed the envelope in a spot other than where she found it.

"I see. I would very much appreciate you making an appointment or giving me the courtesy of a heads-up when you would like to meet."

"Of course. I'm sorry, I wasn't thinking. Do you have time to discuss Deeprose?"

"I'm afraid not."

"Okay, I will contact your assistant to schedule a convenient time." And with that, Sara quickly left the office, hoping her face was not as flushed as it felt. She could hear North slam the door behind her.

CHAPTER 29

North was pleased with his purchase. The Canon PowerShot SX50 HS digital camera was ideal. He had been concerned that he would have to use a large, clunky camera lens and a tripod, which could be difficult to conceal. However, this relatively small camera had a 50x optical zoom, the first of its kind, and could take thirteen shots per second. It also had other high technology options, which virtually made his photography assignment idiot-proof.

By trailing Pendleton over the past two evenings, he had learned that Louis did in fact run the same route, at least on weekday evenings. The challenge with the three mile route was that it was all through residential and relatively secluded wooded areas near Pendleton's home. That made a chance encounter with Ms. Toni in a populated area impossible. Therefore, Ms. Toni would have to don some running shoes and pretend to have an injury of some sort so that Pendleton would stop to offer assistance. She would then have to make all the right moves to make it appear as if they were a couple and intimately involved.

North had selected the most remote area of the route, where he could be concealed ninety feet away and not be detected as he took picture after picture. Giving directions to Ms. Toni was therefore a little more challenging; however, with the aid of several yellow-ribbon tree markings, she should easily be able to find the spot where she would lay in wait, feigning a sprained ankle.

The forecast for tomorrow was sunny and clear and Pendleton was scheduled to be in D.C. Tomorrow would be the beginning of the end of Pendleton's short tenure as director. The pictures would not only serve to dethrone him, but also capture Ms. Toni's face. Even though Ms. Toni had proven to be discreet, letting her live was a risk North could not permit.

He placed a call to the D.C. police chief to confirm she had her eyes on the Conover file. She had sounded annoyed, no doubt by his request to keep the CIA out of the investigation and the news. He took the opportunity to take a jab at the Consolidated Forensics Laboratory, which would be called in to conduct an analysis not only on the cadaver, but also on the broken window in an attempt to determine the time of the break. When the lab was initially opened, it was a hailed as a state-of-the-art forensics laboratory. However, the 351,000 square foot, $22 million operation had been a bust thus far, due primarily to dysfunction, ineptness, and bureaucracy. Reports of mistakes, use of outdated techniques, and labor issues had riddled the lab's short tenure. The last thing the police department needed was the CIA jumping on the critics' bandwagon, given another botched forensics analysis, but North couldn't resist.

The police chief opined, "In reading through the file, all indications were that the subject had indeed committed suicide given his job, personal life, or lack thereof, and his addictive tendencies. In addition, there appeared to be no family or friends interested in the results of the investigation."

The report described the home as untidy and outdated. Pictures of the inside revealed the opportunity for updating and remodeling. A broken window gone unrepaired for a day or two was not necessarily out of character, given what she saw.

"I will have window repair shops local to Conover's address contacted to determine if a repair request was made," she continued. "The taxpayers' money would not be wasted on an unnecessary autopsy and the case would be promptly closed and your precious CIA will not be bothered." North simply clicked off without a goodbye or thank you. He didn't need to worry about Conover being labeled as a homicide, he thought smugly.

❦

Both Sara and Jack had arrived early to the conference room that boasted a large rectangular laminate table and ten meshed-back conference chairs. Jack had made it a point to purchase some new clothes, ensuring he was no longer the worst dressed on the team. Lou continued to hold that distinction. Sara, on the other hand, was dressed in red slacks and vest and an attractive matching scarf.

Jack thought he would take a stab at getting Sara to open up about her brother and the drama the two were handling by themselves. "Has your brother taken in many sights since he has been here?"

"Not really," Sara responded as the pair sat down next to one another.

"What does he do with all of his time since you're so busy with your job?"

"Well, he likes to read and is catching up on the U.S. news and enjoying game shows."

"He must really love his sister to travel all this way to spend very few hours with you in the evening and the rest of his day alone."

"Trust me, he is ready to go home. His visit, was... well, let's say a spur-of-the-moment decision."

"I see. Is everything okay?"

"I think so, but I'm not ready for him to leave just yet."

"Is there anything I can do to help? I'm quite resourceful and have developed many contacts all over the world."

"That is very kind of you, but I think we are fine."

"If you change your mind, don't hesitate. I hope you know that you can trust me. We're on the same team, for goodness sake."

"I'll keep that in mind," Sara said, thinking she was far from trusting him.

As Sara said this, North walked in, looking her up and down as if she were a piece of meat. This did not go unnoticed by Jack and he felt an odd sense of jealousy.

"Where is everybody?" North asked as he helped himself to a seat at the head of the table, adjusting his tie and hair just in case CNN burst through the door, wanting an interview.

"The important people haven't arrived yet," responded Jack, looking to test North's ego. His quip irked North, based upon the steely gaze he leveled at Jack, which Jack returned and held for several seconds until North looked away.

"Is there anything we can accomplish before Mr. Pendleton and Mr. Clapper arrive?" asked Sara.

"Nothing that won't have to be repeated when they get here," responded North.

Pendleton and Clapper walked in together, just in time to hear North complete his comment.

"Well, Mr. North, we've arrived in time such that we can avoid anyone having to repeat themselves," chimed Pendleton. North simply cleared his throat and smiled, thinking that in a few days Pendleton wouldn't be so smug.

"Allow me to provide an update from the Oval Office to begin," stated the DNI. "The emergency NATO meeting will be held via audio and video technology so as to not raise any red flags with our adversaries. We understand that the media will no doubt get wind of it, but it will have less fanfare and coverage if it is not a formal, face to face meeting. It is scheduled for the day after tomorrow, while the primary agenda item, the alleged terrorist union, will not be communicated until the meeting itself.

"As far as the media is concerned, smart defense will be again the primary discussion topic and the information leaked to the press is that little progress has been made, so NATO is taking a more aggressive approach.

"The president and the defense secretary have engaged in a serious dialogue with the Speaker of the House relative to military funding and budgeting. The Speaker is in favor of allocating more to our defense budget, but as one can expect, there is no agreement from where the cuts will come from to make it happen.

"The Joint Chiefs are leaning toward elevating DEFCON again, but the president is hesitant given the impending NATO meeting. The concern is that the media will put two and two together. And you wonder why socialist countries control their media. Sometimes I fantasize about that; our jobs would be so much easier. However, because of the world in which we live, we work within a continual web of deliberate deceit."

Clapper's last comment resonated with Sara. Ever since she had been loaned by Homeland Security to the CIA, she had encountered some level of deceit as a standard operating procedure of sorts; from the way Jack had first introduced himself to her actions relative to her brother's capture. Yes, she was complicit but her deceit was deliberate yet justified.

She then realized she was most likely aware of only the tip of the iceberg. With this thought, she slowly looked around the room and glanced at each participant, wondering if the art of deceit was in their blood and that was how they found themselves working for the CIA at these high levels. The thought gave her a chill, not so much about the others, but the fact that she was arguably now one of them.

"Sara," repeated Lou, "what is the status?"

Lou's question brought Sara back into focus. "I'm sorry, Lou. Could you please repeat the question?"

With a mild look of disgust, he repeated, "What is the status of Abir's crash course in drones?"

"He immersed himself yesterday. We have plenty of internal resources to get him up to speed quickly."

"Given the new intelligence, his knowledge of drones could be his ticket into ISIS's inner circle." Lou then looked at Jack and said, "Let's pray your idea works."

CHAPTER 30

Abir had been somewhat surprised when Jack had called three days before, asking him to handle an assignment alone, but was happy to take it when the compensation was revealed. The fact that the CIA director was behind the request made it more enticing. He found the study of drone technology to be interesting and was eager to put his newfound knowledge to the test.

Abir had anticipated more of a furtive exchange, so when his ISIS contact approached him from the front with a big smile and hand extended to shake, he was somewhat taken aback. The contact, Maysarah, led Abir to a nearby café.

"My job is simply to make the initial contact," Maysarah explained.

"I see. Your job is to determine if I am who I say I am," Abir responded.

"More or less. Your engineering background has piqued our interest, especially your familiarity with drone technology."

"I understand and that is why I reached out to ISIS. Drones can be a game changer when dealing with infidels."

"Possibly. We have considered drones for some time, but given our lack of friendly geography close to the Americans from which to launch them, we cannot use drones effectively."

"What if there was a drone that could travel up to five thousand miles?"

"Hah, we would have heard of it."

"Evidently you have not—no one has."

"Are you serious?"

"Deadly serious. Due to my familiarity with the drone community and the fact I am a Muslim, a representative of a consortium selling the long range technology contacted me."

"And?"

"They want to sell to the highest bidder."

"And how many bidders are there?"

"A limited number, but, given ISIS's momentum and resources, it was suggested I contact you first."

"Who is this consortium?"

"My contact is a Russian. He has been hired by a group of Russian scientists and engineers."

"And why would the Russians give up such technology?"

"The government would not. These are employees who have not necessarily been treated well and are looking to take financial advantage of their development."

"Hmm. Tell me more about the drone."

"It has a range up to five thousand miles, given weather conditions and satellite connectivity, which is four thousand miles more than the current Predator technology. This would allow ISIS to deliver a deadly payload across the seas to the West."

"Can they carry anthrax?"

"Yes. Are you considering anthrax?"

"It just popped into my head. How about missiles?"

"Yes, it can carry many different payloads up to a thousand pounds."

"Very interesting."

"So, my friend Maysarah, what is the next step?"

"I have to review your information with my superiors. If they agree to a next meeting, it will be with some of our military leaders, one of which is a very dangerous man. You need to be absolutely certain of your information and resources."

"There is no doubt in my mind that this will be the tool that is the turning point for ISIS in the quest of the Caliphate."

"Very well. Please notify your Russian contact that we are very interested and will be in touch within a few days."

Less than a day later, Abir received a call from Maysarah requesting a meeting— but with just Abir—in Grozny at the Central Dome Mosque. Abir anticipated what he called a "sniff test" by Maysarah's superiors. He realized this meeting would be the most dangerous part of the operation. If he could convince them he was truly interested in joining ISIS and that he could deliver the drone technology, the rest of the operation would be relatively easier. His thoughts turned to his children and his wife.

***

North couldn't be more pleased with himself. He had purchased camouflage apparel at an army surplus store and decided there was no way anyone could spot him hidden among the trees and bushes ninety feet from the running path. It had been a beautiful sunny spring day. As the hour reached 7:00 p.m., the sun filtered through the trees, creating sufficient light to illuminate his unsuspecting targets. There was a slight breeze that rustled the tree leaves and served to hide whatever sounds North might make.

Ms. Toni had arrived promptly and, using the binoculars he had brought, he could see that she had successfully removed the yellow ribbons from the trees that led her to the rendezvous spot. As he spied her through the binoculars, he found her to be... well... average looking. She was in her mid- to late forties, sporting a bleach-blonde look that exposed her wish to look ten years younger, but the extra thirty pounds she carried diminished any potential of her being described as desirable. She repeatedly looked at her watch, being careful to be in position at the time Pendleton was estimated to run down the trail toward her.

North didn't realize she had added a second layer of leggings as well as a second top to make her appear heavier than she was. She had dyed her hair a hideous blonde, knowing that she would never wear her hair that color after today. She also wore a pair of running shoes one and one-half sizes too large. In anticipation of her being followed after the running encounter, she had prepaid two taxicabs to meet at designated spots, each approximately one-half mile away and in different directions. This would avail her some flexibility if something went wrong.

North steadied his new camera and carefully snapped shot after shot of Ms. Toni, paying careful attention to capture a full facial shot as often as possible. He might need these pictures to help determine her real identity if his primary identification scheme did not work. His preference was to engage a Blackstone surveillance team, but the risk of them identifying Pendleton and connecting him to the impending scandal was too much of a risk.

She sat on the ground, removed her right shoe, and waited for her prey to come within sight before she began her act. On cue, the six-foot Pendleton lumbered down the path, MP3 player, headband, and all. As expected due to his training, Pendleton spotted her immediately, even though she was seventy-five yards ahead. Fortunately, North saw no other joggers, bikers, or walkers as he spied the path from left to right.

Ms. Toni was rubbing her right ankle with vigor, now rocking her torso back and forth as if she were in a significant amount of pain. North had to hand it to Pendleton as he looked left, right, and behind himself as he approached Ms. Toni; a veteran military officer should always be on guard. When Pendleton was within five yards of her, North began shooting photos nonstop.

As Pendleton approached, he slowed down to a walk a few feet before the injured woman, removed his earbuds, bent down, and asked the woman if she was okay.

"Stupid me. I believe I sprained my ankle," she said as she looked up at Pendleton and smiled.

"How bad does it hurt?"

"At first it was a sharp pain, but now it's just a constant throb and seems to slowly be getting better."

"I have my cell phone. Would you like me to call someone?"

"Oh, no, I don't think that's necessary. Do you think you could help me up?"

"Sure. Here, give me your hand."

With that, Toni took Pendleton's right hand and quickly stood, extended her five-foot, five-inch frame as far as she could and put her left arm around his waist and buried her chest into his, thereby pushing him back such that he was looking down into her eyes. She looked up at him and smiled her biggest smile while she was standing on her shoed foot and the socked foot was curled up in the best Marilyn Monroe pose she could muster.

When her lips were inches from his, she said, "You're very strong and I'm so lucky you came along to help me."

At this, Pendleton instinctively pulled back, cleared his throat, put his hands on her shoulders, and extended his arms to create a distance between the two of them. "Well," he began, "I'm happy to have helped. Do you think you could walk to where you need to get to?"

With that, Toni's posture slumped back and she simply responded with, "Thank you very much, I'll be fine. Enjoy the rest of your run." She knew then the damage had been done if the on-site photographer, Doe, had opportunistically captured the moment.

☙

Al-Batal called the gathering to order by standing as the other members remained seated within the circle these five men had formed, and shouted, "Peace, mercy, and blessings of Allah upon you."

"To Allah," the men responded in unison, the sound of which reverberated off the walls of this small, well-hidden cave in the mountain region of Afghanistan.

"My brothers, we are united in jihad against the infidels. We have overcome our differences to unite in the war against our oppressors. In honor of our fallen brother, Osama bin Laden, we are unified!"

"To Allah," responded the quorum, represented by the respective leaders of the Afghan Taliban, Hezbollah, Hamas, al Qaeda, Jamaat Ansar al-Sunna, and the Pakistani Taliban.

Al-Batal continued, "Several of you have traveled far and at great risk to participate, as we all know the importance of our fatwa. Tonight, we will review our respective responsibilities and the status of our forthcoming war against the West."

And for the next several hours, the committee of terrorists discussed their plan to attack the United States with biological weapons. Of all the potential options, botulism and anthrax were the two preferred, and anthrax was eventually the choice, primarily due to its high mortality rate and environmental stability. Obtaining large quantities of anthrax was not a problem thanks to the North Koreans; obtaining the means to distribute it on the East Coast of the United States was the current obstacle.

Hezbollah reviewed the continuing domination of Syria and the status of the recent meeting with North Korea regarding the purchase of anthrax. The plan was to load hundreds of Predators each with 200 pounds of anthrax and have them disburse the deadly payloads into the air over New York, Boston, D.C., and Philadelphia, akin to a crop duster. To date, little progress had been made in obtaining the drones.

Hamas's role was primarily one of establishing and staffing departments of expertise, i.e., IT experts, weapons procurement, policy and procedure, foreign relationships, skills and experience, and financial management. Al-Qaeda took care of opium sales and distribution, etc. Jamaat's focus was primarily recruiting and training. The Pakistani Taliban had the largest membership and their role would be primarily ground warfare following the biological attacks, requiring members to continually enter the United States up until the attack, with a goal of 1000 guerrillas armed with Hazmat suits and guns. Omar's Afghan Taliban was primarily responsible for strategy and leadership, providing ISIS with coaching and direction.

"The infidels believe that they have crushed us with the death of bin Laden. They have no idea that Osama's sacrifice has unified a power greater than the West has ever faced. My brothers, on the anniversary of our most successful attack on the United States, we will unleash our fury. Yes, on September eleventh of this year, a little more than three months from now, we will kill thousands of Americans!"

CHAPTER 31

Sara made it a point to talk with Jack following their discussion about her brother. She found him talking to a good-looking young woman near the elevators and decided she needed to interrupt that as soon as possible.

"Jack, do you have a second?" she asked.

"Sure," he responded as he disengaged from the brunette.

"I have to admit I'm concerned about my brother," Sara said.

Sara was tempted to tell Jack about the kidnapping, but she just couldn't let herself. She didn't trust him entirely; not yet, anyway.

"And why is that?" asked Jack, knowing full well about Habib's abduction. He wasn't going to make it easy for her if she wasn't going to open up.

"The Middle East has become such a dangerous place, especially Pakistan, where my brother lives."

"Why is today different than any other day?"

"I guess I have been exposed to more information as part of Deeprose."

"And that is probably just the tip of the iceberg. There are lots of fanatics roaming the world, believing their actions are justified and rationalize it based upon their religious beliefs."

"Can we talk?"

"I thought we were talking."

"I mean privately."

"Sure, let's go into the small conference room," Jack said as he turned down the hall. Sara followed quickly behind. He closed the door and they sat opposite one another at the small, square table.

"What's up?" Jack asked.

"My brother just didn't come for a visit," Sara began.

Here it comes, thought Jack, "Is that right?"

Sara shared about the kidnapping, the video, and her insistence that Habib fly to America.

"And why was Habib released?" Jack asked rhetorically.

Sara looked down at the table, as she could not look him in the eye. "I gave up Abdul. I told ISIS about Abdul and that he was meeting with Asaryi; that's why Asaryi was killed. I am so sorry, but I didn't know what else to do and I had very little time."

"Why didn't you talk to someone?"

"I was afraid that the response would be no negotiation with terrorists."

"You were probably right. Listen, I would have done the same thing if one of my family members was in danger. And after all, Asaryi was a bad guy and who knows whether Abdul would have ever gotten close enough to get any meaningful intelligence."

Relieved at hearing this, Sara reached across the table and took both of Jack's hands. "Thank you so much for saying that. The guilt has been weighing on my mind. Should I tell Lou?"

"Hmm... in time. He has a lot on his plate and this may just be a distraction he doesn't need right now."

"All right."

"For now, probably best to have Habib stay with you. Since we are sharing secrets, I have one of my own."

"Do tell," Sara said as she sat back in her chair, the tension slowly ebbing from her.

Jack took the next twenty minutes detailing the meadow, his findings, and his suspicions relative to robots and laser weaponry. He noticed the skeptical look on Sara's face when he finished.

"What do you think?" he asked her.

"Forensics was sure it was a laser?"

"It's a logical conclusion."

"Vanishing animal carcasses?"

"Someone didn't want anyone knowing what went down."

"What did Lou say about this?"

"I haven't shared it yet."

"Why not?"

"Because I'm afraid he will look at me the same way you are looking at me right now—like I'm nuts."

"You have to admit, it sounds a little off."

"That is why I have to do some more digging before I talk with him."

"Probably a good idea. Like you said, probably a distraction he doesn't need right now."

"Smart aleck."

❧

Sara's laptop had frozen three times that day, requiring reboots. She knew from experience with and knowledge of computers that the hard drive might be failing or her computer had picked up a virus. She called the help desk and Billy told her he had time now to take a look. She took her external hard drive and cloning software with her, anticipating the need to back up and/or save her data.

Billy had to buzz her into a secure area where the help desk staff worked. She found Billy in a relatively small cubicle surrounded by five monitors. There were six other similarly outfitted desks, their ear budded occupants all talking to internal customers and busily scanning their monitors.

"Hello, Sara. Nice to meet you," Billy began.

"You too. Wow, that is quite a stack of laptops you have there."

"Yeah. We typically scrub fifteen to twenty laptops per day."

"Do you use Blancco?"

"Yes. Are you into computers?"

"I guess so. They still amaze me, as do airplanes, even though we take both of them for granted."

"Let's take a look at what you have," he said as he plugged in Sara's laptop and input her user ID and password.

As Billy manipulated the keys, she noticed the laptop on the top of Billy's stack had a yellow sticky note with Richard North's name on it, along with what appeared to be his user ID and password. "I see you have one of the head honcho's laptops."

"Oh yeah, North. He turns his laptops over every sixty days."

"Really? Why?"

"No idea. I assume it has something to do with security at his level." Sara found that very odd.

"You caught a virus that has been circulating and making the hard drive useless. Let me go and get you a new one and we can get you set up. It will take me a few minutes, as we have the new ones locked up in our inventory room upstairs. Do you mind waiting?" he asked.

"Not at all, take your time."

"Okay, be right back."

After Billy left, Sara's interest returned to North's recycling his laptop every sixty days. She nonchalantly turned on North's laptop, finding sufficient battery power remaining. She quickly input the user ID and password, and plugged in her external hard drive and jump drive containing the cloning software. Even though North had undoubtedly scrubbed the machine to the best of his ability, Sara knew she could recover most, if not all, of his files. It took just short of two minutes to copy the files, turn the laptop off, and return it to the top of the stack. Two minutes after that, Billy returned with her new hard drive. She found herself strangely exhilarated.

CHAPTER 32

Not that he could be linked, but loose ends were unacceptable and unpredictable; he would be sure to clean them up. And one that came to mind was Ms. Toni. North had to hand it to Ms. Toni, Stella, or whatever her real name was—which he would know soon enough as the identification report he ordered from her license-plate number should be in his possession in less than an hour. The GPS tracking devices he had sewn into the yellow ribbons designating the trail to Pendleton was a last-minute idea. He wasn't sure she would remove them as he had instructed her to in an attempt to avoid any suspicion, but she had.

He had easily followed her signal to Union Station, but upon arriving and finding she had hired two models who looked and dressed like her heading in different directions, he knew he was working with a professional. Fortunately, he was able to park and follow the signal to a bathroom in the lower level. When the signal came out of the bathroom carried by what looked at first to be a different person, North thought he had been duped. But upon closer inspection, he realized it was in fact Ms. Toni, dressed now in a different disguise. She promptly dropped the gym bag she was carrying into the nearest trash bin and with it went the yellow ribbons with the GPS tracker. Had North arrived a few minutes later, his target would have most certainly gotten away.

The trick had been to follow her to either her vehicle or a taxi. Ideally, she would return to her own vehicle, which in fact she did five minutes later. Just for insurance, he hailed a cab and followed her to her destination, in case she was staying in a temporary space until the assignment was over.

She drove to Foxhall Ridge, a small community of luxury condominiums. North could not follow any further due to the security gate. He recalled one of the staffer's parents had lived here some years back and there were less than forty units in the development. At the time, North realized if her license check did not generate an address here, it would not be difficult to track her down, especially considering some of the units had been sold.

North continued to be impressed with this woman. The average price tag of a home here was $1.8 million. Such a shame they couldn't be on the same team… then North laughed out loud at the thought.

❧

"Sara? Jack."

"Hello, Mr. Landis. How would I say that in Russian?"

"*Zdravstvooytye, Mistyer Landis.*"

"Wow, that's quite a mouthful."

"How do you ask: *Would you like to have coffee?* In Arabic?"

"*Wswf ykwn ldyk mthl mnh alshfafyh aldwlyh alqhwh?*"

"I would love to. When and where?"

"Very clever, Jack. Well, how about this evening after work? There's a Starbucks in Old Dominion Center. Six p.m.?"

"Terrific. See you then."

"I look forward to it. Bye, Jack."

"Bye."

As soon as Jack hung up, his cell phone rang with a call from Pendleton.

"Jack, the autopsy is in."

"What? I thought this was a slam dunk in terms of cause of death. Who ordered the autopsy?"

"Hey, you know me, always suspicious. Frank was drugged. They used the date-rape drug GHB. It took them a while to find where the needle went in. In further inspecting the body, knowing it was most probably a homicide, they found some bruising around the wrists inconsistent with a cut, but rather from restraints of some kind, possibly handcuffs. In addition, they found a small amount of water in his lungs, indicating his head may have been submerged underwater for an extended period of time."

"Poor bastard. Do you think he could have been waterboarded? Wouldn't that be an ironic twist of fate?"

"It appears Frank was tortured to some extent before being killed, which indicates whoever killed him was seeking information."

"That is very disturbing. That would lead us to believe that we have a leak of some sort. And as I think about it, the one piece of information that Frank had that was most confidential is our capture of an ISIS leader. That then leads me to believe that terrorists were behind this."

"That would be a natural conclusion, given the circumstances. However, it doesn't really fit. I mean, if ISIS believed we were holding one of their own alive, they would be using the media and most likely acts of terrorism to demand his release. But to track down one of the interrogators and interrogate him for that information doesn't make sense."

"I guess the behavior is inconsistent," Jack admitted.

"What the hell was Frank into?" Lou sighed.

"What happens now?"

"The police will initiate a full homicide investigation, assigning two of their best detectives at my request."

"Do you think all of the strange goings on with Deeprose are connected somehow?"

"I don't know, but I wish I had time to find out. Right now we have to concentrate on the growing terrorism threat."

"What time is the NATO conference tomorrow?"

"Six p.m. EST."

"The actions coming out of that meeting will truly tell us how concerned the world is with terrorism."

> *Laura Scheinberg, aka Ms. Toni, is an only child born in 1969 to a prominent New York Jewish family. Her father was an investment banker on Wall Street and her mother a criminal law attorney. They had her late in life and have both since passed, most likely leaving her a relatively healthy inheritance.*

As North continued to read the report, he surmised that Ms. Scheinberg had taken lessons learned from both parents, along with the inheritance, to start her executive escort service. Again, he found himself impressed with the woman. The most important part of the report was confirmation that she did live in Foxhall Ridge. North could not be more self-satisfied and again appreciated how people were so easily played.

The loose end known as Laura Scheinberg would be tied up shortly after the assignment with the media was complete. She had committed to at least one television interview if asked, contingent upon her confidence of privacy. There was no way to know if she would keep this commitment, so North simply had to make a judgment call. He would kill her in three days, regardless of the level of media coverage.

☙

Sara closed and locked the solid metal door to her uninspiring office and began reviewing the files recovered from North's computer. The majority were Word and PDF documents housed in folders, the names of which she assumed to be project- and operation-related. She wasn't looking for anything in particular and was enjoying the fact she had easily obtained the covert files of arguably the second most powerful man in the CIA.

She was randomly opening folders simply based upon how interesting she found the name. Of course, she found Deeprose and briefly skimmed through those documents due to her familiarity. She had perused eleven folders before she opened one titled "Turing Test," which meant nothing to her. Upon opening, she found a sub-folder entitled "ARobotics." With her curiosity piqued, she went about opening and reading the three documents in the folder. The documents were all marked "Top Secret" and were more or less progress reports on the development of AIIR, whatever that was.

The most recent document provided the date, time, and Skype address of a simulation. That date had come and gone, and was unfortunately past the date of the last file recovered. Therefore, if there was a file about the simulation, it would be on North's current laptop. Again, there was no address for ARobotics and no name associated with the documents. She had not heard of it, but that didn't mean anything. Sara would need to do some more snooping. She made copies of the documents to bring home to share with Jack and her brother. Being an aeronautical engineer, maybe some of this would make sense to Habib.

CHAPTER 33

Abir arrived promptly to the mosque and was quickly found by Maysarah, who was accompanied by three men. The meeting was scheduled between the mid-afternoon and sunset *adhan*, or call to prayer. Even so, the mosque was well-populated, providing sufficient cover and distraction. After brief introductions facilitated by Maysarah, the men set out to a truck that was parked near the entrance.

It was obvious who was in command, as Maysarah and the two other ISIS members fell in behind the man with the scar that ran from the corner of his right eye to his jawline. Abir noticed the man, identified as Barraz, leering at him during introductions and deduced he was skeptical, to say the least.

"Where are we going?" Abir asked.

"Somewhere where we can talk privately," Barraz responded.

Abir was instantly on alert, realizing that if he had been made, getting into the truck would be a death sentence, so he decided to push the conversation on the walk to the truck.

"As we are meeting, am I to assume that there is interest in my joining ISIS and the new drone technology?"

"Silence!" Barraz commanded. "It is not safe to talk here."

Abir stole a glance at Maysarah, attempting to read him. Maysarah kept his eyes straight ahead, but made an almost imperceptible nod, which Abir interpreted as a positive, but had to attempt to confirm.

"Maysarah, I very much appreciate the opportunity and look forward to serving ISIS."

Again, Barraz ordered, "Silence, fool!"

Abir decided it was safe to proceed, but regardless, flexed his calf muscle and back muscles to confirm that his ankle holster and knife were there if needed. Abir was instructed to sit in the backseat between the two men he assumed were guards, while Maysarah drove and Barraz sat in the passenger seat.

As the truck began to roll, Barraz turned in his seat. "How do we know you are who you say you are?"

"I trust you have researched my information; otherwise we would not be sitting here."

"I understand that you are prepared to show us the new drone," Barraz continued.

"That is correct. We are making arrangements to divert one en route to a simulation test, but we will only have a short window; otherwise, the Russian government will discover it is missing."

"And when can this happen?"

"Within two days."

"How do we know this is not a trap?"

"Why would we go to all this trouble? If we wanted to capture you, it would have been today, here."

"Please don't take me for a fool. In addition to my two guards sitting here, there are ten more outside. Attempting such a thing would mean death for you and those you have brought with you."

"It is just me and they want to make a deal."

The truck entered a relatively remote area and Barraz waved a hand, directing the driver to stop. The truck pulled over, stopped, but nobody exited. Abir was prepared to thrust his left elbow into the face of the man on his left, while pulling the knife from the sheath hidden at his back. He was confident he could stab the two men in the back and kill them, but he would be an easy target for Barraz, assuming he had a weapon.

Before Abir could contemplate his timing, Barraz pulled a pistol from nowhere and pointed it at his forehead.

"Is this how you treat all of your recruits?" Abir demanded, finding an inner strength.

"Only the ones I do not trust. Are you prepared to join Allah?"

"Of course, but in a way that serves ISIS and the Caliphate—not to be butchered by my brother-in-arms."

"It is believable that you want to join us, but what is your connection with the Russian broker?"

"I have no relationship. All I have been given is his name, and he only speaks Russian."

"So how do you get your information? Who do you know?"

"As I trust your background research has uncovered, I have a significant amount of experience in engineering and technologies related to drones. I was contacted by an insurgent living in Grozny, who speaks Russian, claiming to have been contacted by a broker of the longer range technology. As you, I challenged the information, knowing that no technology had yet been developed. He explained the Russian broker would only share the information with a potential buyer."

"So you have no proof."

"No, but I thought it was worth a discussion and my opportunity to join and contribute. Can you fault me?"

At lightning speed, Barraz placed the muzzle of the gun against Abir's forehead. It took every fiber of Abir's being not to react defensively, as he did not believe it likely Barraz would pull the trigger, at least not at that moment.

"If you deceive me, my friend, you and your family will experience very painful deaths."

"I am here to serve, Barraz. I am not afraid," Abir responded.

"No later than two days from now, or no further discussions."

Apparently satisfied, Barraz lowered the gun, turned in his seat, and again with his hand directed the driver to drive back to the mosque.

"Where and when can we meet the broker and see the drone?" Barraz asked.

"Within two days' time. I will contact the Grozny insurgent and firm up the details and let you know."

"You do remember the consequences for betrayal?"

"You will be learning of the drones at the same time I do. I am willing to take the risk to join ISIS and defeat the infidels."

Abir was driven back to the mosque and given instructions to communicate through Maysarah. Once at the mosque, he called Jack.

"Jack, the second meeting went well. You need to be here the day after tomorrow, as does the drone."

"Shit, that doesn't give me much time. I have to stop in Moscow first to pick up and understand the bogus drone documents, assuming they are ready."

"Not my problem, chief. I did as instructed."

"You did it too well. All right, I'll get things set up on my end. The drone will be flown to a deserted airstrip south of Kandahar." Jack proceeded to give Abir the coordinates. "I'll check flight schedules and give you my touchdown time in Kandahar so you can coordinate the meeting time."

The call ended, and Jack realized he had a bigger interest in finding out more about the robots than he did selling the drone story, but the drones would enable him to get out of the country and do some snooping without Langley knowing.

❧

Lou entered Langley as he normally did at 6:45 a.m., crossing through the main entrance and taking the elevator up to his office on the second floor. What was abnormal about this morning were the strange looks he seemed to be getting from several passersby on the way to his office. After the second strange look, he checked his clothing to make sure he hadn't missed a button or zipper somewhere important. He realized he got a sideways glance once in a while when his tie didn't necessarily match his slacks and sport coat, but he didn't care.

Upon entering his office, his cell phone rang. It was James Clapper. "Lou, have you seen the paper this morning?"

"Not yet. I typically read the *Post* during my lunch hour as a midday respite."

"Well, grab the paper and get yourself to my office, pronto. Do not speak with anyone on the way."

"Yes, sir." *How ominous*, thought Lou as he hung up. Probably another attempt by the media to create fire where there was a distant smell of smoke. Lou grabbed the still-rolled-up paper that had been delivered to his office, sat down at his desk, and opened it. The headline hit him like a punch in the stomach:

CIA Director's Mistress Fed Up, Demands Attention

Lou's heart began to accelerate as he continued reading the article.

> *Ms. Stella Morgan, a forty-three-year-old, self-described career volunteer for multiple causes, claims to have been having a secret affair with Louis Pendleton, the acting CIA director, for several years. Stella Morgan is an alias she is using, fearing repercussions from the CIA. Morgan claims they met while running and have been secretly rendezvousing at least three times per month in several D.C. hotels while Pendleton was supposedly on his weekend jogs. The* Post *spoke to several hotel employees, who were able to identify*

Pendleton and confirm his and Morgan's presence at the subject hotels.

Ms. Morgan stated that she had grown tired of Pendleton's repeated promises to leave his wife to marry her. The picture of Pendleton and Morgan contained in this article was taken by a friend of Morgan's during a recent rendezvous. Morgan realized she needed proof of the affair. The friend has requested anonymity, which is understandable given the circumstances.

When asked what Morgan hoped to achieve by going public with the affair, she simply said, "I was angry and didn't know what else to do." The Post *has placed a call to both the CIA and the Office of the Director of Intelligence for comment, but as of publication time, had yet to receive a response.*

Lou was numb. His first thought was of Kate. Surely she would be receiving calls, if she hadn't already. He needed to call and warn her. But what would he say? This conversation would be difficult in person, let alone over the phone. Still, he had no choice but to call her immediately, then head to Clapper's office.

"Hey, honey."

"Did you forget something?" Kate asked.

"Listen, sweetheart, something has happened."

"Are you all right?"

"I'm fine— well, physically."

"What has happened?" Kate asked.

"This is a conversation I would prefer to have in person, but under the circumstances, I have no choice but to have it over the phone."

"You're frightening me, Lou."

"I don't know how to begin, so I'll just... well, begin. There is an article in the *Post* today claiming I have had an affair." Lou hesitated to allow his words to sink in.

Without missing a beat, Kate responded with a chuckle in her voice. "My dearest Lou, you're many things, but a philanderer you're not. Is this new job worth all of this?"

"Well, I suspect I will not have to worry about the job much longer. I'm on my way to the DNI's office and I don't anticipate it going well."

"Where in the world did the *Post* conjure up such a story? Slander immediately comes to mind."

"Remember I told you about that strange encounter with the woman on the running trail the other day?"

"Yes."

"Turns out she had someone in hiding, taking pictures as I helped her up. The picture they ran in the *Post* can certainly be interpreted that we are together and lends credence to her claim."

"But why go to all this trouble? Who wants to harm you?"

"I have no idea, but am damn sure going to find out. In the meantime, you can expect a media barrage."

"Don't worry about that. I can handle myself."

"I suspect we will be given some strong suggestions on talking points, most of which will begin and end with *no comment*."

"Hurry to your meeting and call me right away with the results."

"I suspect I may be home early today, darling."

"Hmm, maybe I should send your mystery lady a thank you note."

"Love you, sweetie."

"Love you too. Please be careful."

༄

"Sit down, Lou." The DNI was thankful that Lou had shut the office door upon entering. "We have a problem on our hands, don't we?"

"I'm afraid we do."

"Hell hath no fury like a woman scorned."

"Yes, I've heard that. What I want to know is who I have scorned to put this woman up to this."

"Are you telling me you don't know this Stella Morgan?"

"That's exactly what I'm telling you."

"If the *Post* story is true—and the press secretary is all over them as we speak— then someone went to a hell of a lot of trouble."

"Yes, they did. *Why* is the question."

"I think it is pretty obvious. You have an enemy."

"I have been in this job for less than two months and it seems that every time I turn around something bizarre is happening. At first I thought it was a simple streak of bad luck out of the gate. But now this. I'm more convinced than ever that all of the odd occurrences are somehow connected."

"I do have to admit that there have been some strange things that have happened since you took the job."

"Coincidences are rarely just that and if one took the time to dig deeper, one would find a connection. Jesus, I can't imagine what my colleagues, friends, and family are thinking right now."

"What about your wife?"

"I called her immediately after you phoned. She simply laughed at the allegation."

"You're a lucky man."

"Damn right, which makes this story that much more implausible. Doesn't the media have an obligation, or at least the courtesy, to check with us first?"

"Freedom of speech in its ugliest form, Lou. I cannot imagine them printing the story if they had not been able to confirm the information from their sources."

"If that is the case, then people either have mistaken me for someone else or are lying."

"What about the picture?"

"It happened several days ago when I was on my evening run. This Stella Morgan, or whatever her name is, was sitting on the trail, rubbing her ankle from an apparent strain. I had stopped to offer assistance when she jumped into my personal space. Obviously, this was planned, as there was someone hiding in the woods who took pictures when she did that."

"Lou, do you realize how this sounds?"

"Like the truth sounds."

"Okay, we need to manage this, and right now it is by the hour. I spoke with the president and he is concerned about the integrity of the CIA and the administration. I want you to lay low for the rest of the day until we ferret out the *Post* story and determine if and how we conduct our own investigation."

"What about my full plate of assignments?"

"I trust the world is not going to end during the next eight hours. Standard protocol for managing incoming messages will be in place. I'll send an e-mail to your team and other appropriate staff, advising them that the matter is under investigation and that they are to speak with no one, especially the media."

"I'm angry, James. I'm going to need your help finding out who is behind this."

"I would be mad as hell too. I'll call you as soon as I get a report on the *Post* story. Now, please leave the building as quietly as possible and avoid engaging with anyone."

Lou felt everyone's eyes were on him as he exited the building. He was prepared to do whatever it took to clear his name and get himself out of this mess.

CHAPTER 34

Sara had breakfast ready for Habib as he stumbled towards the teakettle, turban-less.

"Morning, Habib. I want to show you something," she said.

"I figured something was up, since you made me breakfast. Won't you be late for work?"

"This won't take long. Here, have a look at these documents. They were housed in a sub-file called 'ARobotics' underneath another file called 'Turing Test.'"

Habib promptly sat up in his chair and blurted, "Turing Test?"

"Yes. What kind of test is that?"

"You don't know and you work in intelligence?"

"Oh, forgive me, oh learned one."

"The Turing Test is not necessarily a test per se, but it is achieved or passed when a robot fools humans into believing it is human."

"Well, these documents seem to deal with robots of some sort, given the name of the sub-folder."

Habib continued to read, the expression on his face changing from mild interest to amazement. "Where did you get these?"

"A colleague had them."

"A colleague?"

"The deputy director."

"And he gave these to you?"

"Well, *gave* is probably a stretch."

"You stole these?"

"Listen, I noticed a peculiar document on his desk and then found out that he was recycling his laptop every sixty days, which also is peculiar."

"So how did you get these?"

"Not important. What do they mean?"

"My loose interpretation is that your government is a few simulation tests away from deploying armed robots into war, which means that they have successfully integrated artificial intelligence."

"But we are not currently at war. We have some so-called peacekeeping forces in several countries, but nothing defined as a formal military campaign."

"Maybe I misread the intent, but it does talk about deployment of hundreds of these AIIRs, which must be an acronym. I would bet my life that the first two words are *artificial intelligence*."

"What about ARobotics? Have you heard of it or them?"

"No, but they are more than likely the developer and manufacturer of the robots."

"We need to find this ARobotics."

"*We?*"

"C'mon, Habib, you talk their talk. What harm can there be in simply trying to find where they are? In addition, there is a guy I work with who can help us and will be very interested in anything to do with robots."

"This is top secret. Getting anywhere near it sounds dangerous."

Sara realized she was getting in over her head, but she couldn't stop herself. She did not like North, nor did she trust him. If anyone was up to no good, it would be him. She caught herself checking the rearview mirror several times during the drive to Langley. She couldn't wait to share her findings with Jack.

☙

Lou called Kate and explained he was on his way home. He inquired if there was any media by the house and learned that, fortunately, there was not. However, he anticipated there would be before noon. He told Kate to pack a bag, as they would be checking into a hotel for the next several days to give this thing a chance to blow over.

He was just entering his neighborhood when his cell phone rang.

"Lou, Hank."

"Oh, Hank, have you heard?"

"Reason for my call, my brother."

"Your connections scare me. My head is spinning. I just left headquarters on a recommended sabbatical of sorts."

"Somebody went to a lot of trouble to make your life miserable."

"I was just trying to come up with a list of those who might, and I honestly have been unable to conjure up one person."

"Doesn't surprise me. You've had a very distinguished career not leaving any dead bodies along the way. I haven't had a chance to give this much thought, but I will."

"Aren't you going to ask me?"

"Of course not. If you had anything to tell me, I trust you would. You, or rather *we*, are dealing with someone or something sinister."

"I appreciate your faith in me. And no, none of it is true, just for the record. When you say we are dealing with something, who is *we*?"

"You and me, partner, and our respective peeps. You got any peeps?"

"I'm afraid it is a short list. The only people I believe I can truly trust now are Kate and Jack Landis."

"Yikes, that *is* a short list. Who is Jack Landis?"

Lou spent the next two minutes parked in his driveway, detailing his past and present relationship with Jack.

"Sounds like a good man. Where is he on all this?"

"We haven't had a chance to talk yet. My first assignment is to get Kate out of the house and book us into a hotel for a few days. I'm parked in the driveway now."

"Good idea. I'll let you go. Once you're settled, I have a tool that may help."

"I'll call you later today. Is this a good number to reach you on?"

"Yes."

"Talk later."

As Lou hung up, Kate came out of the front door with two duffel bags.

"Lou, I asked Sandra Kramly, who lives at the entrance of the subdivision, to call if she noticed any media vehicles entering the neighborhood. She just called—we have two minutes before they get here," Kate calmly stated as she placed the duffel bags in the backseat.

"You are an amazing woman," Lou said, smiling. He started backing out of the driveway while Kate was still closing the door.

Kate and Lou fiercely held hands as he took the long way out of the neighborhood, ensuring he would not encounter the media.

✧

The shooter had been lying prone on the grassy knoll hidden among a grouping of mature shortleaf pines for forty-five minutes, awaiting the return of the target to pass through the gate into the Foxhall community. From that vantage point, he could watch several condominium owners returning home and entering through the gate. The gate was activated by a window decal, as the driver simply had to pull up within one foot of it and wait for the arm to rise to allow them to drive through.

The shooter counted off five seconds between the time a car stopped to wait for the arm to rise and then continue driving. Five seconds was more than enough time to get off a clean and accurate kill shot. The accuracy of the rifle was true up to 400 yards; the knoll was 250 yards away from the gate.

He again used the binoculars to scan the adjacent road, looking for the vehicle. And there it was, turning left onto the complex's drive, slowly approaching the gate. The shooter took into consideration the five to ten mile-per-hour wind and peered through the scope. The car slowly came to a stop at the gate as the electronic eye scanned the bar code of the decal.

The target had eerily and unexpectedly turned and looked directly in the shooter's direction. It caused a nanosecond delay before the trigger was pulled. The target's face then disappeared from the scope view as the impact of the bullet forced the head back and to the right. Confident a second shot was not necessary, the shooter efficiently broke down the rifle, placing its parts in a duffel bag. After ensuring no one was witness to an exit from the pine trees protecting the grassy knoll, the shooter adjusted their wig and glasses and calmly walked away.

CHAPTER 35

"Jack, Sara."

"Z'up?"

"I stumbled onto something you may find interesting. I was in North's office waiting for him to return and I noticed a letter of some sort from a company by the name of ARobotics."

"What did the letter say?"

"I didn't have a chance to read it before North came back. He seemed perturbed that I had seen the envelope. I told him I found it on the floor and was putting it back on his desk."

"Did he buy it?"

"Not sure. Anyway, I did some digging. There is no website, phone number, or listing of any kind with the normal listing agencies, including the Securities and Exchange Commission. I checked with state securities regulator offices. It took me nine states until I located an ARobotics Incorporated, registered in Massachusetts."

"And an address?"

"Yes. I have an idea. My brother is pretty savvy when it comes to technology. I was thinking he could check it out."

"Under what pretense?"

"Looking for a job."

"Not sure how much he would learn, but I guess it's a start."

"Would you be able to go and keep an eye on him?"

"I insist upon it."

"Thank you. I'll talk to Habib and let you know."

The call ended and Jack pondered the possibility of the CIA being behind the events that took place in the meadow. Considering what Lou told him about all of the drone activity around the world, it now didn't seem so farfetched. He still needed more information before he spoke with Lou. Hopefully, the trip to Massachusetts would prove worthwhile.

Sara immediately phoned Habib. "Listen," she said as he answered the call.

"How goes the spy business?"

"I found the information we were looking for. But let's not talk about it on the phone. Can you meet me for lunch?"

"Of course, what else do I have to do anyway?"

Two hours later Sara and Habib were seated together at a deli not far from Langley.

"Did you find anything?" Habib asked as the waitress plunked down two glasses of water trimmed with lemons.

"Yes," she said as she passed Habib a piece of paper containing the address.

"And why are you giving this to me?"

"C'mon, Habib. Make up some reason to knock on the door and ask a few questions."

"Oh, sure. A Muslim turns up on the East Coast of the U.S. and asks for directions to the nearest robotics exhibit."

"I suggest you leave your turban at home."

"And what do you expect to learn?"

"I have no idea. Just get a feel for the place. Look around, if you can. Pretend you are looking for a job. I'm sure they have all kinds of engineers working there."

"Fine. I commit to do nothing more than walk in the door, ask about employment opportunities, and walk out."

"Perfect. Someone is going to go with you, to keep an eye out."

"The guy you mentioned?"

"Yes, Jack Landis. I work with him. He will be right outside and if anything happens, simply call or text him. Here, I'll text you his number."

"Can you trust him?"

"I'm working on it, but this is too important to ignore."

"All right, but this is as deep as I get involved."

"Agreed. Thank you."

Two hours later, Sara was having serious reservations about getting her brother involved, but a knock on the door asking about employment opportunities seemed harmless. She knew Habib would not do or say anything foolish. She considered this the lowest-risk activity she had been involved in since working with the CIA. She hoped to God she was right.

☙

Kate, all 120 pounds dripping wet, drilled Lou with questions the entire drive to the hotel in hopes of creating some thread of rationale to follow. "Have you had any major disagreements with anyone recently?"

"No."

"Is there someone in your past who may perceive something that you did as egregious to them or their beliefs?"

"Not that I recall."

"Have you physically harmed anyone?"

"God, no."

"Could anyone believe that you were, in some way, either flirting with or hitting on their significant other?"

"Really, Kate?"

"I'm serious. If there was some behavior, I know it would have been innocent or not intended to be anything flirtatious, but someone may have mistaken it for something it was not."

"Sorry, but I can't think of any exchange or communication that could be remotely interpreted as anything but business."

"Well, the most logical and easiest explanation is that somewhere along the line you met this woman, she had feelings for you, and you rebuffed them without realizing it."

"Yes, I thought of that, as anything else would require much planning and deliberation. But, for the life of me, I cannot think of anyone. In addition, I know that I never saw that woman before the other day."

"Then this situation is extremely precarious. We need some help figuring this out."

"Once we get to the hotel, I'll give Hank a call back and get hold of Jack. We need to figure this thing out sooner rather than later."

"What's the worst that could happen?"

"I lose my job and my reputation is damaged forever. I'm not sure what the impact would be upon my pension."

"Well, my dear, we have done extremely well financially and don't need your pension to retire handsomely. As far as your reputation, all that matters is that your loved ones and friends believe in you. And, selfishly speaking, losing your job would be a good thing as we could start our retirement sooner rather than later. All in all, things could be worse."

"Please don't say that, honey, because often they do get worse just when you think that they cannot."

As they pulled into the hotel parking lot, Lou found himself feeling relieved. It was if a 500-pound gorilla had been shed from his shoulders. He also felt guilty for feeling that way, but it was a sure indication that he would no longer be the CIA director, no matter how things turned out.

◦∽◦

"Lou," greeted Hank.

"Hey, buddy."

"Are you safely tucked away where no one can find you?"

"We hope so."

"How is Kate doing through all this?"

"Amazingly well. She never doubted me for a second."

"And why would she? You're a man among men, Mr. Pendleton."

"I'm damn lucky, is what I am."

"Do you have any ideas or leads?"

"Not a one. It's very frustrating. We've dismissed this woman acting alone."

"So we have the work of someone fairly sophisticated."

"Evidently. But why and whom?"

"Well, I want to introduce a tool that may help you think through this problem."

"Really? And what would that be?"

"It is called Bluescape. Simply put, it's a think tool. In terms of its physical properties, I like to think of it as a large iPad that fills an entire wall so that multiple people can view it, interact with it, and store information on it."

"Sounds like something from an *NCIS* episode."

"Well, it kind of is, but the difference is this really works."

"How do you have access to something like this?"

"I invested in a tech company in Silicon Valley several years ago and they ended up partnering with a large office-furniture manufacturer. Together they developed this revolutionary new technology. Several showrooms have been set up across North America to demonstrate the product and one just happens to be in D.C."

"Does that mean I can use it?"

"Indeed it does."

"Who is going to show me how to use it?"

"There is a showroom manager; she will teach you. It is uber-simple to use. Like I said, it's like using an iPad. It was designed with the intent of updating the war rooms of old with technology."

"And you believe this think tool can help my situation?"

"I have invested a significant amount of money, so I would have to answer in the affirmative."

"How do we get started?"

"I'll send you the showroom manager's contact information so you can schedule training and book the room as you need it."

"Will the information remain confidential?"

"Yes. You will be given a session, access to which will require a user ID and password."

"Can I invite Jack to join me?"

"I would suggest you invite Jack and Kate, and I would also be interested in helping you decipher this riddle."

"I would be honored, Hank, but I can only imagine how busy your schedule is."

"First of all, you know I would always help you in a jam. Second, I have some skin in the game, if you recall."

"Ah yes, the significant campaign contribution that led to my getting this job. So in other words, this is your fault."

As Lou hung up, he found it absurd that he was holed away in a hotel room hiding from the media. He was fairly certain he would be unemployed within a matter of days, and now a buddy from college had talked him into using the latest technology, when he could barely work the remote.

CHAPTER 36

Glenn Smith had been a D.C. Metro homicide detective for seventeen years. During his tenure many things had changed. A woman was now the chief of police, he handled twice as many homicides as he did ten years ago, and his waistline had grown six inches thanks to ten-hour days and fast food. A couple of the things that didn't change were the brutality of the murders in the city and his partner, Tom Warfield.

Smith was promoted a month before Warfield, each having worked their way up from street patrol to narcotics to homicide. Smith favored pizza and beer and it showed in the spare tire hanging three inches over his belt. What did he care? He was married and didn't care if he stayed married. His clothes were straight off the *Columbo* rack and he shaved every other day—if he felt like it.

In contrast, Warfield was divorced and worked at looking good with daily workouts and a mostly healthy diet. His wore well-tailored, good-quality clothes that were always cleaned and pressed. His six-inch ponytail was like a bumper sticker on a Porsche, but he made it work. His primary vice was swearing, which he was able to indulge in freely as a detective.

The pair proved themselves to be the best at what they did. While Smith was officially the lead detective, but he rarely pulled rank on his partner. They had been discussing the progress of the Conover case, or lack thereof, when Smith received a call from their lieutenant telling them that a body had been found shot and they were to immediately head to the scene.

Upon arriving, one of the uniforms on site shared what information had been gathered so far. "Sir, the woman's body was found by a security guard, that guy sitting on the grass over there. The condo complex's security system's alarm went off when the security gate was stuck in the *up* position. That guy answered the call. He said he had been out here several times for the same issue and thought nothing of it.

"He parked immediately behind the woman's vehicle, walked up to the driver's-side window, and found one eye socket missing and the passenger side smattered with brain residue. He lost his cookies, which you can see next to the car. After five minutes of heaving, he collected himself and had the sense to first call nine-one-one and then his dispatch officer."

"Thank you, Officer," Smith responded. "We'll take a look."

The bullet had entered her skull just above the left eye and cleanly exited near the center of the back of the head and through the passenger-side window, embedding itself into the trunk of a shortleaf pine. The impact of the bullet forced her head back and to the right. Her body slumped to the right in the seat, held up in a 60-degree angle by the seatbelt. There was enough weight from her right leg on the brake to keep the car from moving forward. Her body did not slump forward onto the horn, which would have drawn attention and provided the shooter much less time to exit the scene.

Most of the blood spatter was on the right side of the windshield and the passenger-side window. The bullet had made a clean hole in the window without breaking it. Blood was exiting the headwound and draining into her purse onto an envelope. Smith thought better than to disturb what forensic evidence there might be in her purse, and instead donned latex gloves and opened the glove compartment. He found her name listed on her registration: Laura Scheinberg.

Smith groaned audibly as he and Warfield embarked upon an area search for physical evidence. His instincts told him this was an act of either jealousy or money considering the vic lived in the high-rent district. The fact someone shot the woman in broad daylight was bold. Whoever did this had to be pretty confident in their marksmanship, given the shot was most likely taken from the cover of brush some distance away.

"I haven't seen that much brain matter in a long time," Warfield said.

"Yeah, between that and the guard's pile of puke, I almost lost my appetite," Smith responded.

"Yeah right—*almost*. I can't recall a time you ever refused a meal, especially a free one."

"So what do you make of this mess?"

"Seems pretty dramatic and with an element of risk, given the shot had to be relatively precise." "Agreed. Whoever did this was proficient, which makes me think *hired gun*."

"Makes sense. We better start digging while this thing is still warm."

CHAPTER 37

It was shortly before noon when Lou got off the call with the DNI. Kate could tell by the expression on his face that the call did not go well.

"What did he say?" asked Kate.

"The president asked for my immediate resignation, and I gave it to him."

"Why did you do that?"

"All of the *Post*'s sources were confirmed. In addition, the *Post* provided the script from this woman's cell phone, which was signed *Lou*. The text was from a prepaid cell phone, so there is no way to trace it. This information, in combination with the woman's statement and the picture, is too much circumstantial evidence for the White House."

"Oh, honey, I'm so sorry."

"I can't blame them. Based upon the information, my short tenure, and the serious situations we currently face, I would have made the same decision."

"Are they going to help you get to the bottom of this?"

"Clapper said that the agency would do what it could under the circumstances. But given the media attention this is receiving now, the first thing to be done is for the press secretary to announce my resignation at a press conference this afternoon. I'm hopeful for help, but frankly, once the administration has washed their hands of me, I really don't anticipate much support."

"Who will take responsibility for your job?"

"Richard North will take over on an interim basis until a candidate is identified and nominated."

"And what about Jack?"

"I'm not sure. My team has no doubt been told not to communicate with me while I suspect they will learn of my resignation within the hour. Their phones and e-mail accounts will be under surveillance, so I doubt any of them will try to reach me."

"Well, we need to get hold of Jack right away."

"We have our training scheduled tomorrow morning to learn about Hank's Bluescape. I don't want to compromise Jack. I say we wait until tomorrow morning. I trust neither Jack nor Sara has mentioned it to anyone. We can all catch up then."

"That makes sense. No wonder I married you, you're a smart guy."

"Hopefully, we're all smart enough to figure this mess out. I don't want my long established career to end with a blemish like this."

"Would you be mad if I said I didn't care how it ended, as long as it ended and we could spend more time together?"

"Now, that's a loaded question."

ᐇ

Smith visited the medical examiner first thing the morning following the shooting. He knew he had to push them to finish their work before any possible trail went cold. Smith listened as the ME gave him an overview. "The cause of death appears to be from a single shot to the head. The bullet had been discovered in and retrieved from the pine tree. Ballistics results should be ready tomorrow. As of yet, no one has come forward to claim the body."

Smith knew the police had yet to identify a next of kin, while interviews with neighbors produced nothing other than comments indicating Ms. Scheinberg kept to herself.

The ME continued, "The deceased's possessions included an empty Starbucks cup, a stack of overdue library books, and her purse, the contents of which had been saturated with blood. Beyond the cosmetics, wallet, hairbrush, mirror, and fingernail file, the only contents worth exploring were an iPhone, a prepaid cell phone, and a sealed envelope. If there was an address on the envelope or documents inside, all are indiscernible due to the blood until a forensics analysis can be completed.

"But first things first. We must conduct a full autopsy to determine if anything else contributed to the death, as unlikely as it may be."

Smith interrupted, "We need the autopsy and forensics done yesterday. This is not your average kill. Whoever did this may be a pro and the sooner we have information, the better our chances of catching them."

"I understand, Detective. My assistant and I are prepared to start on the autopsy immediately while all physical evidence has been sent to forensics."

"Let me know as soon as possible."

"Of course."

The assistant coroner went about her business, weighing the organs and taking tissue samples. As she was removing urine from the bladder with a syringe, Smith took a long look at the corpse and believed he recognized the woman from a *Post* article. He asked the ME if he recognized the woman, which he did not.

"Is there a computer with internet access I can use?"

"Sure, follow me," the assistant said as she led Smith to her office, entered the laptop's password, and invited him to help himself.

Smith searched recent articles on the *Post's* Web site. There he found the picture of Louis Pendleton and the woman, who was now lying on the cadaver-dissection table in the examination room. He printed the article and accompanying picture and immediately called Warfield.

"You're not going to believe this, pards…" Smith began as he explained the revelation to Warfield.

∽

Jack and Sara watched the press conference in silence. Jack sighed when North's nomination was announced. When it was over, Sara turned the television off.

"You have a new boss now," said Jack.

"I think he's a creeper; he makes my skin crawl."

"Can you request a reassignment?"

"I guess I could, but I'm fairly confident that there's no one else currently available that has the language skills and background that I have. That's not to say I'm indispensable, but I suspect all other qualified candidates are currently on assignment."

"We need you working this operation, Sara. I need you working this operation. I need to know someone I value and trust will be here while I'm God-knows-where, chasing the bad guys."

"You trust me, do you?"

"I do, and I hope you trust me. But, as we discussed before, you should always have your guard up."

"Come on into the kitchen; making dinner is a team effort tonight."

"Excellent. What are we making?"

"Bruschetta with grilled onions and peppers, Parmesan, and garlic."

"Garlic?"

"No worries if we both eat it," Sara said with an impish grin. "We are then making shish kebabs with large scallops, mushrooms, chorizo sausage, and green tomatoes."

"The tomatoes never make it."

"I know, right? Okay, you're in charge of slicing the vegetables. The cutting board is next to the fridge, while the knives are in the drawer to my left."

Jack grabbed the cutting board to his right, then took a step to his left and reached around Sara to open the drawer with the knives. At the same time, she moved to her left to turn on the range. The result was them bumping directly into one another.

Sara caught a whiff of his cologne as she felt her breasts against his chest. Neither one moved. She remained motionless while he slowly brought his right hand to her face, confident that he wanted her as much as she wanted him. She was determined to go slowly, even though every fiber of her being wanted to grab, smother, and explore every inch of his body.

She moved her cheek into his hand, half-closing her eyes, lips moving toward his. She felt his left hand slip behind her hip and pull her to him. The adrenaline rushed through her; she had not felt this wanting in a very long time. Their lips met slowly and deliberately at first, and after three kisses with their mouths opening wider with each progressive kiss, he plunged his tongue deep into her mouth and she was ready and receptive. It was a long, passionate kiss with each of them pulling the other's body as close to one another as physically possible.

"Oh, Jack," was all Sara could muster between kisses.

He picked her up and perched her on the kitchen counter, moving his hips between her legs. She pulled her shirt off and Jack unclasped her bra. He gently cupped her ample, firm breasts in his hands, bending down so he could take each nipple in his mouth. As he did, she reached between his legs and felt his hardness, wanting desperately to free him from his pants.

She jumped off the counter and whispered in his ear, "Let's go."

Once in the bedroom, they disrobed as if it was a race. She won, helped Jack pull off his pants, and then lunged on top of him.

Their hands explored one another in a frenzy of pleasure and excitement. She was wet and eager as he stroked her clitoris, increasing pressure with each movement. Her back arched and her head fell back. Jack stretched to capture her right nipple in his mouth. The additional sensation pushed Sara over the brink. She cried out in orgasmic ecstasy, riding wave after wave of surrender.

As her shuddering subsided, Sara kissed her way down Jack's chest, to where his hardness eagerly awaited. She took him between her lips, sucking and licking ferociously, bringing Jack near orgasm several times. Only after he said "enough" did she straddle Jack and guide him into her.

Both had every intention of moving slowly, in tandem, to make the moment last as long as possible. But within a minute they were pumping and thrusting as hard and fast as they could until Jack exploded into her and Sara experienced the second-best orgasm of her life, the first one having occurred twenty minutes earlier.

Sara rolled off Jack and onto her back. "Okay," she said with halted breath, "was that as good as I thought it was, or have I simply been missing out on life?"

"No, that was definitely incredible. Come here."

Sara snuggled into his arms and again felt as though he was looking right into her and was able to read her every thought and emotion. She liked it and found herself in... well, heaven—or at least as close to what she thought heaven would feel like.

Jack stroked her hair and lips, kissed her eyes, and complimented her body over and over. She simply smiled and looked at him, wishing the moment would never end.

"Can you stay the night?" she asked.

"If you feed me." Jack smiled.

Sara found herself feeling very hungry, and thinking about round number two.

CHAPTER 38

Lou and Kate were the first to arrive at the showroom housing Bluescape at 6:25 a.m. The showroom was adorned with contemporary office furniture vignettes throughout the 10,000-square-foot space with several glass-walled conference rooms. The floor was a light terrazzo tiling, while high-end leather lounge seats and couches secured the perimeter.

Hank walked in moments later and bellowed across the showroom, "Lou! Kate! How the hell are you?"

Kate raced across the showroom to embrace Hank while Lou saddled up close behind to shake his hand.

"Oh, Henry, it is so good to see you," said Kate, the only person allowed to call him Henry.

"Terrific to see you, buddy," chimed in Lou. "I wish the circumstances were different."

"Hey, the situation is what it is and we have each other to solve it. No worries," responded Hank. "Have you had a chance to see our new baby?"

"No, we just got here," said Kate.

"Is anybody else coming?"

"Well, we're hoping Jack—" said Lou. As he finished his sentence, Sara and Jack walked in together.

"Morning," Jack said.

"Hi Lou, good to see you," added Sara.

"Sara, I didn't expect to see you," said Lou as he gave Jack a raised eyebrow, given he had not asked Lou if it was all right to include Sara.

"I didn't think you would mind, under the circumstances. One more helping hand couldn't hurt, right?"

"I guess not. Thank you two for coming." Lou introduced everyone. The group shook hands and expressed their anticipation for working together. "The showroom manager should be here in ten minutes or so. Oh, here she is now. Please follow me into the new age war room and we will get started momentarily," Lou continued.

After introductions, the manager took the assembled team through the think tool. The manager explained, "It begins with initiating a session, which is a password-protected file that houses all of the inputted data, in addition to data and ideas generated by a team working within the session. Think of a session as a traditional war room, where people gather to strategize about an event, process, product, service, or whatever. Instead of the archaic marker board, yellow sticky notes, foam boards, etc., all information is saved and presented electronically on monitors that are hung immediately adjacent to one another on the wall.

"In the application we have here, there are monitors three high and five columns across, or a total of fifteen monitors. Each monitor is forty-two by forty-eight. As you can see, the effect is that the entire wall behind me is one big monitor and, in fact, they operate as one, similar to an iPad.

"Input data can be downloaded from most any device, while users may interact with it by opening a window with a simple touch of this special pen and making notes, like I'm doing now. The notes then become a permanent part of this session. Data may be moved around within the session by simply touching the object and dragging it to another location, like this."

"Incredible," Lou pronounced.

"What a powerful tool," added Jack.

"Indeed," continued the manager.

"Another advantage," chimed in Hank, "is that it cannot be erased like a marker board, or vacuumed up by the cleaning crew, as some not-so-sticky notes are."

"How much information can it house?" Sara asked.

"One hundred sixty acres," answered the manager.

"Excuse me?" Jack asked.

"Scary, isn't it?" Hank responded.

"I hope we don't need that much space," Lou countered.

"What experience have you had with it?" Jack asked.

"Admittedly limited," said Hank. "The tool is right out of the box. We have several focus groups working on it while an ad agency was the guinea pig. They developed an ad campaign for a high end clothing line. The feedback has all been overwhelmingly positive. That said, like any other technology, it is up to the users to maximize the capability. In a war room, the key attributes are the ability to see, review, interpret, analyze, consider, challenge, add, delete, massage, and expand information and data that has been captured. The real power is the combined intellect of the team using the tool; the tool facilitates the thinking dynamic among the team."

"How do we start?" Jack inquired.

The manager stepped forward. "I would suggest each person identify and organize information that may be relevant to your project. Then, during your inaugural review, each person downloads their respective information into the session. You then review the information together, determine what is relevant, what needs to be investigated, what the flow of information is, if applicable, etc. From there, the power of collaboration and thinking should take over."

"Awesome," Kate chirped, drawing surprised looks from everyone. "What, am I too old to use that word?"

The manager continued, "Why don't you folks spend some time working with the tool this morning? I have connected a laptop so that you can practice downloading information. I have created your session, which you're in now. The user ID and passwords are *Hank* and *Lou*, respectively. You may have this room until eight-thirty this morning, which gives you nearly ninety minutes. If you have any questions, I'll be in my office."

The group thanked her and she left to head to her office. As soon as she was out of earshot, Jack turned to Lou. "Lou, I'm so sorry about what has happened. This is so outrageous; I'm having difficulty finding words to describe it."

"Oh, I have a few words," chimed in Hank, his face flushed with anger.

"I'm so sorry, Lou," Sara offered.

"I very much appreciate all of your support and belief in me. I'm lucky to have you. I'm especially lucky to have you, Kate."

Kate simply smiled, took his hand, and calmly said, "Let's get to work. We haven't much time to learn how to use this thing."

❧

Jack parked the rental two blocks away from the address Sara had given him. It was located in a remote area of an industrial park on the south side of Springfield. There was no sign out front identifying it as ARobotics, while the majority of the windows were tinted, prohibiting anyone from looking inside. The parking lot was full of expensive cars.

"It doesn't look like a factory," Habib said from the passenger seat.

"Not at all; it's a simple two-story brick building."

"Are you sure you have the right address?"

"Yes, it's on the side of the building. Are you ready?"

"I really don't want to do this."

"I understand. I'm happy to do it."

"No, I promised Sara. I will call or text if I need help."

"Roger that."

"Fine." And with that, Habib exited the car, approached the front door, and found it was secured with card access only and security cameras mounted on the corners of the building. He pushed the buzzer next to a speaker and waited. A minute later, a monotone voice asked what was the reason for his visit. Habib simply stated, "Human Resource Manager." And with that, he heard the hum of the release, allowing him to open the door and enter the building.

He was immediately met by two security guards who could easily be moonlighting for the WWE—and twins, no less. They scanned him using a wand of some sort and asked him for his ID. He presented his national-identification number card from Pakistan, assuming that would get him bounced from the building, but the two guards didn't blink. One asked him to follow them, while the other brought up the rear behind Habib.

He was led down a hallway from which he could see what he assumed were scientists and engineers working in several labs full of computers, robotics, and testing equipment. He saw several other guards, all about the same stature as his escorts, as the trio wove their way through the building. They finally reached a suite of offices. All the doors were closed and required a card to access. Upon reaching the third door, one of the guards waved a card over the reader and the light turned from red to green, a faint buzz could be heard, and the guard opened the door, nodding his head for Habib to enter.

Habib slowly sat down in the chair opposite one of the most beautiful women he had ever seen. She was looking down at a file on her desk and didn't seem to notice him. She then looked up and asked, "How did you learn of us?"

"A relative in Pakistan had a friend who traveled to America and had heard that the robotics industry had taken root in Massachusetts," replied Habib, doing his best to maintain eye contact and not belie the fact he was lying. "How did you find us?"

"This friend told my relative that many of the companies are doing work for the U.S. government and that they may be... well, off the grid, to some extent. I checked with the state securities regulators' office for any companies that were involved in robotics. ARobotics was the first one on the alphabetical list, so I started here."

The woman cocked her head left, then right, albeit subtly, as she seemed to ponder Habib's response. At that moment, the TV monitor on the wall to his left came alive with his picture and background information, including education, work history, and family members. Thankfully, Sara's information was captured as United Nations interpreter rather than as an employee of Homeland Security.

"Which relative?" the woman pushed.

"I beg your pardon?" Habib's concentration was thrown by the speed at which his information was obtained.

"Which relative had the friend?"

"Oh, it was my uncle."

"The one who has passed?"

"Ah, yes."

"But he died four years ago. We have been in existence for less than that."

"Again, ARobotics wasn't specifically named, only that the industry was supposedly based here."

The woman again cocked her head left and right, seemingly assimilating this information. After a long pause, she stood, bent forward, extended her hand, and said, "We have no openings at this time. Thank you for your interest."

Habib stood, relieved the encounter was over and took her hand to shake it. The woman's handshake seemed relatively strong and abrupt for a woman's, but he was unaccustomed to working with American women. As he let go of her hand, he again attempted to make eye contact, but the woman's eyes were slightly askew, looking up and a little to the right of Habib's eyes. At that moment, it struck him like a lightning bolt.

CHAPTER 39

Jack had to ask Habib to slow down several times in order to understand what he was saying. The pair had driven to a nearby restaurant for lunch and a debrief of what Habib had discovered.

"They are all robots!" Habib said for the third time.

"Okay, okay," Jack said, attempting to settle him down. "These robots moved and spoke like humans?"

"It was unbelievable, fascinating."

"But how can you be sure?"

"It was the subtleties. The guards moved together, as if they were synchronized. The woman's head movement, handshake, and eye contact were all just a bit off."

"Habib, I don't doubt your expertise relative to engineering and technology, but could it be the guards, as possibly twins, had similar movement tendencies and the woman was simply a bit odd?"

"I guess so. I'd need to see them again."

"Not happening. The deal with Sara was you go in once and you are done. I'll take a second look later tonight. After lunch, I'm taking you back to the airport."

"What do we tell Sara?"

"Why don't we simply tell her that your initial visit was inconclusive and that I'm going to check things out? No need to get her wound up if we don't find anything definitive."

"All right. I'll call her from the airport."

❧

Smith returned to the ME's office later in the day after receiving the call about the possibility that Scheinberg might be Stella Morgan, the woman who allegedly had an affair with Pendleton. If, in fact, Scheinberg *was* Morgan, he knew this could prove to be the biggest case he and Warfield had ever worked.

How ironic, he mused, that several days before they had questioned Pendleton relative to the Conover case. Now Pendleton could be their primary suspect in this murder. Could there be a connection? It was too much of a coincidence, having the same person connected to two corpses within the same week. His boss's consistent warning came to mind: "Make sure your ass is covered and don't get my ass in a sling; no cowboy bullshit. And no media!"

The Medical Examiner led the detective into the autopsy room where the cadaver awaited. Smith was prepared and took out his Vicks VapoRub and loaded each nostril with a healthy dab to cover the smell of death that had seeped into the walls over the years. The ME began, "Time of death was between four-thirty and five p.m. A shot to the head was the sole cause of death. Based upon the wound, we estimate the shooter was between two hundred and three hundred yards away, using a high-powered rifle."

"So, the vic is driving home, and someone is waiting until she pulls up to the security gate. She stops the car for a couple seconds to allow the gate to rise, and the shooter pops her when she's a sitting duck," Smith surmised.

"It appears that way. Any chance this could be an accident?" The ME asked.

"I highly doubt there are any shooting ranges anywhere near the rich and famous community. However, we'll run gun licenses on all neighbors within a square-mile radius. Who knows, maybe somebody was having too much fun, walked outside, decided to shoot their rifle for the fun of it, and the round just happened to find Scheinberg's noggin." Smith said.

"For the bullet to pass through her skull, her car window, and embed itself into a tree, the shot had to be fired from somewhere relatively close," the ME offered.

"Okay, we'll tighten our radius. We'll have to push forensics. We need the phones analyzed immediately for phone numbers and texts."

"Don't be surprised if the blood makes their work more difficult."

"How so?"

"The envelope took the brunt of it, as it must have been on top. Plus, it possesses relatively more absorbent properties."

"Can forensics determine if there was anything written or typed on the envelope or its contents?" Smith asked.

"Hey, I'm a coroner, not a forensics expert. But I suppose it depends upon the quality of the paper, what was used to write or type, and how much blood was absorbed."

"The most intriguing piece of information is the potential that Ms. Scheinberg is, in fact, Stella Morgan," Smith said.

"We took several photos and sent them to the experts to analyze right after we phoned you."

"Terrific, thank you. We'll get the original picture the *Post* received, as well as any other pictures of her we may turn up, including her driver's license, and provide it all to the experts and let them determine if she is one and the same."

"Do you think this has anything to do with the resignation of Louis Pendleton?" the ME asked.

"Given Scheinberg is Morgan, the timing of the two events—the resignation and the murder—certainly gives one reason to pause. However, our job is not to speculate, but to investigate in order to uncover the truth. We have worked homicide long enough to know that there is always more to the story and that things sometimes are not what they seem."

"If you guys need any other information, please let me know."

"If anyone comes forward to identify the body, please contact us immediately."

"Will do. Good luck," said the ME as he turned back to Scheinberg's cadaver.

Smith called Warfield with an update on his way back to the precinct and asked Warfield to meet him in the war room. The murder board they had started for the Conover case was affixed to one wall and they decided to also use it for the Scheinberg murder, due to Pendleton's association with each victim.

When Smith returned to the war room, he started by adding a picture of Scheinberg next to Conover's and noting her time of death and related details. Next came Pendleton with a dotted line connection to each victim. There had been very little information from working the Conover case and it was growing colder by the minute.

"What else do we have?" Smith asked Warfield.

"Given the closest cover are trees approximately two-hundred-and-fifty yards away on each side of the entrance drive, we can assume our shooter is a pro, possibly with military background. Knowing the body would be found sooner rather than later, the shooter had to have a vehicle waiting or someone ready to pick them up. I'll check with the cab companies. Somebody could have seen something. We'll start with the neighbors. We'll get some uniforms to work door-to-door."

"If we're working with a pro, they would most likely blend in to look like they belonged in the neighborhood."

"Possibly somebody heard the shot, not that it would help necessarily," Smith sighed, "but it may help jog someone's memory in terms of what they saw immediately after hearing the shot."

"Anything for the board now?"

"Not really. How about you dig into her financial and employment history? I'll look up any family, check out her place, and talk to neighbors in the complex."

"Sounds like a good start. What about Pendleton?" Warfield asked.

"Probably not a good idea to question him about his whereabouts until we have the experts' opinion on whether Scheinberg is, in fact, Morgan."

"And what about the blood-soaked envelope?"

"Hey, it's forensics calling."

"Shit," Smith blurted as he disconnected the call. "Evidently, the envelope sat so long the blood dried, prohibiting the forensic technicians from deciphering what, if anything, was written on the envelope or the single sheet of paper inside."

"That's it?"

"Nope. The good news is there is a ninety-nine-percent probability that the two women were one and the same, a high enough percentage to overcome a defense attorney's objection."

Pendleton was now suspect number one and Smith couldn't wait to pay him a visit.

∁

North held the meeting with Sara in his office so he could sit behind his desk and look down at her; the seats across from his desk sat four inches lower than his. As he cleaned his fingernails, he patronized her with the obligatory speech relative to the unfortunate dismissal of his predecessor.

"Sara," North began, "any updates from Abir?"

"He's made significant progress in a short amount of time. He's had two encounters with ISIS: The first with a screener of sorts and the second who questioned him on his drone knowledge and experience."

"What is the next step?"

"Abir is to suggest a conversation with the Russian black-market broker, the role that Jack will play, given his ability to speak Russian."

"Promising, I guess."

"What about the interrogations of the ISIS captive?" Sara asked.

North, now finished cleaning his nails, turned his attention to Sara. His gaze began with her legs and slowly moved up her slender physique, hesitating slightly on her breasts before he met her eyes, "We have exhausted the information from him. The DNI will decide what to do with him. Obviously, he cannot be sent to Guantanamo, so I suspect he will be holed up in a very quiet and dark place for his remaining years. Ideally, we can show him the extinction of his breed in the near future."

Sara thought it an opportune time to try to learn more about North's knowledge or involvement in AI and robotics.

"Richard, the more I learn about the atrocities and reach of terrorist groups like ISIS, the more I question the speed and impact of Deeprose."

"Really?" North asked, raising his eyebrows at the unexpected comment.

"Well, as you have said, given the upper hand the U.S. has, it seems that a quick and effective response is justified."

"Couldn't have said it better myself."

"I mean, with our technological and scientific advancements, we should be able to make a significant dent in ISIS's progress."

"What type of advancements are you referring to?"

"I'm certainly not privy to top secret research and development, but with the advent of drone technology and the use of some robots today, I have to believe we are close to using robots to fight." Sara had hoped she wasn't being too obvious, given North had seen her with the ARobotics envelope in her hand.

Sara noticed North's lips pucker just a tad before he responded. "Ms. Fahridi, I can't imagine us deploying robots into battle during our lifetime. That would require a level of artificial intelligence that simply doesn't exist today. It would be nice, but it is not realistic."

"Hopefully, someday, so there is no more loss of life."

"Indeed."

Sara stood, and thanked him for his time. As she was headed back to her office, she couldn't decide if North was bullshitting her, keeping her in the dark, or telling the truth. But, at the end of the day, she didn't trust him, so she tended to lean toward bullshit.

❧

From the comfort of the rental, Jack watched as twelve employees exited ARobotics at the end of the day and drove away in their respective vehicles. He was absolutely certain none of those employees were robots. It was unlikely anyone would develop a robot in the likeness of any of them. By 6:00 p.m., the parking lot was empty and no large security guards or beautiful women had exited unless they had left during the three hours Jack and Habib had lunch and went to the airport. However, Jack had counted the number of cars in the lot before they left: twelve.

Jack had completed some shopping before his return to ARobotics that evening. He was now dressed all in black, with a small duffel bag full of the tools he would need. He strode down the sidewalk toward the front door as if he belonged in the neighborhood. He found four security cameras guarding the perimeter of the building. He pulled the stocking over his head and took the first tool out of the bag.

Jack didn't think he would be able to find a slingshot, but a large sporting goods outlet had everything imaginable. He loaded his pocket with steely marbles, also courtesy of the outlet, and fired them until all of the cameras were disabled. There was only one entry door, which required either a thumbprint or retinal scan to enter. Jack suspected the metal door was at least three inches thick, and he could see it had four hinges supporting it. The next item he pulled out of his bag required some extraordinary shopping. He had placed calls to several SEALs he had served with who were explosives experts. After two hours and many calls, they had located a source of C-4 in Springfield. Jack purchased 1000 grams to be sure he had enough power to blow the door off the hinges.

He quickly divided the plastic explosive into five equal sections, placing one section on each of the hinges and one where he estimated the deadbolt to be. After cautiously inserting a blasting cap into each section, he connected the detonation cord and unspooled it as he walked backwards around the corner of the building to shield himself from the blast.

Before igniting the caps, he looked around the industrial area and found it deserted. Confident no one would hear the blast, he connected the cord to the detonator and pushed the button. The explosion was louder than he had anticipated and he was concerned someone may have heard it and would call the police.

He ran to the front and found the metal door had been blown completely off its hinges and lay flat on the floor inside the building, ten feet from where it once stood. Jack quickly pulled out his flashlight and ran through the new opening, covering his mouth with his hand to avoid inhaling any of the residue smoke.

He found the entryway and adjoining hall as Habib described. Small rooms, or labs, lined the left side of the hallway. They were all equipped with at least three monitors, stainless-steel tools he had never seen before, and varying body parts, many with chip boards and wires protruding out of them. The larger offices were on the right, all with doors closed and locked as he tried to enter each one. He went to the third door on the right, the one in which Habib had met with the woman. Jack removed the crowbar from his duffel and quickly pried the door open.

When his flashlight fell upon her face, Jack instinctively pulled his P7 from his shoulder holster and aimed it at her, or it. She was beautiful, he thought. He found the light switch and re-holstered his pistol, then cautiously approached what appeared to be a mannequin. But the flesh looked real.

He began to cross to the other side of the desk where the robot sat, when it moved. The eyes blinked twice, and its head turned and looked directly at Jack, which caused him to jump back in surprise and once again pull his pistol.

"You are not authorized," the woman robot said.

Jack was attempting to determine what to say in return when the robot stood and its right arm shot out and landed a palm-first punch on

Jack's chest, which sent him sprawling through the office door and into the hallway, flat on his back. He was able to hold on to his pistol, but before he could decide whether to use it or not, a door at the end of the hallway opened and the twin security guards ran toward him.

Jack rolled to his right and, in spite of the excruciating pain in his chest, got to his feet and sprinted toward what used to be the front door. It was only fifteen feet away, but the blow had made it difficult to breathe, and he labored to make it before the guards grabbed him. Fortunately, the guards stopped at the front door and stared after him as he ran to the rental, jumped in, and sped away before any reinforcements were called in. He had to consider his next move very carefully. But first, he had to call Sara with an update.

"Sara, it's Jack," he said when she answered his call.

"Is it true?" Sara asked.

"I believe so. Scared the shit out of me."

"What happened?"

Jack went onto explain his robot encounter and how real they seemed. "Unfortunately, I was unable to get any information or take any pictures. Frankly, I'm not sure what would have happened had they caught me. The female robot had no problem trying to crush my sternum, which still hurts like a mother."

"What's the plan?"

"It all depends on how ARobotics reacts to the break in. If they call the cops, then the operation is on the up and up. If not, then who knows."

"Can you drive by again tonight?"

"Too risky. My rental could have been seen and I can't get a different one until the morning. Considering it's almost midnight, I don't think much is going to happen between now and tomorrow morning. How is Habib?"

"Like a little kid. He is giddy to think that someone has developed AI to the extent it appears that they have. He did some research on how they pulled up his bio so quickly and found there was probably thumbprint technology in one of the doorknobs he touched. He had to provide his prints for his job in Islamabad to be sure he wasn't a bad guy. How ARobotics got his prints is beyond me. This stuff is scary smart."

"Incredible. Speaking of smart, I was inside maybe three minutes, tops, and something brought these things to life—maybe a motion detector of some sort. Have you found out anything from North?"

"Not sure. I spoke with him earlier today, pretending to be a raving fan of a grandiose Muslim extinction via robots."

"What did he say?"

"He said we are a long way from robots and artificial intelligence."

"Believe him?"

"I don't know. The guy seems as slimy as they come. I was tempted to ask him about ARobotics, but thought better of it."

"Good choice. You better be careful. He may be an asshole, but he's not stupid."

CHAPTER 40

Smith and Warfield returned to the precinct house within fifteen minutes of one another, shortly after 8:00 a.m. The fifth precinct was located on M Street in a three-story red brick building. Smith had lobbied for years to have their office moved from the third to the first floor so he could avoid the steps, but to no avail. He attempted to tuck in most of his shirt and pull his pants up to where his waistline should have been before engaging with Warfield, who was neatly dressed in a tan suit, matching striped tie, and brown dress loafers.

"What did you learn?" Smith inquired.

"Financially, Scheinberg inherited a tidy sum from her mom and dad upon their passing, which she used to buy her high end condo. They also left her enough such that she did not have to work, but could live very comfortably. However, she owned a florist shop that did a modest business and turned a very small profit," Warfield responded.

"Have you seen tax returns and bank statements?"

"The tax returns her accountant faxed me appear consistent with what we know. The e-statements received from the bank and investment account, including activity through yesterday, shows a withdrawal in the amount of seventy-five-thousand dollars a few days ago," Warfield said.

"So why that much cash?"

"Who knows. She lives among the rich and famous. That amount of money could be pocket change for her."

"Nobody walks around with that much cash."

"Definitely to be spent on something she didn't want traced. By the way, the accountant was able to provide me the name of her estate attorney, who I have a call in to now. Any luck with her place or family?" Warfield asked.

"No one close. She was an only child, and moved here from New York City following her parents' deaths," Smith explained.

"Has anyone come forward?"

"Not that I know of. However, our little Ms. Laura was getting ready to leave town. We found two pieces of luggage. One contained about a week's worth of clothes, mostly comfort clothing, like sweatpants, loose tops, pajamas. It's as if she was going to a weeklong slumber party. Weird."

"Don't tell me. The other bag contained lots of cash," Warfield surmised.

"You got it. They're counting it downstairs as we speak."

"Had she sold the place?"

"Not that the condominium association is aware of, and there are no listings with the MLS. I checked with the post office. No forwarding address has been recorded, and her mail will be forwarded here henceforth. In addition, the utilities did not have a request to cancel service. I asked for a search of all flights out of D.C. and Baltimore with the names Scheinberg or Morgan, or if there was a no show for any female passengers during the past twenty-four hours. We will continue that no-show query for the next two days, and if there are no hits we'll expand it to all major airports on the East Coast. She wanted to disappear quietly and didn't want anyone to know where she was going or that she was leaving."

"Well, unfortunately for her, she disappeared all right, but not in the way she was planning. So maybe she confronts Pendleton, telling him either he picks her over the missus or she goes public. He responds telling her she had better not, or else. She goes public and he *or elses* her."

"Sounds plausible. Okay, let's get the highlights recorded on the board and then go pay Mr. Pendleton a visit. If we time it right, we might be able to interrupt his dinner," Smith suggested.

"Should we bring him down here?"

"Nah, we don't want to overplay it. Remember the boss's little speech: no cowboy. Let's try and put a little fear of God into him and see how he reacts. Given his career and experience, I suspect this guy has ice running through his veins."

"We can review the phone histories on our drive over."

"Sounds like a plan," Smith confirmed.

"The prepaid cell phone only has a two week history of texts with one number," Warfield said as they got into their standard-issue black Ford sedan to head to Pendleton's residence. "They appear to be the ones exchanged between our two lovers that the *Post* reported. And, of course, there is no way to trace the other prepaid to Pendleton."

"Is there any content that would indicate the two were having a dispute of some sort?"

"No. In fact all are very brief, very lovey-dovey, and signed by their first names, which seems odd. If you and your wife were texting love notes back and forth, would you sign them Glenn and Marge?"

"No."

"So what are your pet names for one another?" Warfield asked.

"Fuck off, Warfield."

"Those aren't very endearing names."

"You made your point. No mention of a squabble and they sign their first names. Very odd. When was the last text?"

"The day before Morgan went public."

"So no further texts and no calls between the two using the prepaids after she talks with the *Post*. So maybe our theory of a dispute is way off the mark. Maybe there was some disadvantage of Pendleton telling his wife about Morgan and it played better for him if she came out."

"He had to figure the agency would let him go." Again, Warfield.

"Maybe he wanted out. He had only been in the position for a short time."

"Doesn't work for me. Why would a man with a very successful career ruin a great track record over a woman?"

"Puppy love does strange things to a man."

"No, not this guy. Remember when we interviewed him about Conover? He was as solid as they get. No, something doesn't jibe."

"What about the iPhone?" asked Smith.

"There were two numbers called routinely. The first, an employee of the flower shop, one Cindy Hoffman, and a Peggy Johnson, who I suspect to be a friend, considering most calls are during the evenings or on the weekends. There are minimal other calls, while there doesn't appear to be a pattern with any of them."

"Please contact the regulars and run the other numbers. We may just find something odd."

"Who put you in charge?" Warfield asked.

"Pretty please, Mr. Mullet."

"Well, since you asked so nice."

"We need to find her personal computer, assuming she had one."

"The boys at the precinct are scrubbing the one from the flower shop."

"Well, here we are at the lovely Mr. and Mrs. Pendleton's residence. I guess we can only assume it will continue to get stranger."

❧

Jack was the first one at the rental counter when they opened at 6:00 a.m. It took nearly half an hour to switch rental cars, as the rental agent was new and slow on the uptake. It took all of Jack's fortitude to not reach across the counter and strangle the idiot.

By the time he drove to ARobotics, it was nearly 7:00 and people were beginning to arrive to work at nearby buildings. There were, however, no cars in ARobotics's parking lot yet and the place looked as when he left it, with the exception of no robots staring out from the hole he had created in the side of the building. There was no police or crime scene tape across the hole. As far as he could tell, no one knew what had happened the night before. He decided to park the car and sit and wait.

An hour later, and still no cars had arrived. Something wasn't right. He donned the brown baseball cap that matched his brown shirt and shorts. He grabbed the empty box from the passenger seat and headed toward the building confident in his disguise as an express deliveryman. Jack looked through the hold and saw the door exactly where it had come to rest last night. He called out, "Is anyone here?"

Upon receiving no response, he slowly entered the building. All of the doors in the hallway were open. He walked down the hall and looked left into the labs—all empty, as were the offices on the right. "Shit," he said to himself. Realizing the building had been cleaned out during the night, he quickly returned to the rental and stared at the empty box in his hands.

What the hell does this mean? he thought. The CIA or other agency could certainly be behind this and had cleaned up the mess before the locals arrived. Or was it not the government, but private industry—but why would they not call the police? Or North was behind this and didn't want anyone to find out. "Shit," he said again. He had stumbled upon a great lead and just as quickly lost it.

As he stewed, staring at the box, an idea occurred to him. He drove the rental around to the back of the building and was rewarded when he found a large trash container. Looking around to be sure no one was watching, he opened the top of the bin, hoping to find some correspondence or other discarded jewels or wisdom. All of the paper documents had been cleaned out. All that remained were four small cardboard boxes.

He had to climb into the dumpster to retrieve them. The return addresses of the first two were from a copier supplier. In reviewing the third one, he hit pay dirt. He scurried out of the trash bin with the empty box, jumped in his car, and sped away, dialing Sara once he was safely away from ARobotics.

"Sara." Jack realized he belayed tension in his voice.

"Jack?"

"We need to talk, but not over the phone. I'm on my way to the airport to catch the first flight back. I'll call you when I land."

"Okay." And Jack clicked off without another word.

CHAPTER 41

The doorbell rang just as Lou and Kate finished lunch. They both thought it must be reporters.

"Should we ignore it?" Kate asked.

"I'll take a peek through the peephole," Lou said as he slowly got up from his seat. He had noticed a lingering fatigue had set in over the past couple days and attributed it to the stress associated with the resignation. He heard himself grunt as he moved toward the front door and swore to himself that he would stop that; old people did that.

He was pleasantly surprised to see the two detectives handling Frank's murder investigation. He was hopeful that they had some new information that would lead to the killer. He promptly opened the door.

"Hello, detectives, please come in."

"Good evening, Mr. Pendleton," greeted Warfield. "You may recall that I'm Detective Warfield and this is Detective Smith."

"Yes, of course, please come in." As the two detectives stepped through the doorway, Lou continued, "I trust you're here with some information on Frank's case."

"Not exactly," said Smith.

Lou caught the tone. "Has something happened?"

"Have you seen the news regarding the murder at Foxhall Ridge?" Smith countered.

"The woman shot while pulling into her complex?"

"That's correct. Her name was Laura Scheinberg."

Lou noticed both detectives watched him intently, waiting for his response.

"Very unfortunate. Why do you ask?"

Kate joined the trio in the foyer. Before Lou could introduce her, Smith explained, "Scheinberg was Stella Morgan."

It took a moment for Lou to register the information, but when it did, he realized this was no social call.

Kate joined the conversation upon hearing Morgan's name. "What's going on?"

Lou quickly regained his composure. "Gentlemen, this is my wife, Kate. Kate, these are Detectives Warfield and Smith."

"Ma'am," the detectives said in unison.

"Lou, what's going on?" she repeated.

"Evidently the woman who was posing as Stella Morgan has been murdered."

"Oh, no..." Then the realization of why the detectives were there hit her. "Oh, my God."

"Maybe we should sit down," Lou suggested.

He led them into the living room where he and Kate sat on the sofa and the two detectives settled opposite them on the other side of the coffee table in matching large lounge chairs that complemented the coziness the home exuded.

"We learned from a call to the CIA that you denied knowing the woman," Warfield commented.

"That's true," replied Lou.

"True that you denied it, or true you don't know the woman?"

"Detective, be assured that as you do your job investigating this murder, you will undoubtedly discover that I have never met this woman. The only time I've ever seen her was while jogging and someone in hiding snapped the picture the *Post* ran."

"Where were you between four-thirty and five o'clock the day of the murder?"

"Let's see... Kate and I were in our hotel room resting, as I recall."

"Yes, that's right," Kate chimed in. "We laid down to rest until approximately five-thirty and then went to dinner at a restaurant close to the hotel."

"A hotel? Where?"

"Right here in the D.C. area. After the Morgan article hit the *Post*, we believed we would be bombarded here at home by the media, which was in fact the case, as confirmed by our neighbors. We thought it best to check into a hotel for a few days until things blew over."

Kate could tell the detectives found this information suspicious.

"So at the time of the murder you were taking a nap in a hotel not far from here?" Warfield asked, the look on his face conveying his skepticism.

"Correct," Lou affirmed, with a challenge in his voice. "I trust there will be cameras on the hotel property that can confirm the times of our coming and going."

Suspicion filled Warfield's eyes, but his tone remained neutral. "Provide us the name of the hotel and restaurant so we can talk to their respective staffs and check out any available video. If what you say is true, we should be able to exclude you as a suspect."

"A suspect?"

"I'm sure you can appreciate our perspective. You resign as director of the CIA following an alleged scandal, and less than twenty-four hours later the woman making the accusations turns up dead. You were also acquainted with the victim in another murder we're investigating. We don't believe in coincidences. Somehow there is a connection between you and the two cadavers the ME has processed over the past week. Please do not leave town. We will follow up with you after we check out the hotel and restaurant."

After the detectives let themselves out, Lou witnessed something he had not seen in more than ten years: his wife crying. As he consoled her, he considered Warfield's comments and could see why the police viewed him as a likely suspect. There had to be surveillance cameras, but could he trust the police to exonerate him even if the videos proved he did not leave the hotel during the designated time?

"C'mon, Kate." Lou jumped to his feet. "We're going to take a ride to the hotel and see for ourselves if there are cameras."

✑

"Lou, Jack."

"Mr. Landis, I thought there was an order not to contact me."

"Yeah, whatever. Is this a good time to talk?"

Lou looked over at Kate in the passenger seat as they raced to the hotel. "Sure, go ahead."

"Listen, something is going on and we—or I—need to know if you are privy to the operation."

"We or I?"

"Shit. Okay, Sara and I stumbled upon some intel that isn't smelling just right and we need you to tell us if it is a sanctioned operation."

"All right, I'm not even going to ask how you and Sara ended up there. What's the op?"

"Robots and artificial intelligence."

"Sure, several agencies are continually trying to one-up one another on the development and execution."

Jack went on to explain the meadow and ARobotics findings.

"Holy shit," Lou blurted.

"I would interpret that as you did not have any knowledge of such operation or operations."

"Damn straight. When I started, I was briefed on all major initiatives. The one you are describing is certainly major and was not on the list."

"Possible you were not made aware?"

"If CIA, no. If another branch, then yes, but unlikely. Why did you wait until now to inform me?"

"I had my own doubts about the meadow and needed more information. I didn't want to unnecessarily burden you."

"Hmm. I guess I would have done the same. But given the ARobotics correspondence in North's office, I'm not sure what to think. You had better go to the DNI."

"We don't have enough. North can simply claim we are making things up out of loyalty to you. I have to go back to Iraq."

"And how are you going to do that without anyone knowing?"

"I haven't figured that out yet."

"Do what you need to do." Lou was tempted to tell Jack about the detectives' visit, but figured that could wait.

❧

During the drive from the Pendletons' to the hotel, Smith received a call from the lieutenant with an update on the case. Smith put his cell phone on speaker. "Go ahead, chief, you're on the box."

"A local noticed a car that was normally not part of the neighborhood landscape parked three blocks from the crime scene at or around the time of the murder. The car is the same model: a sedan, darker color like Pendleton's. No license plate identification.

"We ran the balance of the recent calls from Scheinberg's phone. Most are routine with the exception of several to a plastic surgeon in Houston and to a charter plane pilot based in Richmond, Virginia. We called them and both deny knowing a Laura Scheinberg. They do, however, acknowledge receiving calls from a new client by the name of Amy Steinman. The surgeon admitted that Steinman paid him a bonus to sign a confidentiality agreement and the pilot explained that Ms. Steinman had recently chartered the plane for a flight to Houston."

Warfield joined the conversation. "This woman was scared of something or someone and wanted to get the hell out of Dodge. The plastic surgery explains her bag full of pajamas. But there's no record of a payment to reserve the jet."

"She probably negotiated to pay in cash when she arrived for the flight so there was less of a record to trace."

"Did the pilot say whether Houston was her final destination?"

"The pilot was booked one way only."

"As far as the surgeon goes, Scheinberg was scheduled for surgery today and never showed up. He's e-mailing us the picture she provided him of what she wanted to look like when he was done. Did you call the owners of the most often called phone numbers yet?"

Warfield jumped in, "I was delegated that task by Sir Smith, but haven't had time to get to it yet."

"What are the odds of a similar vehicle being parked in the vicinity at the time of the murder?"

"Small—but, c'mon, this guy is a pro. He's the head spook. Do we believe he is going to drive his own car there and leave it parked out in broad daylight? We'll let you know what we find out at the hotel. If the video shows him exiting the hotel when he claimed to be napping, we should have enough circumstantial evidence to bring him in."

"Let's just take it slow. Let me know as soon as possible. And remember, no cowboy shit."

"Aye-aye, Captain. Oh, by the way, what about the cash?"

"Almost forgot. We counted a total of approximately seventy-eight thousand dollars."

Things weren't feeling right to Smith. The Pendletons appeared to be too Pollyannaish to be killers, and if they were going to create an alibi, it would be a hell of a lot better than taking a nap in a hotel room. "What do you think?" Smith asked Warfield.

"About?"

"The Pendletons. They seem like killers to you?"

"They are smart people and smart people do dumb things sometimes."

❦

Jack and Sara stopped driving in circles and landed at a coffee shop.

"So is it possible the government is involved and Lou was not apprised?" Sara asked.

"Lou thinks not," Jack responded.

"So we circle back to North and the almighty question: Where did all the robots and animals go that roamed this field of dreams in the farmlands of Iraq?"

"Funny. I need to go back."

"Don't you think you should speak with Clapper?" Sara asked.

"I'm not comfortable going to the DNI yet. The fact Lou knew nothing doesn't necessarily mean it is not in play, but would the DNI acknowledge, regardless?"

"If you and I can stumble upon it, our enemies certainly could."

"Good point. Are you up for it?"

"Yes, I'll request a meeting."

"He would certainly want to know, but again, ego may get in the way of acknowledging it. But if North is up to his eyeballs in this, he can't do this alone. He has to have some help, some very powerful and influential help. Any chance you could do some more sniffing around?"

"Of course, but I don't know what I'm looking for."

"I would start with any significant relationships or associations that he has. Granted, they may be secretive, but it's worth a try."

"Will do. And you?"

"I need to find a break in my Deeprose responsibilities to make a return trip to the meadow, and quickly."

❦

Having lined up Abir and the ISIS meeting, Jack now focused on Iraq. As expected, when he told North he would be leaving early, North couldn't have cared less. He got the impression North didn't care if he came back. He now needed to leverage Sara's connections.

"Sara, Jack."

"I heard that the ISIS meeting is set up. They must have bought the drone story."

"Evidently. Abir must have done a good job. I need your help with something."

"Name it."

"I'm going to make a stop in Iraq after the ISIS meeting."

"Who knows?"

"Only you and Abir, and he is going with me. Do you think you can work your magic in Homeland Security so I can get a UHF radar metal detector onboard a commercial flight without any trouble?"

"What's that for?"

"If I am going to find something that the drones couldn't pick up from the air, I'm going to need some help. If there is some type of facility in the woods beyond the meadow, it will have metal somewhere in its construction—and it could be an underground facility."

"Smart. How big is it?"

"Approximately eight inches by twelve inches. I want to carry it on and there is a chance it could be misidentified as a detonator of some sort."

"I doubt there will be an issue, but I will make some calls. Send me your flight information as soon as you can. What happens if you find something?"

"Good question. Will cross that bridge later. Any more interaction with North?"

"No. I know he is suspicious, based on our last conversation."

"Better leave it alone for now. I'll contact you after we search the area."

"Be careful, Jack. I want you back in one piece."

"Trust me, I want that as badly as you do."

CHAPTER 42

The hotel manager had to be all of twenty-five years old. He was still battling acne—and losing the fight. His suit was a little small at the shoulders and the top button of his shirt could be seen beneath his clip-on tie. His face darkened upon seeing the detectives' badges.

"Can you confirm that a Louis and Kate Pendleton checked in two days ago and checked out this morning?" Smith asked.

"Of course, give me one second. Let's see. Ah, yes... they checked in without having a reservation at nine-oh-five a.m., originally planning to stay one night, but requested a second night at four p.m. yesterday."

"Are you able to confirm that both husband and wife checked in?"

"There are no notes to that effect, but we can check the video recording for that time."

"Okay, but first, can you give us an overview of the hotel security, specifically the surveillance cameras?" Smith began.

"Of course. We have a network video recorder system that allows us to view whatever is captured by our cameras over the internet, from anywhere. I believe the system is a wireless one and we have four cameras. You can see one behind me—there—which monitors the front desk. One is for monitoring the front door. The third one monitors the largest parking lot, which is just out the front door to the left, and the fourth one monitors the exit door at the rear of the building."

"Are there any other exit doors?"

"No."

"Is there a parking lot in the back?"

"Yes. It's much smaller than the side lot."

"Why don't you have a camera monitoring that lot?"

"As I understand it, we had the option of purchasing a four- or eight-camera system, and we opted for the four since we didn't need eight."

"So there are no cameras by the elevators or staircases?"

At this comment, some of the manager's exuberance wilted. "No, sir."

"All right, we would like to see the recordings at the time of check-in as well as for yesterday."

"No problem. Can you please wait here while I get an associate to watch the front desk, then we can go back to the office and pull the memory cards we need to watch?"

"Please hurry."

At this, the young man scurried through the door adjacent to the front desk. And a moment later, the Pendletons came through the front door.

"Detectives," Pendleton said.

"Well, well, if it isn't our primary suspect," cracked Warfield.

"Mr. Warfield, I don't appreciate your tone or your attitude," Kate said coolly.

"And I don't appreciate having to work another thirteen-hour day because somebody killed somebody."

"Then get another job," Kate shot back.

"Whoa, lady."

Lou intervened. "C'mon, folks. Gentlemen, we need your help and your respect right now. Any surveillance video will show that Kate and I went out for lunch around noon and returned at two and that I—or rather, *we*—did not leave until around five-thirty for dinner."

"Well, you're just in time. The hotel manager should be back shortly and we can all watch the main feature together."

"Excellent. I'm eager to get this behind us. We've been through hell the past few days."

"And by the way, do you still drive your dark-colored, four-door sedan?"

"Yes, why?"

"A neighbor of Scheinberg's saw a car matching that description parked three blocks from the crime scene around the time of the murder. Claims she never saw the car in the neighborhood before."

"God knows how much cars resemble one another these days. It wasn't my car."

"I guess just another coincidence, then?"

"I don't believe in coincidences, Detective. Whoever got me kicked out of the agency went to a lot of trouble. It wouldn't be hard to believe they have gone even further to set me up as a murderer."

"It is not our job to judge. We simply investigate to determine the facts."

The hotel manager returned, introductions were made, and the group made its way back to the manager's office to find out what the video recordings would reveal.

ॐ

"Hello, Mr. Director."

"Eric, can you talk?"

"Can I say *no* to the man? Congratulations. Weird deal with Pendleton."

"Thank you. And yes, Pendleton's indiscretions have given the agency a black eye, but with any luck, it will be old news in a few days and we can move on."

"I doubt that will happen, based upon the news report I just watched."

"What news report?"

"Channel Seven reported there is a high probability that the woman shot in her car was the one having the affair with Pendleton. She evidently used an alias when she spoke with the *Post*."

North couldn't believe his luck; they had identified Scheinberg as Morgan. "Eric, listen, I better get off the phone, as I'm assuming the shit will hit the fan any moment and I best be accessible. I want to meet in the next day or so. Can you be in D.C.?"

"Yes, my current projects allow me to work remotely. I'll book a flight tomorrow morning. Simply call when you have time."

"Sounds good. Talk to you soon."

North was grinning ear to ear when he clicked off. *This should make Pendleton's life interesting,* he thought.

⁓

Eric's cell phone buzzed as soon as he hung up with North.

"Commander Covington, how goes the battle?"

"The Springfield location was vandalized."

"Vandalized? How the hell could anyone get inside, given the security?"

"Plastic explosives."

"What? Jesus. Are the cops involved?"

"No, sir. The interior motion activated the robots you had shipped there, which determined there was an intruder, and evidently scared them away before our assets could arrive to secure the building. No one else saw or heard anything. We were able to dispatch a unit to empty the building and remove all evidence of activity within three hours of the breach. The unit will be up and operational in two days. All employees have been briefed accordingly."

"Did we catch anything on video?"

"Unfortunately, the perpetrator destroyed the cameras. All we saw was a figure in black wearing a stocking mask."

"Someone knew we were there?"

"Hard to believe. There was no evidence to suggest anything but a rogue burglar in a relatively deserted industrial area attempting to loot the place."

"Anything else strange happen?"

"Not really. Some guy knocked on the door looking for a job, but he was screened and our fingerprint technology found him to be simply an engineer based in the Middle East."

"The Middle East? What the hell was he doing in Springfield? What was his name?"

"Hold on, let me check. His name was Habib, Habib Fahridi."

"Okay. Let me know when it is up and running again and keep me abreast of any additional issues."

"Will do."

Eric, compelled to update North, called him back and filled him in on the break in.

"Do we have any suspects?" North asked.

"No, just some guy who had stopped in looking for a job."

"Looking for a job? Have a name?"

"Yes, hang on. A Habib Fahridi. F-A-H-R-I-D-I."

"Fahridi?" There was a long pause as North digested this information. "We may have a problem on our hands. Call me when the unit is back up and running."

North ended the call and immediately turned on his laptop and checked his confidential file on Sara's brother's abduction by Blackstone. There it was: A Habib based in Islamabad. It was too much of a coincidence that Sara was asking about robots and her brother shows up at ARobotics. Sara was now a liability he could not afford to ignore.

❧

Smith needled the manager with questions as he prepared the videos. He wasn't surprised that the surveillance equipment did not fully catch the perimeter of the building. Frankly, he was impressed that the video cameras actually worked and were not placed on the building simply for show.

After watching the video confirming both Pendletons checked into the hotel on the day and time they claimed, the manager put in the memory card for the following day, the day of the murder. At 12:10, the couple could be seen leaving by the front door, then were picked up by the parking lot video getting into their car and heading out to lunch. At 1:48, the parking lot camera recorded their car entering the main lot, which was mostly full, and proceeding to the lot at the rear of the building. The manager then input the memory card for the rear exit door so that they could view the Pendletons entering, assuming they would not walk all the way around to the front, which Lou confirmed when asked by the manager.

"That tree is blocking most of the view," Warfield complained.

"We have asked the landscaping company to trim the tree for several months now, and they claim that their contract only covers shrubbery maintenance and lawn maintenance. I have looked at the language myself and it clearly states maintaining grounds foliage to include fertilizing, trimming, and replanting as necessary. Basically, we have a dispute and are at a standstill."

"Just terrific."

"Look, there we are." Kate pointed to the computer monitor.

"All I see are a woman's lower half and most of a man's legs."

"Oh, c'mon, those are the clothes we were wearing. We all saw what we were wearing earlier," Lou barked.

"Agreed, but we can't see your faces or enough of you to know it was you, had we not known what you were wearing. Let's jump to the parking lot camera for the hours three o'clock until four-thirty," Smith responded.

"Yes, sir," chimed the manager.

After studying the video, all agreed they never saw Pendleton's car drive through the lot to exit.

"Okay, let's view the rear exit footage from two o'clock until four-thirty."

The hotel manager fast-forwarded the film up until someone exited, and then the group would scrutinize the individual or individuals. During the two-and-a-half-hour time period, ten people exited the rear door: six men and three women, one of whom was accompanied by a young child. Warfield asked to take a second look at two of the men, whose height was similar to Pendleton's based upon how much leg they could view. All of the other men were shorter and stockier. Lou did his best to keep his mouth shut so as not to antagonize the detectives.

"Okay, here comes mystery man number one. He appears to have a little bit more spring in his step than you, Mr. Pendleton, as if he naturally walks that way, or possibly this guy is in a hurry."

"I don't own a pair of pants like that," observed Lou.

"Coming from your line of work, you can appreciate the relative insignificance of clothing ownership before or after a crime." Lou said nothing. Smith continued, "And like you, he does not wear a wedding ring. The shoe size appears to be about the same, but I do notice this individual walks somewhat pigeon-toed. Play that back again."

"Yeah," Warfield joined in. "I definitely see the toes landing inward with each step. Could be an act for the benefit of the camera."

"Let's go to mystery man number two," Smith directed. "Okay, this guy's gait is similar to yours, no wedding ring, but he's got some boats. I'm betting he is wearing a size thirteen or fourteen. What size do you wear?"

"Eleven and a half," responded Lou.

"Again, easy enough to don a pair of shoes several sizes too big to throw off the camera."

"If I follow your logic, Detective, I scouted out a hotel that I knew had no camera for the back lot and that the rear door camera's view would be obstructed by a tree. I did all of this upon leaving Langley to head home, pick up Kate, and drive to the hotel to check in.

"As you recall, I was alerted to the *Post* article by the DNI after I arrived at Langley. Be assured my departure time will be captured accurately by our—or rather the CIA's—surveillance equipment. Since you just gave me credit for understanding the significance, or lack thereof, of clothing ownership, I trust you will give me the benefit of the doubt that if I did plan a homicide, I would have considered the possibility of security cameras. Can we please stop screwing around?"

"Those are excellent points. However, I have to exhaust every possibility. From my years of experience, I know that very smart people do incredibly stupid things under duress. Based upon the analysis of the video recordings, I believe we have one potential match leaving the building at two-thirty-five p.m."

Yet even as Smith said it, he began to get an overwhelming feeling that they were wasting precious time.

CHAPTER 43

"Chief, Smith here."

"Whatcha got?"

"A bunch of circumstantial mixed with coincidence with a couple of maybes on top for good measure."

"It's late, Detective. Can we get to the facts?"

Smith reviewed the findings from the hotel videos and noted the fact that the restaurant next door had no security cameras. "So, should we bring him in tonight?"

"No, it's late. Tell him to come in first thing in the morning, say seven o'clock. That will give us all a chance to digest this overnight and come at it fresh in the morning."

"Roger that."

"So what is your gut telling you?"

"It's not Pendleton, nor his wife for that matter. Not to say that he couldn't have hired someone to do it, given his background and access to people with shooting skills. No, I think someone went to a hell of a lot of trouble to make his life miserable."

"That's a good thought. We should check into his background for anyone who is or was a sharpshooter or sniper. Have you taken a look at it, other than vengeance? Who would benefit from her death?"

"We haven't gotten hold of the estate attorney yet to review the will."

"Well, what's the problem?"

"Working on it, Chief."

"And one more piece of trivia for you to chew on: In reviewing the books of the flower shop, we found forty percent of the deliveries were to three high-end hotels. The hotels did not order them; the orders came from the individuals staying in the rooms. And they were all—I mean, every single order—paid for in cash."

"That is odd. Repeat customers?"

"Not a single repeat in five years. Every order is from a different person. We're now checking with the hotel to find out if they were involved in or aware of the flower orders."

"Weird."

"Let me know how the conversations go with the regulars from her cell phone. I'm now especially interested in the manager of the flower shop."

"Will do."

⁓

North had to assume that Sara had somehow discovered that he was involved in robots, but so far she must be keeping it to herself. He decided in the near term, he needed to be proactive in order to give him time to think about how to deal with her. After discovering Habib had been to ARobotics, he had called the DNI requesting a meeting.

"Come in, Richard," the DNI said as he removed his suit coat, hung it on the back of his high-back leather chair, and took the seat behind his desk.

"I just had a very strange conversation with Ms. Fahridi."

"How so?"

"I had the impression that she was... well... somewhat passive when it came to military doctrine."

"Passive?"

"I mean, she seems to support Deeprose and its intent to keep any potential bloodshed to a minimum."

"I would agree with that assessment. So what's changed?"

"She stopped in my office earlier today and expressed a strong interest in an aggressive campaign using robots and artificial intelligence, given the technologies were available."

"Really? Where did that come from?"

"I have no idea. But I assured her that we, or any other branch of government, is a long way from deploying robots with artificial intelligence, and that even if we had the technology, there is not a unified position on using it."

"Interesting. Are you concerned?"

"I just thought it important you be aware. Granted, I acknowledge that I tend to push for a relatively more aggressive approach, but I believe Sara has been watching too many sci-fi movies and should focus on her role within Deeprose."

"I agree. Let's keep an eye on her."

CHAPTER 44

Upon landing in Moscow, Jack was taken directly to the Kremlin.

"General Makarov, nice to meet you, sir," Jack said with a forced smile, admiring the man's height and girth. Makarov was six-four with a broad chest and close-cropped gray hair. Jack guessed he was approximately sixty years old, but based upon the size of his arms, he could take on a man half his age.

"And you, Mr. Landis. Does your president truly believe this scheme will work?"

"Well, if you want to blame someone, blame me."

"This was *your idea?*"

"More or less."

"And you are but a Navy SEAL, no disrespect intended."

"None taken. Our team thought it believable that the Russians would and could develop the next evolution of drones."

"Please don't—how do you Americans say?—stroke me, young man. You know as well as I that when push comes to shove, we've no real proof of a longer range drone and that is where this plan unravels, in my opinion."

"Agreed. My job is to learn as much as I can about their organization, leadership, and plans. I trust the falsified engineering, design, and test documentation you brought me today should buy us some credibility and time."

"We did the best we could, given the short notice. When is your meeting?"

"This afternoon in Grozny. By the way, what is the price of a black market drone these days?"

"And why would I have knowledge of such things?" Makarov asked, not wanting or expecting a response. "What are your lists of demands other than cash?"

"If I'm to be believed as a black market agent of Russian government employees gone rogue, I cannot make demands on behalf of Russia. For example, insisting the terrorists exit the Democratic Republic of Georgia or that there will be no support of oil distribution that negatively impacts Russia's exports to Europe."

"Unfortunately, you're correct. But if your plan actually works and you're able to unravel and destroy the leadership of this so-called larger organization, then we should ultimately achieve the same results."

"That is our objective and to do such with minimal collateral damage."

"We're about to embark upon an operation wherein collateral damage, as you call it, might be a necessity."

"Agreed and understood."

"And what assurances do we have that if and when we see your ships and planes nearing our borders this entire operation is a ruse and Russia is, in fact, your ultimate target?"

"If we do engage in any military action, you will be notified well in advance and be part and parcel to any military planning in this regard."

"Please let your president know that even though the trust and dialogue between our countries is the best it has been, we'll be on full military alert during this operation."

"We would expect nothing less, General."

Makarov spent the next sixty minutes reviewing the falsified documents in detail so that Jack could regurgitate the information later that day. Jack was pleasantly surprised and impressed with what the Russians had prepared.

As he was preparing to leave the Kremlin, the general stood and approached Jack so that he was only two feet in front of him, and looked him directly in the eye. "Mr. Landis, it may become critically important in the future for you and I to maintain a dialogue that is based in logic rather than political posturing. I'm sure you can appreciate that if for whatever reason this mission unravels and somehow places the U.S. and Russia on opposite sides of the fence, we may not depend upon our respective presidents to do what's best for all."

"I understand and agree, General. Cooler heads must prevail. Saber rattling does no good but to dull the sabers."

"Indeed. Good luck."

"Thank you. I'll contact you later today to provide you a status update."

"Again, please use the alternate number I gave you. We cannot have anyone connecting me or the Russian government to this mission. Otherwise, we will disavow all and place blame solely on the United States."

❧

When Kate showed up alone to the showroom looking like she hadn't slept all night—which she hadn't—Hank was the first to ask where Lou was. Kate shared the revelation about Scheinberg and that Lou was the primary and only suspect at this time and was ordered to appear at the precinct this morning for further questioning.

"How was Morgan—I mean, Scheinberg—killed?" asked Sara.

"Shot. Believed to be a high-powered rifle from approximately two-hundred yards."

"Does or has Lou ever owned a rifle?"

"No. Several handguns, but never a rifle."

"Does he know or has he ever worked with anyone who was good with a rifle?"

"No, we discussed that last night."

"I suggest we all get busy loading the information we prepared and put it onto the big screen as we go along." Sara entered the user ID and password they were provided to open the session. She used one of the e-pens to begin writing.

Sara uploaded the victims' pictures as she provided an overview. "All appear to have been murdered by people that are in the business of killing. Frank's murder was set up to look like a suicide, while no one has claimed responsibility for Asaryi's death. And now we have a third murder in Scheinberg."

"Who is Asaryi?" Kate asked.

"He is, or was, a member of a terrorist organization that we were attempting to develop a relationship with, and we were doing a pretty darn good job of it. And then he was killed. We assume he was killed by his own, as they believed he was wittingly talking to us, but he thought he was recruiting an ISIS member."

"After Frank was killed, Lou explained that he was working on some high security projects?" Kate said.

"Yes."

"Well, I can't begin to understand the spy business, but Scheinberg's murder is devastating, at least until the police can clear things up and dismiss Lou as a suspect."

Hank joined in, "Without a motive or motives, it will be hard to connect all three murders."

"Indeed. We need to think like homicide detectives."

"What about asking Smith and Warfield to join in?" Kate asked.

"Would that be a conflict of interest?" Sara asked.

"I'm not sure how it could be," Kate said. "The communication may be a one-way street in that we would be sharing information, and they may not reciprocate. But at the end of the day, if it helps solve this mess and gets Lou off the hot seat, how could it hurt?"

CHAPTER 45

After arriving in Kandahar from Moscow, Jack notified Abir so that he could arrive at the meeting location ahead of Jack. Given they had positioned themselves as unable to communicate due to a language barrier, it would be extremely odd for them to show up for the meeting together. If they pulled this off, Jack thought, they should be nominated for Academy Awards.

Maysarah and the two guards were waiting for Abir outside the designated café, but not Barraz. The café was specifically selected due to its proximity to the airplane hangar where the drone was parked. Jack arrived twenty minutes later and was easily identified, given his Western dress and turbanless noggin. After brief introductions facilitated by Maysarah, Jack and Abir were searched for weapons before the men entered the café and found Barraz sitting at a table in the rear. Jack was anticipating encountering Barraz, given Abir's experience. He found the man to be as sinister-looking as Abir had described. Barraz stared at Jack as he took his seat at the table.

Maysarah spoke both Arabic and Russian and began the conversation explaining to Abir that Barraz would be questioning Sergei about the missiles in detail and asked if Abir would like a full interpretation. Abir declined, requesting only that he be made aware of any abnormalities in the responses, details of any agreements, disagreements, and future contacts.

"Sergei, Abir tells me that our Russian friends have developed advanced drone technology and that you're empowered to negotiate the terms of sale on their behalf," Barraz began.

"Let's just say that Abir is mostly correct. Yes, the Russians have indeed developed a Predator-type drone that will travel approximately five thousand miles, given relative payloads and conditions. *Empowered* may not be the appropriate term relative to my position; I believe *opportunistic* would be a better choice of words. I haven't been sanctioned by the Russian government to meet or negotiate with you. Rather, due to my close relationship with those that have developed the technology, I have access to the technology and can arrange to have it delivered to the highest bidders."

"What exactly is your relationship, if I may ask?"

"During my decade of supplying and working with the Russian team, I've developed some very good associations. The engineers and scientists that work on the team are grossly underpaid and, frankly, treated very poorly by the government that funds their development program. They saw this breakthrough in the range as an opportunity to be justly compensated for their hard work and success."

"And why would the Russian government allow them to do such a thing?"

"The government would not allow it."

"So you're telling me that this development team would be able to ship us drones right under the government's nose?"

"Shipping the drones is impossible, as it would be uncovered. The group I represent is willing to sell you the technology to build your own drones."

"You expect us to build the drones?"

"With your vast resources and the information you will be given, you will be able to accomplish it."

"And how long will it take?"

"I am told five months, given the facility can be outfitted with the proper equipment within three months."

"I am not a scientist. How am I to believe you?"

"As I trust Abir has told you, I am empowered to sell the long range drones. I am simply a broker and will share the technological information I was given. Today you will have the opportunity to view the new drone, but we will only have thirty minutes to do so if we leave within the next hour; otherwise it will be gone."

Barraz interrupted Jack, directing a question to Maysarah, "And why was he chosen to be the broker?"

Maysarah interpreted and Jack responded, "They had no one else to turn to who they could trust." And before Barraz could challenge him again, Jack made a statement: "Having the ability to make them is invaluable, I would think."

"That is a very interesting proposal, indeed. But we do not have the talents to build them."

"I know of several experts who would be happy to join your team for the right price. As a vendor of the government for so long, I have come to know the other key suppliers of materials for the drones. I know they'll supply product, materials, and related technology to anyone. There is no need to make them aware of the new range capability."

"And what is in this for you?"

"A lot of money. As the front man for this consortium of technicians and engineers taking the most risk, I'll be compensated very handsomely from the purchase price."

"You sound like an American who only cares about money. The natural next question would be: Where is the proof?"

"Of course. I have brought with me engineering documents and schematics for your review, which include testing of the computer routines in wind tunnels and structural laboratories and results of using enhanced Kevlar and glass epoxies. Obviously, a few pieces of information are missing, which would be provided upon an agreement. However, there is enough here, I'm told, to convince anyone of the new development."

"We do have specialists on our team, but I'm not sure they have the knowledge and experience to not only interpret your data but also attest to its feasibility."

"I cannot help you there, other than attempt to find experts for hire that help validate the information."

"We will consider the offer."

"There are a few conditions the consortium I represent insist upon."

"Please tell me."

"Many participants have friends, family, and loved ones who live in Russia with a few having some in Georgia. Obviously, no one wants to sell the weapons that will kill their own."

"It appears we share the same dilemma relative to proof: Yours with targets and ours with capability."

"Indeed. The Russian rumor mill tells me that a new, much larger alliance of those supporting your objectives has been formed. Is this true?"

"It is. Why do you ask?"

"My constituents want me to witness an agreement among the leadership that Russia and Georgia are not intended targets."

"Impossible! And why would that provide assurance?"

"It is no secret that there have been differences among the sects with which you align yourself. For me to witness an agreement among these varied sects would suffice."

"Do you realize what you ask?"

"Yes. Personally, I couldn't care less who or what your targets are. I'm a businessman. Unfortunately, human behavior and emotion sometimes intervene, but must be addressed as logically and expeditiously as possible to achieve the end result."

"And how do we, as you say, logically and expeditiously address the need to confirm that you and your consortium have successfully developed longer-range missiles?"

"Given the technological and scientific acumen, the proof is in the briefcase that I have brought for you. In it are plans for the Predator drone, a ground-control system, a data-distribution terminal, and all of the related technology, connectivity, and satellite requirements."

"Witnessing a test would seem to be the simplest way to verify."

"Without a doubt. However, it would be difficult to cover up such a long range test from the rest of the world as the drone could span several continents. Secondly, and most importantly, the Russian government is not aware of this development."

"I see. So, to summarize: A highly talented, underpaid, and poorly treated group of Russian technicians and scientists has banded together to sell this new technology on the open market, unbeknownst to their employer, and you represent this group."

"Precisely. My job is to negotiate the highest price with the lowest risk of harm and highest probability of payment."

"And what happens if and when the Russian government learns of this sale and how can we be sure that they won't obtain the new technology?"

"With regard to the employees, frankly, it is not my concern. Personally, I'll be able to disappear quietly and without a trace. As far as other governments, entities, or interests obtaining this technology, there is no guarantee. Yours is the first organization that I have met with to discuss this opportunity. I trust you can appreciate that the world powers would not sit down and negotiate such a purchase, so my target customers are relatively limited. It is not difficult to speculate who else I may approach."

"No, not difficult, given certain countries' continuing efforts to develop a drone program. Is there any potential scenario wherein your group would sell the technology only to us?"

"We anticipated this question. However, there was not a consensus on the response. Trust was a common part of a business transaction's vernacular years ago; today, not so much. As you can imagine, the group I represent is a very conservative one. They are not born risk-takers. The fact that they have banded together in this way is truly amazing."

"What if we were to pay the group's target sum and have the ability to resell the technology to others, thereby minimizing your efforts and risk while creating a payment scenario that all but eliminated risk of collection?"

"That question we did not anticipate. However, given my job to get the best price—and yes, we do have a target number—I believe I'm empowered to agree to such an arrangement."

"Empowered or opportunistic?"

"Let's say both."

"So what is your number?"

"What do you believe the value of the technology is?"

"To be brutally frank, it is invaluable to our organization. What I or we do not understand is the cost of purchasing the supplies, tools, technology, and other items necessary to construct the drones, ground controller, and terminal. In addition, we will have to hire the talent and expertise to support the manufacturing and oversight. Granted, we believe our financial position is fairly strong, but we cannot afford to underestimate these costs."

"Understood. I have also brought with me a breakdown of the costs you have mentioned."

"You are indeed prepared."

Sergei opened his briefcase in the middle of a small café in Kandahar and began to review the bogus information the Russian government had prepared.

Jack stole a glance at Abir and through eye contact conveyed that things were progressing well and then asked Maysarah to communicate the same to Abir. *Round one to the good guys*, thought Jack. He found he had a chill running up his spine despite the fact that the temperature hovered near ninety-five degrees.

CHAPTER 46

"Chief, Smith here," Smith said as he carefully wiped the jelly filling off his shirt that had oozed out of the doughnut he had just bitten into.

"What's up?"

"I stopped by the estate attorney's office and picked up Scheinberg's will. The attorney is out of the country on a mission of some sort. Her reluctant assistant appeared to be taking full advantage of the fact her boss was out of the office. I noticed mail was piled up on the desk and the assistant evidently read my mind, offering that she could not do anything with it until her boss returned."

"What about the will? "

"Two potentials. One, Peggy Johnson will be inheriting the majority of the financial assets, the value of which we are still determining. The second, a Cindy Hoffman, will be inheriting her business."

"Are they related?"

"Not that we can tell. We ran DMV information and didn't find any connections."

"No relatives named at all?"

"Nope, just those two."

"How soon can you interview them?"

"Today, given they are available."

"Well, make sure they're available. And remember, no cowboy!"

"Yes, sir, partner."

"Just hurry up and figure out who did it."

Smith found himself bordering giddy now that they had two more potential suspects with plausible motives. With enough good detective work, they would quickly figure out if it was Pendleton, Johnson, or Hoffman.

Precisely at 7:00, Smith met Pendleton at the front desk of the precinct house and led him to an interview room, where he left him with a uniformed officer. Smith thought Pendleton looked like any Joe off the street dressed in jeans and a polo shirt—any guilty Joe. The only furniture in the interview room was a simple desk with two wood-framed, upholstered chairs on one side for the investigators and a metal folding chair on the other for the detainee. The room couldn't have been more than eight feet square and the small size served its purpose to make one feel claustrophobic. The overhead fluorescent light provided twice as much light as the space required. The two-way mirror was encased in the wall opposite the single door.

"Good morning, Mr. Pendleton." Warfield smirked as he entered and remained standing so he could look down at Pendleton. "May I call you Lou?"

"You're killing me, Detective. Please start."

"Very well. In your long established career in the military, one would have to believe that you came to know those who specialized in using high-powered rifles, and were proficient and accurate in using them. Do you know anyone who fits that description?"

"No. The majority of my career was spent in the Navy and rifles are not a common weapon of choice."

"I have to believe that over the years you must have encountered someone, possibly from another branch of service, who excelled with a rifle?"

"No, no one that I specifically recall. I assume from your line of questioning that I'm no longer a suspect, at least one that pulled the trigger?"

"I'm afraid I can't say that, Lou. We're exploring all avenues. How are you and your wife getting along?"

"What?"

"Just answer the question."

"Like a hand in a glove, Detective."

"So if I were to summon her down here for questioning, she would stand by her man, right?"

"Be my guest. She wouldn't be too happy with the inconvenience, but she would be happy to tell you the truth."

Just then, Smith entered the room and sat in the remaining chair. "Good morning, gentlemen. Do we have a signed confession yet?"

"I was just about to get it before you came busting in and ruined the mood," Warfield retorted. "I guess we will have to start at the beginning."

The detectives watched the blood rush to Pendleton's face.

"Relax, Pendleton." Warfield smiled when he thought Pendleton's ears would spit fire. "Just a little humor at your expense. What do you have, Glenn?"

"Our video experts are ninety-five percent sure that mystery man number one and Mr. Pendleton are not one and the same. They were able to make estimated measurements of the leg below the knee joint, ankle motion, foot size, and some other metrics that couldn't be faked. So we can discount you were the one that pulled the trigger, but how do we discount the fact you could have hired someone?"

"You guys know damn well that I had minimal time from when I found out until the murder. You have my and my wife's cell phone records. Neither of us had our laptops and the hotel did not have a business center with a computer that I could have accessed. And the most important fact is I did not know this woman!"

"Okay, settle down."

"Fuck you, Detective. I've gone out of my way to be cooperative. You have circumstantial evidence at best. You're wasting time busting my balls while the person behind this is out there, possibly ready to kill again."

"So if you were us, where would you start looking for someone with a motive? Because right now, you're the only one we can identify," Smith lied, given the recent discovery of two additional suspects.

"I have an idea on how we may work together, but I need to call Kate first."

"Fine by me. Okay with you, Tom?"

"Never want to refuse help. Do you need some privacy?"

"Yes."

"Okay, we'll step out for a minute while you make the call."

Lou placed the call to Kate to tell her he was going to take her up on her suggestion to invite the detectives to join the Bluescape sessions. In another minute he knocked on the precinct conference room door to let whoever was outside know he was finished with his call. Smith and Warfield entered.

"Well, what's the plan?" Smith asked.

Lou explained his relationship with Hank, the offer of the new technology, and the small team attempting to figure out who was behind his forced resignation and now the murder.

"Our little team thought it would be appropriate to invite you two to join our discussions, and your participation would be a big advantage," Lou continued.

"Had this come from anyone else other than the former director of the CIA, I would have either been insulted or amused to tears. However, giving you the benefit of the doubt regarding this team's credibility, this big screen TV technology piques my interest. What do you think, Glenn?"

"I have to admit the new technology interests me. We could at least check it out," Smith responded.

"Am I free to go?"

"Yes. I'll walk you out. And as they say in the movies, don't leave town."

"I'm assuming you have had me under surveillance since this began."

"Hey, the CIA isn't the only organization with secrets."

Lou smiled as he exited the conference room and walked shoulder to shoulder with Warfield toward the entrance of the precinct.

"Hurry back, Tom, we have a date with a florist," Smith yelled toward the two departing figures.

℣

As the convoy of two Jeeps headed toward the hangar, Jack thought back to the brief argument among the Joint Chiefs about providing security for the Predator. Probability-based logic drove the decision to land it and remotely drive it into the open hangar bay, unguarded. The worst that could happen was that a roaming band of jihadis would witness the landing and have time to gather a cache of weapons to destroy it. Given the remote location of the hangar and the brief amount of time the Predator would sit on the ground, it was low-risk. It would be worse if security were discovered and Jack's cover was blown. It wasn't as if Barraz and his henchmen could steal it.

Jack was not comfortable with the fact the ISIS gang had grown to six men and Abir was riding in the other Jeep, but he supposed he would have handled it similarly if the shoe was on the other foot. The men in his Jeep rode in silence. Jack wished he had brought VapoRub to pack his nostrils—the Muslims stank. He was grateful when the thirty-five-minute ride ended and the Jeeps parked next to the hangar. Jack checked his watch. The drone would fire up and take off in approximately twenty minutes, which he conveyed to Maysarah, who in turned interpreted for the other men.

The Predator selected for the ruse had just been delivered via aircraft carrier to the U.S.'s Afghanistan location and looked like it was straight off the assembly line. Jack kept his eye on Barraz, looking for a reaction, and he wasn't disappointed. Barraz's total attention was on the glimmering Predator drone, which had been painted with Russian decals the day before. The drone's seven-foot-tall, twenty-seven-foot-long, and fifty-five-feet-wide wingspan had everyone's attention.

Jack pulled the spec sheet from his pocket and began reading slow enough so Maysarah could keep up with interpreting: "The long range Predator has 115 horsepower thrust and a ceiling height of 25,000 feet. The major differences between the older model and this new, long range model is the addition of combustion engines and the cavity redesign to account for 650 gallons more fuel to enable it to go up to 5000 miles, nearly eight times the original capacity, and a larger payload capacity of 1000 pounds, 650 pounds more than before."

Jack stopped to gauge the interest and understanding. The men were oblivious to Jack and Abir as they stared and babbled among themselves, the interpretation of which Jack could not wait to learn from Abir. Jack was sure he and Abir could have jumped into a Jeep and left and no one would have noticed.

The group had moved closer to the Predator and were now pointing at the two laser-guided, 114 Hellfire missiles. Jack checked his watch. The Predator was scheduled to leave in less than one minute.

"Maysarah, have the men get back, it is about to leave," Jack called out.

As he said this, the running lights on the wings illuminated, and two seconds later, the turbocharged engines roared to life, sending the ISIS gaggle scrambling for the hangar exit. However, they couldn't keep themselves from looking back as they ran to watch the aircraft line up to exit the hangar door and successfully take off, creating a cloud of smoke and dust in its wake. Although Barraz was thrown to the ground, Jack noticed he was smiling.

CHAPTER 47

Cindy was arranging a wedding bouquet when Smith and Warfield arrived at the flower shop.

"Good morning. I'm Detective Smith and this is Detective Warfield with the metro police department. We're looking for Cindy."

"You found her. How can I help?" Cindy said, then continued, "Oh, you must be here about Laura. Just horrible. What is this world coming to?"

Smith thought her comments less than sincere.

"Yes, a tragedy. Would you have a couple minutes to answer a few questions?"

"Of course," she responded as she set the bouquet aside, wiped her long-fingered hands on her green apron, and let them come to rest on her slender hips.

"How was your relationship with Ms. Scheinberg?"

"Excellent. We have—or rather *had*, I guess—a very good working relationship."

"How about personally?"

"How do you mean?"

"Did you do things socially together?"

"No, our relationship was strictly business."

"Are you aware that you stand to inherit the floral shop?"

"Yes, Laura has been very kind to me."

"Do you intend to keep and run the shop?"

"Oh, yes. I love working here and she would want me to continue what she started."

Smith believed he had hit the hot button when discussing her owning the shop.

"Any idea why anyone would want to kill her?"

"Well, that CIA guy she was having the affair with comes to mind."

"So you knew about the affair?"

"Not until the other day when her picture appeared in the *Post*. She told me about it later that day and that she had decided to uproot and leave town."

"Did she tell you where she was going?"

"No, she didn't want anyone to know. She was afraid there could be trouble over going public with the affair."

"Did anyone else have access to her condo?"

"She gave me a key the day before she was killed."

"Really? And why did she do that?"

"I actually suggested it, you know, in case she needed me to take care of anything while she was away."

"Have you been to the condo?"

"No."

"Our IT forensics people will need to scrub your computer."

"Of course. The only computer we have is a desktop that we keep in the office."

"No laptops?"

"No," Cindy lied.

Smith noticed that Cindy looked away and to the left, usually the indication of a lie.

"Where were you at the time of the murder?"

"I would have been at home preparing dinner."

"Was anyone with you or did you see or speak with anyone shortly before arriving home?"

"Ah, no. I closed the shop at five and went directly home."

"How long does it take you to get home?"

"On a good traffic day, fifteen minutes. I did stop and talk with my neighbor when I got my mail upon getting home." She provided the neighbor's name and address.

"Any other information you think is relevant that we should know?"

"Not that I can think of."

With that, the detectives handed Cindy their cards and requested she remain available for the next week.

As they pulled away from the floral shop, Warfield began, "You thinking what I'm thinking?"

"Yup. Cindy learns of the affair, offs her boss, then points the finger at Pendleton."

"We'll have to confirm her alibi."

"Don't you find it interesting she didn't ask what time the murder happened?"

"Not necessarily. But, let's double check the news reports to find out if they reported the approximate time of the murder."

☙

Smith and Warfield found Peggy Johnson at home and answering her door twenty seconds after Smith rang the doorbell. She was a frail-looking forty-year-old, shoulders bent over, wearing a sweater when the outdoor temperature was in the high eighties. She couldn't have weighed a hundred pounds.

Smith's instincts immediately dismissed her as a possible suspect, simply given her diminutive frame and feeble appearance.

"May I help you?" Johnson asked.

"This is Detective Warfield and I'm Detective Smith." Both detectives held their badges high for Peggy to see.

"Is there a problem?"

"We're here about Ms. Laura Scheinberg," Smith began.

"Has something happened?"

"I'm sorry to inform you that Ms. Scheinberg was murdered," Smith told her.

"No! Oh, my God. No, no."

Peggy stumbled backwards into her home and covered her mouth with both hands as tears began streaming down her face. She shook her head back and forth so her medium-length, strawberry-blonde hair covered the lower portion of her face. The detectives closed the front door behind them and allowed Johnson to continue her sobbing until it subsided enough to resume the conversation. Smith was sure the tears were not an act.

"Are you up to answering a few questions?"

"Yes, yes, of course," she managed. "Please, come in and sit down."

The Cape Cod–style home was small but clean. Pictures of family adorned the walls and most available flat surfaces. This woman lived very modestly.

Johnson forced herself to make eye contact, gently rubbing her hands together as she spoke. "I love Laura like a sister."

"How long had you been friends?" Smith continued.

Hearing her friend referred to in the past tense made Johnson start bawling again. After two minutes and six tissues, she regained her composure and answered the question.

"Eleven years. We met at a book club and instantly hit it off. I have no idea why. We were so different in many ways. She was a business owner with lots of smarts and money, and I… well, I'm just very simple. I like things simple."

"Do you know if she had any plans to take a trip?"

"No."

"Did you get together or talk often?"

"We spoke several times a week and often got together for lunch or dinner, mostly dining out, as it was our treat to ourselves."

"It's somewhat hard to believe, given your close relationship, that you were not aware she had been murdered. Had you not tried to call her in the past few days?"

"Well, no. I probably would have today."

"Don't you watch the news?"

"Not much. It's always bad and depressing."

"Where were you at the time of the murder?" Smith hoped liked hell she wouldn't start crying again with the question.

"What? Why would you ask me that? Do you think that I had something to do with it?"

"Just a routine question."

"When was she murdered?"

"At six p.m., two days ago."

"Uhm... I was home, reading."

"Can anyone confirm that were home?"

"What do you mean?"

"Did you have any visitors? Did you speak with anyone on the phone at that time?"

"I didn't have any visitors—I rarely do—and I doubt I spoke with anyone."

"Is there anything else that you can think of that was out of the ordinary? Had she met anyone new, any changes to her routine?"

"No, nothing."

"How about any next of kin?"

"None. She was an only child, as were her parents, and they have both passed."

"Are you aware that you stand to inherit all of her financial assets?"

"I don't care about any of that."

"Really?" Warfield asked as he looked around the room.

That question put Johnson back over the edge and she began sobbing again. The detectives thanked her for her time and quickly exited to avoid having to listen to weeping.

"Whaddya think?" Warfield asked when they got into their car.

"Not a chance," Smith responded.

CHAPTER 48

Jack had cleared his carry-on through customs in Moscow and Kandahar airports and now the Kirkuk Air Base in Iraq without incident. The UHF radar metal detectors were never an issue, and Jack had thought to bring an extra one for Abir. Abir had arranged to have a car waiting for them at the airport and the two wasted no time in heading to their destination. Jack felt more assured knowing that Abir was there. He knew he could count on him.

They again parked at the same deserted farmhouse and made their way to and through the meadow to the woods beyond. Given the detectors' detection range was only forty feet and they planned to sweep an area the size of four football fields, they would have to make several back and forth passes to effectively cover the terrain. Since at any one time they were only eighty feet from one another, they could coordinate moves via hand signals, thereby avoiding alerting anyone within shouting distance. The woods were dense, which at times made signaling difficult.

One hour into their search, eagles appeared, circling an area to their immediate right. Jack, concerned about the limited time they had, made a judgment call and signaled Abir to abort their grid search and head in the direction of the eagles.

Twenty minutes later, the needle on Jack's detector bounced slightly. He looked over to Abir to give him a thumbs-up and found Abir's thumb already up. The men moved cautiously ahead, the needles on their respective detectors becoming more active with each step. The eagles were flying in a large circle, a circle wherein Jack and Abir found themselves dead center. Jack's instincts were *pinging*. He signaled Abir to stop, dropped his detector, and pulled his pistol. He slowly moved ahead, swinging the pistol to the right and left as he went.

On the second swing to his right, Jack saw a man aiming a gun at him and dove to the ground, arms extended, pistol pointed at the target. As he did this, the target did the same thing at the same time. "What the hell?" Jack said to himself. A nanosecond later, Jack realized he was looking at a reflection of himself. With his sudden movement, Abir had pulled his weapon and was moving in Jack's direction. Jack slowly stood as Abir reached his side.

"What is it?" Abir asked.

"Look that way," Jack answered.

"Is that a mirror? I can see parts of us through the trees in front of us."

"Sure looks that way."

The men moved closer and found themselves standing in front of large mirrored panels extending twenty feet high, twenty feet to their left, and as far as they could see to the right.

"Invisible architecture. I've read a little about it," Jack stated.

"And this is why the drones never picked it up?"

"Right. In these dense, high woods, the mirrors reflect the foliage so it appears there is nothing here but more trees."

"This building is huge."

"Yes, like a factory."

"Exactly like a factory."

"What now?"

"First we call Sara to give her an update, then we find a way in."

Jack called Sara, one of the few people he was able to call on his CIA-issued international cell phone, and provided her a status update as Abir searched for surveillance cameras, but did not find any.

The two men, weapons drawn, began walking the perimeter of the mirrored structure, looking for an entrance. They found the length of the building to be over three-hundred yards, and upon turning the corner, discovered a well-worn two-track leading to a camouflaged bay door in the side of the building. If there was a bay door, Jack figured there had to be a side door of some sort. And there it was, again mirrored like the rest of the building, but the handle and card scanner gave it away.

"Now what?" Abir asked.

"I brought C-4, but don't think it's a good idea to blast our way in. The most important thing is that we found it. We'll capture the coordinates, inspect the rest of the structure, and plan another visit if need be with the appropriate resources."

As Jack said this, an approaching vehicle could he heard rumbling down the two-track. Abir and Jack immediately took cover in nearby, low-lying bushes.

"This may be our best opportunity," he whispered to Abir. "Are you game?"

"I think I need to ask for a raise."

"Okay, a fifty-percent increase in your contract rate."

"Let's go get 'em, Captain."

They could now see the camouflaged Humvee slowly making its way toward the bay door. As the Humvee came into the clear, they could see a second Humvee behind the first, retrofitted similarly to a limousine. At seeing that, Jack and Abir stole a glance between themselves. The first word that came to Jack's mind was *incredulous.*

Pistols drawn, the pair patiently waited as the bay door opened and the vehicles slowly entered the building. They could see through the windows that the large Humvee was full of passengers—Jack could not tell if they were military or civilian. Upon the rear wheel of the larger vehicle passing their hiding spot, the two, crouching, quickly covered the twenty-foot distance and were now behind the Humvee, keeping pace with it as it moved forward.

Jack was hoping that vehicles would move some distance into the building before the occupants disembarked, giving him and Abir a chance to find cover without being spotted. Although not the preference, he and Abir had agreed to stay together as they had no way to communicate if separated. Jack was to make a split-second decision upon entering the building on whether to move left or right. Abir kept his head low so Jack could see in his direction.

With the first step, Jack looked right over Abir and saw shelving. As he looked left, he saw large drums, which he assumed contained diesel fuel. He signaled Abir to move left and the two men scurried behind the drums and waited in silence to learn if they had been detected. The only sounds that could be heard were the Humvees driving off and the bay door slowly closing. Jack realized he hadn't considered how they were going to get out.

The pair peered out from the drums. Jack couldn't believe his eyes. Before him was a ginormous operation of some sort—all high-tech, using manufacturing robotics to assemble what he assumed were robots; robots that killed animals with lasers. As he looked left, there were small, window-encased enclaves, each occupied by two or three people working together. Each enclave appeared to have at least five computer monitors.

To the right were several assembly lines, but Jack couldn't discern what was on them as whatever was being produced was relatively small. Straight ahead appeared to be racks full of what he assumed were raw materials; many shelves appeared to be filled with a metal of some sort.

"Now what?" Abir asked for the second time.

"Boy, you have that question nailed down."

"Well?"

"We need to get to the person in charge and find out who is behind this operation."

"And how do we figure that out?"

"I can see there are a mix of civilian and military people here based upon the service khakis—these are Navy personnel. I trust there is a commanding officer and I will be able to pick him out by his uniform. The challenge is how do we find him."

"Describe how the uniform is different and let's split up and meet back here."

"Good idea."

Jack described the rank insignia patches found on the collar, sleeves, and shoulders. He explained that based upon this level of operation, Abir should be looking for three stripes on the shoulders and sleeves that represented a commander. They agreed to meet back at the drums in thirty minutes. If one didn't return, the other had the choice between finding a way out to get help or attempting to rescue the other. The two men shook hands and set out to their assigned portion of the factory.

CHAPTER 49

The detectives walked into the showroom. Lou formally introduced Smith and Warfield to the small group, then asked, "Okay, who is the most adept at this thing and can show the detectives how it works?"

"I would be happy to," Sara said, beaming.

She opened the data that had been created thus far. The wall came alive with the pictures, documents, and notes.

"You can manipulate the size of the displays, much like your smartphones, depending upon the need at the time," Sara demonstrated, moving to the wall and shrinking the information so that it all could be viewed at one time. She then expanded one of the windows containing text.

"Holy crap," Smith muttered.

Warfield nodded. "This is unbelievable; it's like an iPad on a wall."

"I know, right? I can also move the information to the left or right and create space in between as more information is gathered or creatively determined. It really is a tremendous tool for strategic and creative thinking and problem solving."

Warfield walked up to the wall and began to manipulate the display with his finger.

"How long has this been around?" Smith asked no one in particular as he simply stared at the wall.

"Not long at all," Hank answered. "In fact, this is one of the first installations in the United States used as a demo unit."

"I have to admit I'm eager to give it a whirl. Mr. Director, how do you suggest we start?"

"I missed yesterday's meeting due to being inconveniently disposed, as you may recall, so I'm not the one to ask," Lou responded. "Sara?"

Sara reviewed the information, explaining their approach and rationale on how the data was currently displayed.

"Determining the relationships between and among the players is a good start," commented Smith.

"Where we stalled last time is motive," Sara said.

"Motive or motives?"

"Either-or. If in fact all of the murders are connected somehow, which none of us have been smart enough to figure out, then there could be a single motive, but if they were independent then one would assume there would be different motives for each murder."

"Logic works. Were you able to make any connections?"

Kate spoke up. "Yes. All of them had a negative impact on Lou."

"Mrs. Pendleton, I appreciate you coming to the defense of your husband under the circumstances, but—"

"Just hear me out, Detective." Kate cut him off and then took the detectives through the connections of Conover and Asaryi; Scheinberg was a no-brainer.

"All right, there is a possible connection, but quite a stretch for someone to go to a lot of trouble to make grief for your husband."

"*Grief?* Are you calling the president asking for one's resignation and being accused of murder *grief?*"

"Beg your pardon, ma'am. I didn't intend to discount what you two have been through over the past few days."

"I believe the key to solving this is finding out why Scheinberg was in such a hurry to leave town and change her appearance, given the assumption the affair was a ruse and Lou was not to be feared," Warfield said.

"Who else could instill that level of fear?" asked Sara.

"Whoever put her up to it," said Smith.

"And who has the most to gain from the alleged affair?" Again, Sara.

"Assuming Lou is bounced from the job, the next in line," Smith said.

"Richard North!" exclaimed Sara.

"Now that's a leap," said Lou.

"It is simply one more scenario we have to investigate. Was North hostile or uncooperative?" Smith asked.

"No, to the contrary, he was professional and helpful," said Lou.

"He makes my skin crawl," offered Sara.

When everyone nodded, Smith continued: "Okay, let's start with any similarities, regardless of size and scope, between Conover and Asaryi."

"The obvious one is the CIA connection. More specifically, both were connected to a covert operation and were killed within days of one another," Lou said. "We know how both were killed and we're pretty confident we know why Asaryi was killed."

"And as I move our open session over to Asaryi's profile, I see he was killed, most likely by his own, for being a traitor."

Sara interrupted the detective and explained her role in Asaryi's death, believing it was a good time to come clean. She expected a reprimand from Lou, even though he was no longer with the CIA, but none was forthcoming, leading her to believe he already knew.

"Okay," Smith continued. "Ms. Fahridi, under duress and out of fear for her brother's life, leaked false information that most likely led to Asaryi's execution."

"Which really creates another connection in that both Frank and I were working on the same operation," Sara stated, almost to herself.

"Indeed it does. So our connection is layered: CIA to operation to team members. Did you and Frank have any other common assignments, interests, or experience?" Smith asked.

"Not that I'm aware of. I had only met Frank in the operation meetings and otherwise did not talk with him."

"What was Frank's role?" Smith asked again as Sara glanced at Lou.

"Gentlemen, I'm afraid that information is confidential," Lou said.

"*Whoaaa*, wait a minute, Lou. Tom and I are sticking our proverbial nuts on the chopping block here," Smith reminded him. "We don't expect there to be any secrets."

"It's complicated," Lou barked

"So is a life sentence for murder."

"Point taken. Okay, Frank was responsible for working with detainees to learn whatever information he could to help our military efforts."

"In other words, he interrogated military captives," Smith said.

"Yes."

"That wasn't so hard, was it? Now, I won't ask how he interrogated them because I'm sure the answer is why you were so reluctant to share this in the first place. So, we've got another potential connection. Frank is interrogating bad guys while bad guys abducted Sara's brother. Was there any way for the bad guys to know what Frank did or that he and Sara were working on the same assignment?"

"Odds are highly against it."

"Unless somebody in the know let the cat out of the bag."

"That's a stretch," Lou said.

"Oh, really? Did you think it was a stretch before Sara hung Asaryi out to dry?" Smith asked.

Sara's skin went cold as she felt everyone's eyes turn toward her.

"No! You can't think I shared what Frank did!" Sara said loudly in self-defense.

"All I know, Ms. Fahridi, is that you were worried about your brother's life and you were instructed to share some secret intelligence in return for his release."

"But I only gave them the information regarding Asaryi."

"Can you prove this?"

"I can," Lou offered. Everyone turned in Lou's direction with a look of surprise. "I had hoped not to share this, but your point about transparency is well-taken, Detective. When I first began as director, one of the primary operations I was responsible for was called Deeprose. There were a number of strange occurrences that were more than likely coincidences, but deserved a closer look. As a result, I asked a colleague by the name of Jack Landis to maintain surveillance on both Frank and Sara to ensure that we did not have a rogue agent among us. As part of the audio surveillance, we heard Sara explaining to Habib exactly what she did to gain his freedom. There was never any mention of Frank and there was no reason for her to hold this information back."

"You guys are just one big, happy family," Smith opined.

Lou turned to Sara. "I'm sorry, we felt it necessary at the time. You must be wondering why we never questioned you."

"No, I understand. Given what I did, I am surprised that I'm still here," Sara admitted, while not letting on that Jack had already told her about the surveillance.

"You were, and continue to be, a tremendous asset to the CIA. Asaryi was not a for-sure thing and I trust that whatever current operations may be underway have a greater chance of success than Deeprose ever did."

"They do."

"Okay, enough with the spook double-talk," chimed in Smith.

"Let's get back on track," Warfield interjected. "Okay, now consider any connections between Conover and Scheinberg."

"Lou's a connection," Hank stated.

"Lou's been a connection among all of them from the beginning," Kate said.

"That's why you jumped to the top of our bad-guy list." Warfield looked at Lou.

"Well, they were both brutally murdered at someone's hand, as opposed to Asaryi, who was blown up," Kate continued.

"And one was made to look like a suicide and one a blatant kill," Warfield commented. "We have no record of them knowing one another as colleagues or personally. Their paths never appeared to cross."

"But they crossed someone who took it personally," Lou observed, "again assuming we have one person behind all three deaths."

"All right, let's shift to our final couple: Scheinberg and Asaryi."

"They were both outside the fence, so to speak, from the CIA operation. In other words, they were most likely not aware of the operation and could have been innocent bystanders of sorts. Well, *innocent* is not exactly the right adjective for Asaryi. However, given the revelation about the alleged escort service North had uncovered and that some of the clients were supposedly high-ranking government officials, Scheinberg could very well have known about the operation. She could have been murdered because one of her clients wanted to ensure it was never known he was a client."

CHAPTER 50

Jack estimated there were at least seventy-five people working in the factory. The majority were civilians wearing white lab coats, while the enlisted carried sidearms. Even if he could score a lab coat in an attempt to blend it, the fact he was wearing shorts and jungle boots would give him away. He could see quite far down the walkway that aligned the small labs and did not see anyone wearing officers' insignias. He thought it best to find the Humvees in addition to the CO, as that would probably be his and Abir's best way out.

His first challenge was to cover an open area of approximately thirty feet between the drums and a bank of lockers, which presumably housed workers' personal items. Maybe he would get lucky and find one unlocked that had clothes that fit him. He successfully made it to the lockers and edged his way to the end to peer around the corner.

Just as he was about to peek around the corner, a voice behind him said, "Don't move, I have a weapon pointed at you. Hands up and lock them behind your head," said Ensign Patrick Culver.

Jack did as instructed.

"I'm now going to remove the pistol from your shoulder holster and search for additional weapons," Culver continued.

"Yes, sir," Jack responded.

Having removed the pistol and not finding any additional weapons, Culver instructed him to turn around while continuing to aim his weapon at Jack's chest.

"You can relax, Ensign, I'm not here to harm anyone, only to learn who is behind the operation. Is there a commanding officer on site?"

"It's your lucky day—that is our next stop."

"How did you find me?"

Culver nodded in the direction of the corner of the floor. Jack looked down and saw the surveillance camera.

"I checked the ceilings where the cameras are typically placed, but not down. Rookie mistake. None outside, so I didn't look too hard inside," Jack said, shaking his head.

"We should have your friend by now. Are there any more than two of you?"

"Nope, just us two dumb-asses."

"All right, we are going to take a left beyond the lockers and head straight until we come to a cluster of offices. I don't want to alert the employees, so I am going to holster my sidearm and stay six feet behind you."

"I understand the drill, Ensign. I'll be a good boy. I want to speak with the CO."

It took Culver and Jack ten minutes to reach the CO's office. Abir was already there, handcuffed with hands in front and an armed sentry standing behind him.

"Have a seat," said Commanding Officer Covington.

As Culver moved to place handcuffs on Jack, Jack blurted out, "Hey guys, I'm a decorated retired Navy SEAL. How about a break with the cuffs?"

Culver stopped, turned, and looked at the CO, who nodded at Jack, giving him a chance to explain. Jack quickly gave a career synopsis, concluding with the disaster in Iraq that ended his career.

"So what the hell are you doing snooping around my factory?" Covington asked.

Jack decided he was in no position to hold anything back, so went on to explain his findings in the meadow, the eagles and his suspicion of robots, artificial intelligence, and lasers, as well as his role in Deeprose.

"If you are working for the CIA, why not just ask them instead of sneaking out here on your own?"

"I did, more or less, and no one is claiming knowledge of this operation."

"More or less? What the hell does that mean, son?"

"Lou Pendleton is a friend as well as a colleague and boss."

"I see. Well, given Pendleton's disgraceful exit, did it occur to you he may have not been in the clue shack?"

"Yes, sir. I approached the DNI."

"I can assure you my orders come from the highest levels within the CIA."

"Richard North?"

"Son, you're pushing your luck."

"Have you ever communicated with or seen correspondence that included the DNI relative to this operation?"

"What are you hinting at?"

"Sir, we have reason to believe that North may be working autonomously and without the government's knowledge."

"Are you out of your fucking mind? I think that explosion in Iraq jostled some of your marbles. Look around. You think someone can make all this happen on their own?"

"Would you be willing to call the DNI just to confirm?"

"Hell, no, I'm not willing. That's insubordination, son, and I'm a soldier who follows the rules, whether I agree with them or not. Maybe you should think about doing the same thing."

Jack realized that he had gone too far too fast and was losing any opportunity to gain the commander's help. In that split second, he decided it was now or never if he and Abir were going to make it out of there.

Covington's face reddened as his anger increased. He bent down and pointed his finger in Jack's face as he continued to berate him for his behavior. Jack stole a quick sideways glance at Abir, then rammed his right elbow into the crotch of Ensign Culver. As Culver bent over from the pain, Jack quickly stood, moved behind him, and pulled his pistol from the holster. As Jack elbowed Culver, Abir planted his feet and pushed his chair back into the sentry behind him as hard as he could, resulting in the sentry's inability to quickly pull his weapon. Jack now had Culver's weapon out, safety off, and was pointing it back and forth at the sentry and Covington. Culver was curled up in the fetal position on the floor.

"Abir, take their weapons and set them on the floor in the corner over there," Jack directed.

"You're making a big mistake, son," Covington said.

"In the end, I hope you're right, sir. But if I am right, this operation is not sanctioned and could be leading us into a war we are not prepared to fight."

Abir found the keys to the handcuffs in the sentry's pocket, removed them, then handcuffed the sentry to the metal desk. He then took the cuffs intended for Jack and did the same with Culver, while taking Culver's gun and aiming it at the sentry.

"And what are you going to do with me?" Covington asked.

"You are going to give us a quick tour, the keys to the Humvee, and help us leave without incident."

"Bullshit!" Covington roared.

Jack rushed Covington, pushing him back and down into his chair and placing the barrel of the pistol up Covington's left nostril.

"We can do this nice or not nice. Either way, we are going to confirm what we believe is going on here, leave, and provide the information to the DNI. If I'm wrong, then I'm in a hell of a lot of trouble. If I'm right, then I suspect *you'll* be in a hell of a lot of trouble."

"Fuck. Let's go. First, let me give my men a heads-up; otherwise, it could get ugly."

"Be sure to let them know that Abir and I will be up close and personal with you the entire way, just in case someone thinks they're a good shot."

Covington placed a call to his lieutenant commander and ten minutes later all of the enlisted knew there were hostiles inside, the CO was hostage, and they were to stand down. The trio left the CO's office with Jack now wearing a lab coat to conceal the pistol he had pointed at the CO.

The tour began with a review of the labs, where teams were tasked with writing code to overcome identified flaws in the artificial intelligence. Next were the twenty-three assembly lines outfitted with the latest robotics manufacturing technology, each assembling different parts of the robot. The final assembly line ran the entire length of the factory and was used to assemble the final product.

The trio reached the end of the line as the last section was being added: the head. Small soldering arms were moving at lightning speed, connecting hundreds of wires to the neck cavity. When complete, the head was moved into its place and welding arms completed the attachment. The final product was lifted off the assembly belt by a large winch that swung it to a holding area, which Covington explained was a quality checkpoint before it was placed in inventory. Jack was amazed and frightened at the same time. He began to pray he was wrong.

They moved to where the inventory was stored. It was intimidating. The six-foot-six robots were lined up as an infantry would be, eight robots deep and a line at least fifty long.

"How many are there?" Jack asked.

"Four-twenty," Covington responded.

"But I thought you said all of the programming glitches were not worked out. Why are you continuing to produce them at this level?"

"Orders."

"Doesn't that strike you as odd?"

"The remaining issues are relatively minor ones. The last thing you should see is a video."

"Robots in action?"

"Yes. Follow me."

Covington led them to a small conference room, turned on the computer, and fired up a video of the most recent field simulation. The robots could be seen moving like humans and communicating with one another with hand signals as they converged upon PackBot tactical robots, which served as the enemy, based upon their artificial-intelligence programming. The seven robots surrounded the PackBots, then in unison fired their lasers, destroying the PackBots.

"Holy shit!" Abir exclaimed.

"It's the future of hand-to-hand combat, gentlemen. No more parents grieving for the loss of their child in battle," Covington said.

"How many simulations went poorly?" Jack asked.

"A few."

"Anyone killed, animals?"

"Unfortunately, one incident early on where a few engineers were killed and then another time when we didn't program properly for animals."

"And that is the carnage I found in the meadow."

"Yes."

"How did you remove them?"

"We have a helicopter at the other end of the factory. We loaded the carcasses into a net, hoisted them up, and buried them two miles away."

"What happens if we forget to program something else, or worse, the artificial intelligence takes over and we lose control of them?"

"Son, people smarter than I am take care of that. My job is to keep this facility secure and operational. I've obviously failed at securing it."

"When I share this with the DNI and he explains the CIA is supporting this, I will take full responsibility and exonerate you as best I can."

"How sweet of you."

"Okay, time to go."

Jack grabbed Covington's left arm and pinned it behind his back, holding the barrel of the gun to the base of Covington's skull. The trio briskly walked to and entered one of the smaller Humvees.

"Tell your men to have the bay door open. We will drop you off once outside and the bay door is closed. Any trouble, then you're taking a ride with us."

Once released, Covington stood and watched the Humvee as it raced down the two-track out of sight. Jack watched him in the rearview mirror, wondering who Covington would call first, his commanding officer or the DNI. Given he had taken orders his whole life, Jack bet it would be his commanding officer, which meant the shit was going to hit the fan, and hard.

Driving a Humvee all the way from the factory to Kirkuk would only be asking for trouble, so Jack and Abir stopped and switched to the car at the farmhouse. Jack checked the rearview mirror often during the one-hour drive from Makhmur to Kirkuk, but found no one chasing them. He deduced Covington figured his odds were better in letting Jack escape and tell his story, rather than create a scene that could potentially jeopardize their cloak of secrecy and the operation. Once back in Kirkuk, Jack would provide Sara a full debrief of his findings, requesting she share it with the DNI and await the next step in the drone dance with ISIS.

CHAPTER 51

Smith wanted to run through what they'd uncovered so far, so he dragged Warfield to the lieutenant's office.

"We are taking a look at North," said Smith.

"*North?* You're telling me a thirty-year CIA man with a stellar record and major influence within the intelligence community got a little green with envy and started offing people?"

"Not just *some* people. These were strategic kills that had a negative impact on Pendleton."

"Okay, let's play this out. Starting with Conover, what's the motive?" the lieutenant challenged.

"Frank was involved with obtaining information from a relatively high-profile detainee to support a mission that North did not back. Frank was just beginning to make progress when he shows up dead. At that time, this particular mission experienced some other setbacks and Frank's death seemed to highlight the failure of the mission under Pendleton's watch."

"And the CIA shared this information with you?"

"Well, actually Pendleton did," Smith confirmed.

"Of course he did—it takes the target off his back."

"Chief, we are ninety-nine-percent sure he didn't do it, based upon our investigation. Pendleton was simply helping us figure things out."

"So North kills Conover, makes it look like a suicide, to make Pendleton look bad? Really? Are you guys losing your touch?"

"That taken alone seems like a stretch. The timing of the abduction of Sara's brother seemed coincidental at the time, but now seems intentional. Sara was blackmailed into giving up secret intelligence."

"But how would North know what intelligence she would provide, if any?"

"Being relatively new to covert ops, it was more than likely that Sara would provide information. As far as what information, it really didn't matter. Once the information was leaked, I trust North had a way to tie it back to Sara and then the mission, and therefore one more demerit for Pendleton."

"So how did Sara get away with it?" The lieutenant's face belied his doubt.

"Sara was especially clever in the information she provided, in such that it resulted in the killing of one of the terrorists' own, versus harming any of our people or jeopardizing a significant campaign."

"You really need to provide a shovel with this shit. And now Scheinberg?"

"North sets Lou up on the running path, takes some pictures, and coerces her into talking to the *Post* and sharing the now-infamous picture. And twenty-four hours later Lou's out and he's in."

"That's quite a story."

"Do you think it's feasible?"

"Most things are feasible, but probable is another thing. However, you've made a connection between all the vics—albeit very loose—and very imaginative, I may add. I can buy into North ordering the hits, but how does he round up ISIS members to take Sara's brother hostage?"

"Imposters, maybe?"

"This thing is getting pretty farfetched," said the chief, exhaling a loud sigh.

"So what now?"

"I don't think we can go storming into Langley and drag North out for questioning. Given that we had a probable suspect in Pendleton and could not build a case, gunning for another CIA guy is not going to play well with the agency or the media if they get hold of it."

"We need to smoke him out somehow."

"Any ideas?"

"How about if we visit the North residence under the pretense we want to ask the mister about the Conover case knowing he won't be home and take the opportunity to chat with the missus?"

"Gotta start somewhere," concluded the lieutenant.

☙

While en route to McLean, Smith left a relatively ambiguous message with the main operator at Langley, requesting North return a call to the precinct, but understood the deputy director was probably very busy and there was no hurry. Smith and Warfield found a Bentley parked in the circle drive by the Norths' front door. The house was a grand brick colonial, boasting a large set of double front doors, three stories, and a garage able to house seven automobiles. Smith guessed it must have over fifty rooms. A doorbell and two minutes later, Patricia North answered the door.

"Good morning. We were hoping to catch Mr. North at home. We left a message at his office, but got the impression he might not be in today," Smith said.

"I'm Pat, his wife. Can I help you?" Pat had answered the door in a dark green pantsuit and matching heels with a pearl necklace. It appeared she had just come from the hairdresser.

"This is Detective Warfield and I'm Detective Smith with the metro police department. We stopped by on some routine business relative to a case involving one of Mr. North's colleagues."

"Are you referring to Frank Conover?"

"We are."

"What does this have to do with Richard?"

"Oh, nothing other than some additional background checking we're required to do as part of the investigation."

"I thought Frank committed suicide."

"Well, regardless of the cause of death, we still have to dot the i's and cross the t's, if you know what I mean."

"Yes, I guess so. I'm sorry, but you drove out here for nothing. Richard is at work today. If he wasn't in his office he might have been at a meeting."

"That's no problem. We were in the area on another matter and it was convenient to stop by."

"I wish I could help you."

"Well, actually, you may be able to help with some of the routine background information and eliminate the need for us to bother Mr. North. He must be extremely busy with his pending nomination and all."

"Yes, he is. We're all so proud of him. He's worked very hard to achieve that position. Where are my manners? Please come in. I have to leave on an overnight trip shortly," Pat said.

"We will only be here briefly, ma'am," Smith said.

She led them to her husband's office. Smith and Warfield were immediately struck with the taxidermy that adorned the walls.

"May I get you something to drink before we start?" she asked.

"Ah, yes, I'll have water."

"Me too, please," concurred Warfield.

When Pat left the office, Warfield turned to Smith. "Are you seeing what I'm seeing?"

"Holy shit. I doubt our Mr. North purchased his *Wild Kingdom* menagerie."

"Which means he shot them all and most likely with a high-powered rifle."

Pat returned with their glasses of water. "So, what can I tell you, detectives?"

"We simply need some background information on Mr. North's work history," Warfield explained.

"Well, that's all public record, isn't it?"

"Most of it, yes. We're simply looking for the length of time he and Frank worked together. The psychologists who work on similar cases believe that additional insight can be gained from colleagues even when there isn't much of a connection with the deceased. And frankly, some of the information that is public record is not necessarily always accurate or correct. For example, Frank was listed as working in Human Resources, when in fact we have been told he also worked in other areas of the agency."

"I see. I'm afraid I don't know the answer to that. Richard does not talk about work much, which is somewhat of a mandate by the CIA, as you can understand."

"Of course. I have to tell you, this office is very impressive. Is your husband a hunter?"

"Oh, my gosh, yes. It's probably his favorite hobby. He has been on countless guided hunts all over the world, as you can see by some of the relatively exotic animals in here."

"He must be quite the marksman," Warfield continued.

"He is. Of course, he buys the most expensive rifles on the market, which probably helps his accuracy."

"Does he keep his rifles here at the house?"

"Yes, but don't worry, they are unloaded and under lock and key. He has a license for all of them."

"Oh, I wouldn't doubt it. I'm interested as a fellow sportsman. I prefer shotguns when I hunt."

"Would you like to see his rifle collection?"

"That would be terrific. Are you sure it's okay?"

"Of course. Richard is very proud of his kills and his guns. Follow me to the study."

Housed within an ornate wood case with unbreakable glass sat ten high-powered rifles. "May I take a picture to show my hunting buddies?"

"Why not?"

"Great." As Warfield snapped pictures with his phone, Smith did his best to take a mental inventory of the brands of the rifles without appearing overly interested. "Does Mr. North have any other rifles?"

"If he does, I don't know where they would be. He has several pistols." Pat opened a felt-clad drawer containing two revolvers: one a long-barrel and one a snub-nosed."

"Does he ever shoot for practice?"

"Yes, he has some targets set up on the north end of the property out by the lake. He really hadn't used them much up until a week or so ago when he went shooting for a few hours. He said it felt good and helped him relax."

"What a terrific setup." Warfield checked his watch. "We've really wasted a lot of your time, Ms. North."

"Please, call me Pat. And no, it was nice to have visitors. I cannot wait to tell Richard he has a firearms soulmate."

"Well, my collection is humble compared to what I've seen here today."

"Let me walk you two gentlemen to the door."

"By the way, is that your beautiful car out front?"

"Yes, it is."

"Do you and Mr. North drive matching Bentleys?" Warfield joked.

"No, he prefers the German engineering of the BMW."

"Is his black like yours?"

"No, he prefers white."

"Those are easier to keep clean, I think."

"Yes, he is definitely the smarter one. I have to take mine through the wash three times per week."

"Thank you for your time. Ms.—I mean, Pat."

"You are so welcome. Have a wonderful day."

"I have to tell you our visit here was definitely not only the best part of the day, but I trust it will be the best part of the week."

"Well, how kind of you. Bye now."

As Pat closed the front door, Smith and Warfield couldn't help sharing a grin. They quickly jumped into their car, giddy with the excitement of unexpected, but potentially significant, information.

"I think the fact that I went to church once last year is finally paying dividends," Smith joked as he put the car into gear.

"Talk about opportune."

"Now, c'mon, that's just good old-fashioned detective work."

"Right. Do you really think it's possible he did it?"

"If she had said his car was a dark-colored BMW sedan like the one near the crime scene, I think we would have enough to bring him in."

"Let's talk this thing through while it's fresh."

"Right. Scheinberg was killed with a high-powered rifle, most likely a Remington, based on ballistics. Distance of shooter estimated at two hundred to two-hundred-and-fifty yards. There were no Remingtons in North's case to match the ballistics report, while he is allegedly a sharpshooter of sorts, based on his wife's comments. In addition, he coincidentally practiced shooting for the first time in a long time right before the murder."

"And why would he use any of his guns that could be traced?"

"Of course he wouldn't. He would borrow one or pick one up that couldn't be traced."

"What about the car?"

"Yeah, that is a wrinkle, unless he used her car that day. But a Bentley is not your ordinary sedan and one that would be identified as something special by the witness."

"Maybe he borrowed a car."

"Or possibly rented one."

"Check with the local rentals?"

"We'll get our boys on it. What else did we learn today?"

"They're rich and the missus is not plugged in too closely with what's going on."

"No, certainly not like Kate. So what does that mean to the investigation?"

"Not sure, just worth a mental note for now."

"Okay, let's also get the boys checking on Remington sales within a two-hundred-mile radius."

"I'll call it in now."

"If in fact it is North, once his wife tells him of our little visit, he'll have a pretty good idea that he leapfrogged to number one on our hit list."

"Which means he'll be even more guarded and careful."

"Do you think there's any chance we can get his schedule for that day?"

"Out of the spook palace? Not likely until we have something more concrete. We need to place him at or near Scheinberg's place—and quickly."

CHAPTER 52

North surreptitiously took his cell phone from his pocket to check the incoming text. Normally he wouldn't be so rude during an important strategy session, but he couldn't afford to miss any information now.

Oh brother, he thought. It was his dumb-ass wife. She rarely texted him during the day, and when she did, it was some innocuous message. He was tempted to just delete it without reading it, but she might ask him about it later.

> *Hi, honey. Two nice detectives stopped by today. They are investigating Frank's case and wanted to ask you a few questions. While they were here, they showed interest in your hunts and I showed them your gun collection. They were very impressed. Anyway, they said they left you a message at the*

office and it was not urgent, just call when convenient. See you later. X-X-O-O

Oh my God, he thought. *That stupid bitch let them in the house and showed them my rifles.* He had to get out of there and think.

The DNI noticed North's discomfort. "Richard, are you okay?"

"Ah, yes. Well, no. I just received a disturbing text from home that I need to address immediately. May I be excused?"

"Of course. Is everything okay?"

"It seems Pat is feeling extremely ill and wants me home as soon as possible."

"Good luck. Just give me a call later when you have time."

"Yes, sir."

North strode out of the conference room and headed straight to his office, where he told his assistant Jake he was heading home to look after his wife. On the drive home he considered whether he needed to be concerned about the detectives snooping around. He had an alibi for the time of the murder, so he turned his thoughts on how to deal with Sara and her silence.

❧

Covington sat and stared at his monitor screen, debating what to do next. Why would Landis go through all the trouble of finding the factory, breaking in, and fabricating such a cock-and-bull story? Covington realized he had three options, one of which was to do and say nothing, which was really not an option. His military training and experience told him to call his Blackstone contact, Eric. His gut told him to go around North and contact the DNI directly. What was the worst that could happen? Assuming Landis successfully got his message to the DNI, then why should Covington risk his position?

He picked up the phone and dialed, recognizing the nine-hour time difference. Eric answered on the second ring.

"Commander, do you realize what time it is?" Eric said as he looked at the clock on his nightstand, which read 2:00 a.m.

"We have a situation." Covington went onto explain the break-in, but did not convey Landis's claim that the operation was not sanctioned.

"First of all, how in the hell did someone find it? Second, why were they even looking for it? Third, how did they manage to get in and, most importantly, how did you let them get away?" Eric was screaming into the phone. He was thankful his wife was away; otherwise she would now be awake and asking annoying questions.

"Sir, they managed to disarm us during questioning and seemed to know what they were looking for."

"That's impossible. No one knows what is going on there. Shit, did you capture them on surveillance video?"

"Yes, sir."

"Send it immediately. I suppose there is no point in going after them now, but initiate a perimeter detail. Make sure everyone is out of sight if and when any drones are in the area."

"Yes, sir." Covington once again stared at the monitor, wondering if he had done the right thing. Time would tell.

❧

Eric had immediately called North and shared the factory news and that he was sending him a video file of the intruders. North closed the door to his home office and sat down at his desk as his laptop *pinged* with the announcement of a new e-mail. He quickly opened the e-mail from Eric and clicked on the video file to open it.

"That son of a bitch!" North yelled at the screen as Landis was seen peering out behind oil drums, then making his way to a bank of lockers. North realized he now had a serious problem and his timetable for deployment would have to be accelerated. He had no doubt that Sara's brother's visit to the Massachusetts office and Landis showing up in the middle of nowhere, Iraq were connected. They had somehow put two and two together and now jeopardized everything he had worked for over the past several years.

And he was only a month from having all of the artificial intelligence bugs worked out.

North paced his office as he thought through the scenarios. Every scenario required him to keep Sara quiet, knowing Landis would be providing her updates. North had no choice but to put his plan into play immediately and hope that whatever issues remained with the artificial intelligence did not create a problem. He called Eric right back.

North began, "Eric, the men that broke in are believed to be ISIS sympathizers. Given our cover may be blown, we need to accelerate our schedule."

"We are really contemplating deploying the robots? The bugs are not completely worked out."

"The glitches that are left are relatively minimal. We cannot afford to lose the advantage."

"The AI is still dominant over any programming. The consequences and related collateral damage will be extremely large."

"Only for those who are working feverishly and diligently on staging an attack against the U.S. The question is: Should we sit around and wait, or should we act preemptively to avoid death and destruction on our soil?"

"You make a compelling case."

"It's not my case. This is coming straight from the president, Joint Chiefs, secretary of defense, Foreign Relations Committee, and the director of national intelligence."

"But it doesn't sound like you have enough evidence to convince the world stage of a preemptive strike."

"No, but I'm feverishly working on it. I need you to coordinate the deployment of four hundred robot infantry first to Mosul, then onto other ISIS strongholds in the Middle East."

"Has the president really thought this through?"

"God, I would hope so, given the gravity of the situation, the threat to our national security, and the forecasted casualties. This is not to be taken lightly. Blackstone can look forward to very lucrative contracts if we are successful. I know the president can count on you, Eric. There is a lot at stake here. Time is of the essence."

"I hear you loud and clear. I'll talk to Covington and get back to you with a status ASAP."

Eric called back in twenty minutes, explaining it would take at least thirty-six hours to complete the necessary programming, including rest time for the programmers. North quietly laughed to himself as he disconnected the call. He considered himself a master manipulator. In a few short days the world would be a different, much better place. *All hell would break loose on ISIS and its precious Caliphate*, he thought.

CHAPTER 53

Sara was dressed for her early-morning run and eager to work off some of the stress of the past several days. The forecast was for another hot, sticky late spring day in Washington, with temperatures and humidity both hovering near ninety degrees. However, at 6:00 a.m. it was an ideal sixty-eight degrees. She eagerly opened the front door to her brownstone, pulled it tight behind her to lock it, and bent down to tie the key to the laces of her left shoe.

As she straightened up to begin her run, she found North standing two feet away, smiling eerily. He was dressed in a running suit, ball cap, and sunglasses. She was instinctively on guard and felt panic surge through her. She looked left and right, debating whether to make a run for it.

"Sara, I apologize for showing up unannounced, but I was unsuccessful reaching you on your phone and the president has asked for a briefing as soon as possible," North began.

"Oh, I apologize for that. Okay, let me change clothes—"

"I'm afraid we don't have time for that," he interrupted.

Sara wanted to get inside, lock the door, and call for help.

"It'll only take me a minute," she insisted. But as Sara turned away, she looked over her shoulder and saw him pointing a small revolver at her.

She froze, but her mind raced wildly. What were the odds of him shooting her?

Why did he find her a threat? Had he somehow found out about her suspicions of him?

As if he could read her mind, he told her, "Unfortunately, Sara, I believe there's been a misinterpretation of my intent and related actions to ensure the security of our nation." His eyes roamed up and down her body, clad in a skintight running shirt and short-shorts. Sara was both frightened and repulsed. "I simply need to detain you for a few hours until some things are accomplished. I cannot afford anything or anyone to interrupt the implementation of the next phase of my mission. I trust once you have all of the facts, you'll understand why I had to do this."

"Where do you plan to detain me?"

"Given the short amount of time I had to prepare, you'll be a guest at my home."

"What? Me and the missus will have tea and crumpets and discuss the weather in Paris?"

"I applaud your bravado under the circumstances. My wife and two of her friends are headed to their favorite spa in the mountains for the next several days. You'll have the house to yourself, so to speak." The eerie smile returned to his face. "Now, I need you to walk down the sidewalk to your left to where my car is parked. Move!"

Sara slowly walked down the path, praying that one of her neighbors would pass by so she could give them a signal of some sort. However, since moving there she had only run into a neighbor at that hour once. And she wasn't close enough to any of her neighbors that they would notice if she didn't return from work.

As North zip-tied Sara's wrists and ankles, duct-taped her mouth, and placed her in the backseat of his car, he imagined binding her limbs and splaying her naked body face down on his bed. His juices were flowing now. He loved the adrenaline rush of the kidnapping, the anticipation of annihilating the fanatics in the Middle East, and having his way with her.

❦

North parked at the rear of his large home so no one could spot him removing Sara from the car.

North opened the back door. "Out," he commanded.

Sara flipped him the bird, even though her wrists were zip-tied together.

"Really, Ms. Fahridi? Listen, I could shoot you now for treason. Yes, I am aware of your sharing information about Asaryi with the enemy. Now, like I said, I simply need to detain you for a few days."

Sara realized she did not have any options, so she scooted across the backseat so she could exit.

"Now, I'm going to cut the tie around your ankles so you can walk— no funny business."

Sara cringed at seeing the box cutter and was quickly relieved when the only thing he cut was the tie. North then ripped the duct tape from her mouth, which hurt like hell.

"Now, we are going through the back door, take a left, and head down a flight of stairs into my wine cellar."

"I'm claustrophobic," Sara explained.

"Not to worry. The size of the cellar fits the size of my home. It is very spacious. Now, move!"

Sara slowly began walking, thinking this may be the last time she saw the sun. She slowed in an attempt to turn to make a plea, but North shoved her forward before she could turn. Now they were at the stairs and Sara's heart was racing as if she had just run three miles. She also found she was sweating from fear.

Thirty minutes later, with Sara locked in his wine cellar with food, water, sleeping bag, pillow, and toiletry necessities, North was on his way back to Langley. He was confident no one had seen him at or near her home and there were no security cameras in the vicinity. He would decide what to do with her later. His first priority was the deployment of the robots. His second priority was to dispose of Fahridi, and the idea of how to do such began to crystallize. Today could be the best day of his life. He cranked up Coltrane as he drove to Langley.

CHAPTER 54

"Detective Smith, this is Patricia Hunt's office calling. Ms. Hunt has returned from her mission and instructed me to provide you a copy of a letter Ms. Scheinberg mailed right before her death," the legal assistant explained.

"When can we expect it?" Smith asked.

"I can get it to you later today. I, uhm... have other appointments outside of the office most of the day."

"This is a homicide investigation and any related information should be considered urgent in nature."

"I understand, Detective. I'll scan and e-mail it to you as soon as I can."

Great, Smith thought, she probably has a date tonight with an insurance salesman making six figures and she was not about to change a hair appointment for a letter from a dead woman. He considered driving to the attorney's office to pick up the letter, but Warfield walked into his office, interrupting his thoughts.

"Let's review what we have regarding North," Warfield began.

"We have motive, familiarity, and arguably expertise with a high-powered rifle and ownership of the rifle type used."

"Is it enough?"

"In any other case, I suspect the chief would support us going in with guns a-blazing. But the political nature requires us to conjure up more crud." Smith frowned.

"We need to place him at the scene, which means we need to make an inquiry into his schedule."

"And that means the lid comes off this thing and we better be damn sure he's our man."

"What do you think?"

"The jealousy angle works for me, but why would North go through all the trouble of setting him up? Why didn't he just shoot him instead?"

"Too direct," Warfield said. "Someone would have questioned North as the killer, considering the job pass-over. No, he needed to distance himself."

"Well, if we're not prepared to request his schedule," Smith said, "we need to work the car angle."

"Agreed. So, if you're North and you're going to rent a car that matches Pendleton's description on the off chance that someone may see it in the vicinity of the murder—which they did—how do you get to the rental agency?"

"None of the rentals are reporting a white BMW parked at their site, while it is highly doubtful he would have someone drop him off," Smith related.

"Cab?"

"Yup. I'll get the boys at the precinct on it, pronto."

"Still doesn't work for me. He's too smart to have a cab pick him up at his home and drop him at the rental agency. Even if he walked a mile from his home, it would still be too close to his house."

"He would need to have created a legitimate excuse for renting a car that day on the off chance that someone ever checked," Smith said.

"Why do you rent a car?"

"When my car is unavailable, like in the shop."

"Bingo," Warfield agreed. "Considering he drives a high-end BMW, there can't be that many dealerships in the area."

"And you know he is not going to take his car to Joe mechanic on the corner. I'll have that checked on also."

"We need to move quickly. If he's our boy, he knows we're onto him after our chat with his wife and will be double-checking his tracks to make sure they're covered."

☙

Jack was now calling Sara every thirty minutes with no response. He knew something was wrong and felt helpless. The international phone the CIA provided allowed him to call only three numbers: the field liaison, Sara; her boss for the operation, North; and General Makarov. He couldn't call North—he didn't trust him. Abir's phone allowed him to call only Sara and North, so his next-best method was e-mail.

As he pulled out his laptop, he realized he did not have Lou's personal e-mail address. He would have to send a general e-mail to the metro police, hoping that Smith and Warfield would get the message. He then realized he could use Bluescape. He quickly opened the session using the ID and password he had been given. He then opened a window and began typing.

> *I've been unable to reach Sara all day and am fearful that something may have happened to her. If she is not with you, please immediately attempt to contact her and let me know. I'm unable to call you on my international cell phone, but you may call me. The number is 011-7-92-555-1...*

He expanded the window that contained the message and saved the session, such that when it was opened the next time, it couldn't be missed.

ॐ

Sara found her prison cell to be oddly comfortable, given the circumstances. The only pain she'd experienced so far was when North ripped the duct tape from her mouth. She would have liked the opportunity to ask him questions during the car ride, but doubted she would have received any substantial responses. Plus, he had the music turned up so loud she could barely think straight.

She sat on the sleeping bag he provided, with her legs crossed in front and her back leaning against the wall. She perched in the corner furthest from the locked door, believing that whatever additional distance she could put between herself and his inevitable return increased her odds of survival.

Over the past hour her thoughts and emotions had run the gamut. The hope she experienced when searching every nook and corner of the wine cellar for an escape route or some clever way to hide gradually subsided to anger when thinking about her situation and inequity of it all. Here she was, a victim, without having put herself in harm's way. It was simply bad luck that she had been assigned to the CIA at a time when a self-absorbed egotistical lunatic was in charge.

Sara wasn't a wine connoisseur, but based on the labels, she was sitting amid tens of thousands of dollars' worth of wine. In her moment of anger, she thought of breaking every last bottle, but that might incite North to do something to her that was more painful than whatever he was currently planning.

As she sat staring at her hands, she resigned herself to the fact that the odds of surviving this were slim. *How ironic*, she thought. She had trudged through the rungs in her life as she was supposed to. She had moved to the United States, established a successful career, taken good care of herself, loved and cared for her family, and had not wished ill will upon anybody. But here she was, trapped like an animal awaiting slaughter. She had no misgivings about North's intent. She was confident he was behind at least one, if not all, of the murders. Sara couldn't shake the painful irony from her mind: She had finally met somebody who turned each day into anticipation rather than just another check on the calendar. Now she might not see too many more days of the calendar.

She made the decision there and then that she would not go down without a fight. She stood and took a running start at the locked door and threw her left shoulder into it. She bounced off like a rag doll and fell to the floor, then slowly got up and canvassed every corner of the cellar, looking for an air vent or crack of some sort and found nothing that could help her escape.

She looked around the cellar again, but this time her intent was different. As the idea formed, she felt energized and quickly went to work, not knowing when her executioner would return.

CHAPTER 55

Smith and Warfield again arrived early to the showroom, bringing coffee and a continental breakfast with them.

"We should have the results of the BMW dealership search by nine a.m.," Smith said as he fired up the computer and Bluescape.

"Did we get anything from that attorney's office?"

"Nope. Her assistant must have gotten busy. We may have to run over there to pick it up."

"Jesus Christ. What is so hard about scanning and e-mailing a letter?" Warfield complained.

"We're not billable hours and therefore last on the priority list." As Smith said this, Jack's message filled the entire wall and caught both detectives' attention.

"What do you make of this?" Warfield asked.

"Looks like a message from that Landis guy. Just when I think this case can't get any weirder, it does. Well, in another ten minutes we should know if Ms. Fahridi is MIA."

Just then Smith's cell phone buzzed. "Hey, chief."

"I got a call from the admin pool upstairs stating they had a fax without a proper cover letter and wondered if I recognized the contents," the chief explained.

"And?"

"The fax is from Scheinberg's attorney. There are some pretty juicy tidbits in a letter that Scheinberg must have mailed the day she was killed. In it, she alleges that Richard North is behind a plot to disgrace Pendleton, she is being used as a pawn in the plot, and that if anything happens to her, look first at North."

"Holy shit. That plays right into our current thinking."

"The letter also alleges that he was behind the murder of a young woman by the name of Francine Fulbright, evidently a model of some sort. In addition, it appears our little Laura was worth several more million than we thought; the majority of it stashed in offshore accounts."

"The floral business is very lucrative."

"Given the circumstantial evidence you already have, I believe you now have enough to knock on the CIA's door."

"We may have more than we need as of this morning. Sara Fahridi may be missing and North would be our first suspect, given what we know now."

"What do you mean, *may be missing?*"

Smith had to think quickly, given they had not shared the use of Bluescape with their boss. "Lou remains fairly well connected with his former staff members and he hasn't been able to reach her. He's worried. Do we have clearance to visit Langley?"

"Let me have a call placed there first, and let me know when you guys are on your way there."

"Will do."

"Just catch the bad guy—and don't ruin my career doing it."

As Smith hung up, he realized the Pendletons and Hank had arrived, but no Sara. They were all reading Jack's message and looking anxiously at the entrance to the showroom.

"Let's call this Jack Landis," Smith said quietly to the group.

⁂

After a restless night—at least, what she assumed to be night, due to her circadian rhythms—Sara continued putting her plan in motion. She had broken several wine bottles in the cellar's darkest corner to create cutting tools. Her goal was a five-inch-long piece with a thin profile at one end and a thick one at the other. Using the sleeping bag to protect her hand, she held onto the thicker end and used the thinner end as a knife to create a groove in the sole of her running shoe at the center of the toe area. Her plan was to wedge a piece of razor-sharp glass into grooves in each sole to make her shoes a weapon. Ideally, she would get the opportunity to launch a kick or two at North.

The expensive shoe was proving to be worth what she paid, as it was extremely difficult to chip away at the sole. She ended up having to break ten bottles to yield enough glass tools to create the wedges. She'd been at it for two hours and had finished just one shoe. She had no idea how much time she had before North returned, so she continued to work at a feverish pace.

⁂

Jack was debating his next move when his phone rang, displaying an unknown number; his heart sank.

"Mr. Landis, this is Detective Glenn Smith with the Washington metro police."

"Is it Sara?"

"I'm afraid that Sara's not here at the showroom with Lou, Kate, and Hank and no one has been able to reach her."

"Have you tried her place?"

"We dispatched a squad car immediately before we called you. No answer, but her car is there. We are preparing to break in."

"Any ideas?"

"Based on new information that we've just received, we believe that Richard North may be involved." Smith gave Jack a recap of what they had learned from the attorney.

"Can you pick him up?"

"You can appreciate we have to make sure we have every i dotted and t crossed."

"Which means what?"

"We have a fair amount of circumstantial evidence now. The remaining, strong piece of the puzzle is to place him at the scene of Scheinberg's murder, which we hope will be one of the BMW dealerships telling us he had his car in for repair that day."

"How long?"

"Mid-morning, latest."

"Then it's a go?"

"Not exactly. We have to get clearance from the Tower, meaning the metro chief has to speak with a head spook as a courtesy of sorts."

"And give North a chance to get away?"

"No. We'll be waiting outside Langley with backup and will be notified as soon as the call has been made."

"Not good enough; this is taking too long."

"Believe me, Jack, if it were up to us we would go in now."

"I know, I know. Find her, Glenn."

"We will, Jack."

"Call me as soon as you hear something."

"Can you tell me any more about your situation that may help us?"

"North is heavily involved in my mission. He's running the show, more or less."

"Good Lord. That can't be good, based upon what we've learned, can it?"

"Not sure. I can't imagine him sabotaging a mission that could potentially make him and the agency look like heroes."

"I believe our Mr. North may be capable of anything while his rationale and justification may make sense only to him."

"Please find her, Glenn," he repeated.

"We'll do our damnedest."

Jack hung up, knowing what he had to do. He dialed General Makarov.

[space break]

Five minutes later Jack met Abir in the hotel lobby.

"I still cannot reach Sara," Jack said.

"Now what?" Abir asked.

"You with that fucking question."

"Jeez, what's up your ass?"

"Sorry. I think Sara is in trouble and I'm half a world away. So I'm heading back. General Makarov has agreed to help us keep the dialogue going with ISIS by having an agent pose as a Russian engineer and join you for the next meeting if I can't get back in time. He is also flying me back overnight in a jet."

"What do you want me to do?"

"Keep an eye on the factory. Depending on what Covington does, North may already be on to us and doing whatever he can to keep the factory under wraps. I can't imagine him attempting to move it, but he managed to move the office in Massachusetts in a matter of hours without a trace."

"We still don't know if North is behind it."

"True, but we need to operate as if he is."

"Given the situation, what would you do if you were North?"

"The thought scares me."

☙

Smith updated the Pendletons and Hank on the call to Landis and promised to advise them of any new developments. The priority now was to find Sara, followed closely by picking up North for questioning. But first, they had to get the metro chief of police to make a call to Langley.

Smith arrived at City Hall to find the chief tied up in the mayor's office in budget talks and not to be disturbed. *Goddamn bureaucrats,* he thought. What was he thinking? Eighty percent of his job involved what he referred to as the *whirlwind,* or the administrative bureaucracy that stole precious time from the real job, which was catching criminals. The metro chief was the only one who should and would make the call to Langley.

The mayor's administrative assistant was less than pleased that Smith was insisting on interrupting the budget session she'd been told should be disturbed by nothing other than an emergency.

"Listen, we're working a very high-profile homicide investigation and it is imperative that the chief be made aware of new developments as soon as possible," Smith pleaded.

"Who died?" responded the assistant.

"You're killing me. I'm not at liberty to say, you know that."

"If you're blowing smoke up my ass, I'll make sure this office has yours, understand?"

"Understood. Now, can you please get me in?"

"Hang on."

Forty minutes later, the metro chief of police exited the conference room, looking less than pleased. "What do you have?" she asked as she approached Smith.

Smith took less than five minutes to review the progress and related circumstantial evidence he and Warfield had uncovered. The chief agreed that a call to the DNI was appropriate and that she should make the call. She thanked Smith, acknowledged his good decision-making for interrupting her, and told him that they better be right. The metro police were about to storm Langley.

છ

North checked out one of the agency's black Suburbans to head home. After checking on Sara before work and finding her asleep, he had changed into slacks and a sports coat and it wasn't until he reached Langley that he noticed that the tie he wore did not match well. He spent the morning anxiously awaiting confirmation that the robots were programmed and ready for deployment.

He left his office at 1:00 p.m. and told Jake he had an offsite meeting but would be reachable by phone. As North headed out of Langley, he noticed two patrol cars and what he suspected was an unmarked vehicle. Must be another unimportant *important* dignitary visiting their fair city that demanded unneeded and costly pomp and circumstance, he thought. Little did he realize they were there looking for him.

His thoughts returned to the mission and Sara. After the successful attack in Mosul, he could celebrate by having his way with her. Based on the latest update from Eric, the robots should be deployed in approximately twenty hours. He reveled in what he had accomplished. He was the pending director of the CIA. He was almost singlehandedly curbing the threat of global terrorism. A day from now he would be in the midst of directing the eradication of terrorists throughout the Middle East using artificial intelligence. What would the world do without him?

ℜ

Sara heard someone in the house. She wished it was North's wife coming home early from her little vacation, but she knew it was a man by the footsteps. She had successfully implanted sharp shards of glass into the bottom of each shoe. Two inches protruded from the toe area and could produce a fairly serious wound if her kicks found major arteries. She needed to create a distraction. "Think," she whispered to herself.

North unlocked and opened the cellar door with his left hand, while holding the revolver in his right. He stood back and to the left in case Sara decided to throw a few wine bottles in his direction. After a few seconds, he heard her say, "Hey, asshole."

He peeked around the door, remaining several feet back from the entrance, and saw Sara curled up in the sleeping bag, leaning against the far wall. The sweet smell of wine filled his nostrils. To her left were two wine bottles with the tops broken off. One of the bottles was empty and the other was half empty. In her hand was one of the water bottles he had left her, but it appeared to be half full of wine, not water.

"Where the hell have you been?" Sara slurred. "I've been stuck in this fucking hole. What kind of asshole leaves another human being like this? I'll tell you, a fucking dickhead, that's who."

North couldn't help but be amused. His hostage had turned to booze to help relieve her anxiety and fear and the alcohol was providing her an inebriated sense of strength and resolve. Sara noticed him relax his guard just a little as he entered the room and came to stand three feet in front of her.

"Well, my dear, I see you're enjoying a vintage red from the Italian winery Francia located in Serralunga d'Alba."

"Whatever, asshole."

"Ha-ha. Well, I do admire your taste. How did you come to select that particular wine?"

"I hoped it was the most expensive, based upon the year and amount of dust on it." She bobbed her head ever so slightly.

"Very clever. But no, there are many that are much more expensive. We have a little bit of a problem, my love. Turns out I'll be working the balance of my day here. I may possibly have some uninvited guests who may be looking for you."

Sara's heart leaped, but she kept her composure.

"That means we'll have to find another place for you to hide until I have time to deal with you."

Sara let the water bottle half-filled with wine slip and spill onto the floor. Her eyes closed and her head fell forward.

Time stood still as she did her best to make her breathing slow and deliberate. She heard North step cautiously toward her and command her to stand. She ignored him. He yelled at her, but she continued to ignore him. She was very conscious of her shoes, hidden underneath the sleeping bag.

Deciding she was in a stupor, he reached down with his free hand and grabbed her right arm to help her to her feet. Sara made a feeble attempt to pull away from his grip and mumbled, "Let go of me, prick."

He released her arm and slapped her hard across the face. She wasn't expecting that and it took every fiber in her body to maintain her intoxicated guise. She knew this was the moment.

"All right, all right, you bastard. Give me a minute."

Sara clumsily attempted to stand, ensuring that the sleeping bag covered her feet. She put her palms flat and back against the wall as a brace and slowly pushed herself upright. Just when she was almost standing, she started to slide away and down from North. As he instinctively grabbed her arm to keep her upright, she kicked the sleeping bag away, pushed him back with a straight arm, and brought her left foot into his groin, kicking as hard and deep as she could. One inch of the glass shard tore through North's scrotum and embedded into his abdominal wall.

It wasn't enough to create significant damage, but it was enough to catch North off-guard, giving Sara a chance to step back and attempt to connect with her right foot. Bent over from the blow to his groin, North saw the second kick coming and deflected it with his left arm and lunged forward, swinging his right hand in Sara's direction. The handle of the revolver caught her square in the temple and she fell unconscious.

North looked down at his hand holding his crotch. Blood oozed through his fingers but not at a rate that was life-threatening. But when he took a step he realized a shard of glass must have broken off inside him. He'd need a doctor to remove it.

Goddamn bitch. Shit, he did not have time for this.

He wished he could just shoot her dead as she lay there, but he needed to assess his situation and alternatives. Decisions based upon emotion typically were bad ones. He took off his shirt and stuffed it in his pants to block the blood flow, closed and locked the cellar door, gingerly headed upstairs, and called his doctor, who agreed to see him immediately. North placed a call to the DNI, letting him know about the doctor visit but certainly not the reason why. Two hours later, he left the doctor's office and headed back to Langley.

❧

An hour after he spoke with North about his small medical emergency, the DNI received a very disturbing call from the metro chief of police. He insisted on speaking with the homicide detectives handling the case before he did anything, and said he'd be available at 5:00 p.m., in a little over an hour.

Clapper hung up, wondering if North was really capable of what the police were suggesting, just to become director, and decided to wait until he spoke to the detectives to apprise the president. *Jesus, the agency can't afford another debacle.*

Smith and Warfield arrived at Langley twenty minutes early for their appointment in case they had to complete security clearances to enter the building. But with a simple showing of their badges and driver's licenses, they were led to a first-floor conference room and told the DNI would arrive shortly.

"We already have probable cause to question and detain and enough to obtain a warrant to search for the weapon," Warfield complained.

"You're right. But it'll be easier with the CIA's cooperation. Considering the Pendleton mess, the last thing this guy needs is another media fest," Smith opined.

"Well, he should look at it as if we're cleaning up one of their messes. We turn one bad guy into a good guy—Pendleton, and there is still one bad guy at the end of the day—North."

"Please don't consider a second career in politics—you'll never make it."

"Thank you. I consider that a compliment," Warfield said, smirking.

The DNI walked in looking especially serious, thanked the detectives for patiently waiting, and then listened as they laid out their case that

Richard North had murdered at least one individual and was possibly behind the murders of two others.

"Gentlemen, I cannot emphasize enough how bad your timing is," said the DNI.

"We appreciate the fact that North is slated to be the next director," Smith said.

"That's only part of it. Politics aside, there are significant initiatives in play now that Richard is intimately involved with."

"Care to share?"

"I wish I could. I think it would help buy me a day or two. So what happens now?"

"The first thing is to question North. We ordinarily would have knocked on the front door asking for him, but considering the politics you just referenced, our team thought it better to give your team advance notice."

"I very much appreciate it and it will obviously work to gain our full cooperation."

"Can we speak with North now?"

"He is not in the building."

The detectives exchanged glances.

"Are you sure about that, sir?" Warfield asked.

"Fairly certain. He called me not long ago, explaining he had an accident and needed to visit his doctor, but planned to be in later today and would check in with me. He has not checked in with me yet, so my assumption is he has not arrived."

"We began light surveillance once our evidence pointed in his direction and we haven't seen his car leave the premises today."

"In that case, he most likely checked a vehicle out of the car pool. I'll call his assistant to find out if he knows."

Thirty seconds and a brief phone exchange later, the DNI confirmed that North had indeed taken an agency vehicle.

"Why would North take a company vehicle?"

"Typically they're taken when conducting agency-related business. However, I'm not aware of any assignments North had out of the office today."

"Do you find that suspicious?"

"Not necessarily. We should do a better job of monitoring the personal use of the vehicles, but we don't."

"Can you call him?"

"Of course, hang on." After twenty seconds, the DNI explained he had gotten his voice mail.

"Do you have his doctor's information?"

"I'll have Jake, his assistant, get it for us. I'll also have Jake notify us when he arrives."

"We'll also need his phone numbers—all of them."

***

North felt amazingly well for getting five stitches to close the rip in his lower abdomen and four more stitches to close his scrotum. The doctor said the local numbing could last up to four hours. He parked the agency Suburban back in the lot and called the DNI's assistant to find out if he could get on his schedule within the next hour. What he heard stopped him in his tracks. The DNI was tied up with two homicide detectives from metro and was expected to be free within the next hour.

"Want me to book you for then?" the assistant asked.

"No, I'll try him later."

"Yes, sir."

As soon as he ended the call, his phone rang. It was the DNI, who had to be calling from the meeting with the detectives. He couldn't pick up; he needed time to think. First, he had to get out of there without being noticed. He returned to the Suburban and quickly exited the premises.

He drove home and found Sara passed out. At first he thought it another ruse, but after checking her over while avoiding her feet, he was convinced she was still unconscious. He couldn't carry her—the doctor explained any lifting could result in the abdominal stitches tearing.

He parked the Suburban in his garage and made sure there were no lights on in the house, as if no one was home. He had decided to shoot Sara in his backyard near the lake the next morning. He would use a pillow to muffle the sound of the gunshot. North prepared his crime scene, laying a sixteen-by-sixteen-foot tarp on the grass, which would capture any blood that escaped from the bullet wounds to her chest. Not that there were any neighbors close enough to see anything or decipher a gunshot, considering the size of his property, but why take any chances?

In addition, if any police were out on the street keeping an eye on the place, they would never be able to see in the backyard, let alone all the way to the lake. And if anyone stepped foot on his property, his alarm would go off and notify the pager he carried with him.

He had anchored his flatbed fishing boat adjacent to the tarp, so he would only have to move the body a few feet to get it into the boat. He had brought his large wheelbarrow to help if necessary. In the boat he had assembled chains linked to eighty-pound boat anchors. He also had four locks to secure the chains in place, once wrapped around her body.

He would drop her in one of the deepest areas of the lake farthest from his house. Any dredging would be extremely difficult at that depth, and if the police actually went to that extent he would be long gone, taking advantage of fake passports, money in offshore accounts, and clandestine contacts he had made during his career. At the end of the day, he was smarter than anyone he had ever met or would ever meet. Once the preparation work was complete, he ate a light meal and turned in early. He had a big day ahead of him.

CHAPTER 56

Before dawn the following morning in Iraq, Abir switched from the car to the Humvee at the farmhouse, realizing his chances of escape were much better in the Humvee. The meadow and woods, once serene and quiet, had taken on an ominous air. The sun's rays were beginning to slice through the tree line as he parked the Humvee a quarter mile from the factory and slowly began to make his way through the woods. No eagles about this morning. He took up a position two hundred yards away, which provided him a clear view of the bay door, and he used his binoculars to keep a lookout. He quickly discovered there was now an exterior security detail comprised of two men who circled the perimeter every thirty minutes.

The morning came and went as the temperature rose above ninety degrees. Abir wondered if today would be the longest day of his life. He had just finished the snack he had brought and settled in for more long hours of boring surveillance. He wanted to call Jack and give him an update, but realized he would be in the air for another thirty minutes, landing in D.C. around 5:30 a.m. local time. An hour later, Abir, having fallen asleep, was awoken by a loud noise.

Upon focusing, he blinked his eyes several times to be sure he saw what his brain was telling him he saw. A hundred-foot-wide section of the factory wall had fallen outward, the mirrored panels breaking upon impact with the ground. In the gaping hole of the factory stood the robots, shoulder to shoulder, the sensors in their eye sockets lit an eerie red. Abir crouched down and hid as best he could. Then—all at once and in unison—the robots began moving slowly, in formation, out into the woods. There were hundreds of them. Abir turned and ran toward the Humvee.

As he jumped in and started the engine, he could see the infantry to his left approximately fifty yards away, the sun glistening off their steel exterior. They were all out of the factory now and had begun to run at what he estimated to be twenty miles per hour, zigzagging through the woods, hurling bushes and anything else in their way. Abir could feel the ground shake as he sat in the Humvee.

They were headed toward Mosul, and assuming he had guessed their speed correctly, they would be there in approximately two hours. As the last wave of robots passed, he swung the Humvee behind the stampede, followed from a safe distance, and called Jack.

"Jack, can you hear me?"

"Barely. My plane just landed. What's all the noise?"

"I'm in the Humvee following the robots."

"You're what?"

"Hundreds of them, running toward Mosul. They're alive; their eyes are on."

"North must have given the order to attack." As Abir listened to Jack, he did not notice the two robots that had taken up flank positions to his left and right. As Abir began to respond to Jack, both robots fired their lasers at the Humvee. It took a nanosecond for the beams of green light to reach the vehicle. The result was an enormous ball of fire as the Humvee exploded. The phone connection died along with Abir.

"Abir, Abir?" Jack called out, but received no answer. Jack called Abir right back after the line had gone dead, but found it went immediately to voice mail. Given what Abir had told him, he feared the worst, but he would have to place his concern on the back burner and deal with the emergencies at hand.

Jack sprinted down the jet's stairs onto Reagan National's tarmac and into the car he had arranged to be ready. He started the engine and sped to the security exit; the guards had been given notice of his impending arrival and need for speed and quickly waved him through. Given it was early morning and the D.C. traffic was not at its peak, Jack was able to speed at will. He punched in a number on his cell, which he was relieved to be able to use now back on U.S. soil.

"Hello," Lou answered groggily.

"Lou, it's Jack. Wake up."

"Are you back?"

"Yes, now listen. There are two situations I need your help with and they both need immediate attention and action." Jack realized time was of the essence and he had to be as succinct as possible. "Lou, you trust me, right?"

"Of course."

"This is going to sound farfetched. I am certain North is behind the development and manufacture of robots with artificial intelligence armed with laser technology. I discovered an office in Massachusetts and a factory in Iraq. Abir just called me and told me the robots have been deployed, like an infantry, and are marching—rather, running— from a farm in Makhmur toward Mosul, approximately forty-five miles southwest. They have to be stopped." Jack paused, allowing Lou to ask a question. When none was forthcoming, Jack continued, "I cannot reach Sara and I believe something has happened and I'm certain North is behind it. Sara and I were working together, pursuing leads about the robots, and North was suspicious she knew something."

"You should know that the police have uncovered a significant amount of circumstantial evidence that points in North's direction relative to the Scheinberg murder."

"Have they picked him up?"

"No. I received a call from the detectives late yesterday, explaining that North had to have some unexpected medical attention and is staying with a friend and no one knows where he is."

"What a crock of shit."

"Everyone knows it, but nobody is willing to stick their neck out, given the political backdrop."

"Have they checked his house?"

"They have and no one appears to be home."

"No warrant to enter?"

"Not until later this morning. When did you get back?"

"Twenty minutes ago. Can you get in touch with Clapper and let him know about the robots?"

"Yes, I'm certain he'll still take my call."

"Do you have North's address?"

"No, I don't. All I know is that he lives in McLean."

"I need that address ASAP."

"Hang on. I'll get you the detectives' numbers. They'll know. What do you plan on doing?"

"Breaking and entering, what else?"

"I believe it's justified. Good luck, Jack. Please keep me informed."

"You got it."

Two minutes later Jack was on the phone. "Detective Smith, Jack Landis."

"It's six o'clock in the morning."

"Sorry, emergency. I need Richard North's home address."

"Excuse me?"

"We have little time, Detective. We believe that North has misled the CIA with false information that will result in an unsanctioned attack in the Middle East. In addition, I suspect that he has abducted Sara or did something to her."

"And why do you believe all of this?"

"Because I was the primary in the operation, providing the intelligence that now has been somehow compromised. Sara was assigned to receive my intelligence and now she is missing."

"And what do you plan to do with North's address?"

"C'mon, Detective, quit jerking me around. You don't have a warrant, we have precious little time before the weapons are to be deployed that could ignite a holy war, and I'm fearful that every second counts for Sara. Also, I strongly suggest you order any uniforms watching his place to call it a day."

Armed with North's address, Jack was now speeding toward McLean. He had no idea what, if anything, he would find, but he had to do something. He wanted to call Lou to find out if he had successfully reached Clapper, but he thought it best to stay focused on the road as he raced 100 miles per hour down the George Washington National Parkway.

CHAPTER 57

"Lou, there is no way North could have orchestrated this, let alone funded it," the DNI said as he angrily looked at the clock on his nightstand, which read 6:07 a.m.

"James, what is the harm in sending a few drones?" Lou pleaded.

"First I find out North may be a murderer and now this?"

"James, please, now!" Lou barked into the phone.

"All right. We have a fully operational system in a remote area of northeast Syria. The four drones can be over the target area in fifteen minutes."

"Will you let me know?"

"Lou, that would be breaking agency protocol, given the situation—but, yes, I will let you know."

"Godspeed."

☙

Twenty-five minutes later and forty-five minutes after the robots had left the factory, two of the drones were providing a live feed of the robot stampede to the ground- control station and primary satellite link communication suite. The pilots looked at one another, sharing a look of disbelief, and uploaded the feed so it could be seen in the White House's situation room, where the DNI and the chief of staff sat impatiently, both unshaven and dressed in jeans, having left their respective homes as quickly as possible to get to the White House.

After viewing the live video for a minute, the DNI turned to the chief of staff and said, "Wake the president. I'll call the chairman of the Joint Chiefs and the secretary of defense. We need to do this by conference call, given the lack of time to react."

Thirty minutes later and seventy-five minutes after the robots had left the factory, the military leaders of the United States were convened on a conference call, many of whom could now see the live feed dispatched to their personal devices.

"Gentlemen," the President began, "it is estimated that the robots will reach the outskirts of Mosul in little over an hour. We do not have time now to discuss how and why. Suffice it to say, we cannot allow them to reach the city. We assume their target is ISIS; however, there is no way to know if the artificial intelligence is developed to the extent that innocent people will not be killed. The U.S. will be held responsible and the reaction may be unprecedented. To that end, what is our best offensive response?"

The chairman of the Joint Chiefs responded, "Our air base near Baghdad provides us the best and closest strike capability. Given the robots' numbers and their relatively large geographic footprint, we will need to drop bombs with a relatively large blast radius. We cannot afford to engage in a shootout, especially if they have laser technology—we will lose. The air base is equipped with the Hammer, or Mark 84. It has a blast radius of four hundred yards and is our best option. Recognizing speed is of the essence, we have two attack helicopter options: the Chinook, which flies one-hundred-and-ninety-five miles per hour and the Apache, which flies one-hundred-and-seventy-five miles per hour. I ordered their deployment as soon as I saw the video feed, sir, in the essence of time."

"That's fine, commander. Can they get there in time?"

"The air base is two-hundred-and-twenty-five miles from Mosul as the crow flies. They've been airborne for fifteen minutes—so, yes, we can engage when the robots are approximately ten miles from the outskirts of the city, given the robots' speed estimate of twenty-five miles per hour is reasonably correct according to our drone surveillance."

"What is the probability of preventing any of the robots from getting into the city?"

"Again, their laser capability is an unknown. I honestly cannot give you an accurate assessment. If we had some particulate we could drop above the kill zone prior to engaging, it would interfere with their lasers; unfortunately, there was nothing available when we deployed the helicopters. The recommendation is to send all twenty available Apaches first to engage from what we perceive to be a safe distance, each carrying sixteen Hellfire missiles. The intent is to delay the robots' progress as they encounter the missiles. Five minutes later, the ten available Chinooks, each carrying three Hammers in their payloads, will be in position. The debate we are currently having is whether to drop all of the Hammers at the same time, or in sequence."

"Why the debate?"

"If the artificial intelligence and laser technology are advanced enough, the Hammers could be destroyed before reaching the ground. If thirty are dropped at once, there is a chance that a few will get through. The other thought is if we drop them in sequence and the first round is destroyed midair, the explosion may interfere with the laser's ability to detect and destroy the next round."

"Jesus. What about two rounds of fifteen?"

"We've considered that."

"We don't have time to consider anymore. Do it: two rounds of fifteen. I want everyone on this call to hightail it here and stay on this line until you get here."

"Sir," the chief of staff said as he looked to the president.

"What?"

"We are getting calls from Russia, the U.K., Saudi Arabia, and Israel. They've detected the movement and are screaming for answers."

"Shit! Get them all on a videoconference immediately and we will simply tell them the truth—unless somebody's got a better idea. Maybe they can help, somehow."

CHAPTER 58

The robots, synchronously moving across the terrain toward Mosul, remained in precision formation, twenty robots in a line, twenty lines deep. They had encountered fifteen humans thus far. The robots in the front row had vaporized them with their lasers without missing a beat in their forward progress.

Twelve miles from the city, the first line of five Apaches were a quarter mile from the pack and fired four laser-led Hellfires before peeling off to take up position in the rear to make a second sweep; each line was positioned to do the same. The robots detected the incoming missiles and immediately broke into two units of 200. One group of 200 continued its march to the city, while the other fanned out in a large circle and easily detected and destroyed the missiles in midair.

The result was radioed back to the situation room. Two of five Apache lines were directed to engage with the group still advancing. As before, the pack divided itself in half; 100 remained to engage, while 100 maintained pursuit of the city.

"The Apaches are useless," the President said.

"Not necessarily," replied the chairman. "We can use the Hellfire explosions to our advantage, given our timing is good. Remember, the laser's effectiveness is reduced significantly with any particulates in the air, such as smoke or the metal fragments from the midair explosions."

"I see. If we can time the Hellfire explosions with the Hammer drops, some may get through."

"Exactly."

With that, the Apache runs were called off, allowing time for the general and his staff to coordinate the timing of the weapon launches. Five minutes later, the respective helicopter pilots were given their instructions. The major concern in the attack plan was that the Apaches had to get closer to the robots to ensure the midair explosions happened above the robots, which could expose them to laser fire. The pilots were instructed to fire one missile from a safe distance, and fly near and above the midair explosion, prohibiting the laser from detecting the helicopter and allowing them to fire a second round of missiles closer in.

The Chinooks were divided into three teams. Three remained with the group of 200, three were assigned to the stationary group of 100, and four were following the remaining 100 that continued to run toward the city. All hovered 1000 feet above their targets, ready to deploy each of three Hammers when they received the *go* from their partnered Apache. Given it would take the Hammer 5.5 seconds to drop 1000 feet, the Apache pilot would have to give the *go* command as soon as the second Hellfire was fired.

The Apaches, similarly divided per robot pack, were given the green light. The pilot engaging with the group of 200 had timed it perfectly as he flew through the smoke from the explosion, yelled *go*, fired the second missile, and successfully peeled off and up to avoid laser fire. The second missile was detonated 300 feet directly above the circle of 200, and a split-second later three Hammers hit the ground within a ten-foot radius in the center of the circle. The explosion created an eighty-foot crater in the ground and sent metal fragments 400 yards in every direction. The metal fragments, which were designed to penetrate fifteen inches of steel, easily bore through the robots and shredded them apart.

The timing of the pilot converging on the stationary 100 was not good. He had flown too close behind the first missile and the explosion damaged his ability to fire the second missile. He was a sitting duck as he saw the laser beam a split second before it struck his fuselage and the helicopter exploded, falling to the ground.

"Apache down," came the voice over the conference phone in the situation room.

The timing of the pilot covering the moving 100 was excellent in terms of the missile launches, but his *go* command was late and the Hammers were detected and detonated 500 feet above ground. However, the shrapnel successfully destroyed seventy-five of the 100; twenty-five continued their pursuit.

"Approximately two-fifty down, a hundred and fifty to go. Targets are estimated to be five miles from the city," was heard through the conference phone.

The pilot next in line covering the stationary 100 timed his missile launches and *go* command well enough that one of the three Hammers successfully reached land and detonated, creating another heap of scrap metal and electronics.

"Twenty-five remain and have just subdivided into five groups of five; estimated three miles to city," the phone announced.

"We're running out of time," the President urged.

"We are continuing with the same attack strategy, sir; we have time," responded the chairman coolly.

The Apaches and Chinooks regrouped and deployed into five groups. The same missile and bomb approach was used. Within five minutes, four of the five robot packs had been destroyed.

"Five remain, one mile from the city," again the box squawked.

"We are too close to the city to drop the Hammers," the chairman said.

"We don't have an alternative," the President said in desperation.

"We have one, sir."

"The five Predators are in position in five, four, three, two..." the phone announced.

Each of the robots fixed on a separate Predator coming in at them from the front and fired their lasers, instantly destroying the drones. What they did not have time to detect were the nineteen Apache helicopters flying at 275 miles per hour to their rear, firing a combined 100 Hellfire missiles, all of which successfully hit their targets.

"Zero remain. Last five destroyed one-half mile from city limits. One Apache lost. Out," and the box finally went silent.

The situation room exploded with yells and clapping at the announcement. Men hugged each other in the moment of victory. They settled back into their seats, wearing the anxiety and fatigue on their faces like Halloween masks.

"Gentlemen," the President began, "I congratulate you on your superior performance here today. I'm proud to say that human intelligence beat artificial intelligence. Next, I want that cocksucker North, and I want him now."

CHAPTER 59

Sara realized that North had slipped something into either her food or water. She began to feel extremely light-headed and it felt like she was moving underwater. Whatever North had planned, he wanted her drugged and unable to put up a fight.

She heard the door open and watched as a blurry figure she assumed was North enter the room. His voice had an eerie echo to it and she shook her head, as if trying to dislodge something stuck in her ears. She felt as if she was floating as she watched her feet ascend up the stairway and through his house. North had a grip on her arm and was leading her outside.

Every now and then he would say something, which she thought might be *You're doing great*, but she wasn't sure. For a minute she thought she had lost him, but then swung her head back to the right and there he was. She could see his hand on her arm, but she couldn't feel it. She almost enjoyed the sensation. She knew somewhere deep in her mind she should be afraid, but wasn't.

Sara could now smell the outside, but she couldn't see anything. It was dark. Then she heard a strange buzzing sound and turned in its direction. North released her arm and she felt unstable, but remained standing. She watched as the blurry figure reached for his belt for the buzzing noise. Whatever it was also had a red blinking light.

She then heard North yell something and began to run away from her. He then returned and pushed her and she felt herself falling, but it was as if she was in slow motion. She felt the wet, dewy grass on her face and neck, but she couldn't feel any other parts of her body. She decided to close her eyes and rest.

❧

Jack could not see North, but heard his pager go off and then him yell "Fuck." Jack figured his presence had somehow triggered an alarm, which alerted North via the pager. He assumed North had a weapon.

Jack decided to make his presence known in an attempt to locate North in the dark and yelled, "Freeze, asshole," from where he lay in hiding in the thick brush surrounding the lawn.

"If you had anything to stop me with, you wouldn't be yelling from a hiding place," North shouted in the direction of the voice.

Get him talking, Jack thought, *to better locate him.*

"It's over, North. The CIA and the police are on to you; the murders and the robots."

"Who the hell are you and why are you trespassing?" North walked swiftly in the direction of the voice.

"You know who this is, North. The police are on their way now."

North fired a round in the direction of Jack's voice. The bullet hit an oak tree twenty feet to Jack's left. Jack picked up a rock and threw it in the direction of the oak tree, causing North to fire a second round in that direction.

"C'mon out and let's figure this thing out before someone gets hurt."

"The only one getting hurt in this scenario is you, North."

Jack knew the sun would be coming up soon and he would lose his cloak of darkness. He had to create a diversion and make a move. All he had brought with him was a knife that the Russian pilot had given him. He was fairly adept at throwing, but not from more than ninety feet. He needed to get within forty feet for both accuracy and visibility. And he would have to throw while on the move, which would make a kill that much more difficult. North was helping him by moving in the direction of his voice, but Jack still couldn't see him.

He took out the knife and picked up another rock. Jack got down on his stomach and slowly crawled toward where he thought North was. It was a gamble, but one he needed to take if Sara was still alive and in need of help. Whoever saw one another first would have the advantage. He figured North's line of sight would be straight ahead and not down to the ground, thereby giving Jack a split-second advantage.

He moved several feet, then stopped to listen. North had not moved. He continued this pattern for another ten feet when he noticed the sky beginning to lighten to his left. Time was up. He crawled faster, methodically looking to his left and right as he moved. After fifteen more feet, Jack spotted North approximately fifty feet away, down on one knee in a shooting stance, slowly sweeping his extended weapon back and forth.

Jack moved to a crouched position as quickly and quietly as he could, then threw the rock. It landed in front of North and as he turned to fire in the direction of the sound, Jack took off in a full sprint directly at him, then aimed and threw, burying the knife's blade deep in the thigh of North's right leg.

North screamed and fired two quick rounds in Jack's general direction. But having anticipated North's reaction, Jack had already dived to the ground, rolling several feet to the right before getting up. He ran directly away from North's position, then made an arc, intending to come up behind him and engage in hand-to-hand combat if necessary.

The dawn's early light illuminated the lawn. Jack saw North attempting to run, but limping badly toward the lake sixty feet to his right. North still had a gun. When Jack saw the boat he started running toward the lake. After just a few strides, he had to hurdle Sara to avoid trampling her. He knelt beside her and yelled her name. His first thought was that she was dead and he was too late.

But Sara's head slowly turned in his direction and her eyelids fluttered. He saw her pupils were dilated and her confused expression made it obvious North had drugged her. He checked her over quickly but did not find any wounds, other than a bruise on the side of her head.

As Jack prepared to resume his pursuit of North, someone—or rather, *something*—came out from behind North's house. At first he thought it was another man, but as the sun rose, he could see it was made of a metal substance of some sort, but had a human form and moved like a human. *Shit, one of the robots*, he thought.

Behind him he could hear North start the engine to the boat and push the throttle to the max. North shouted above the engine as he sped away from shore: "Man versus machine, Landis—kiss your ass goodbye."

The robot began to run directly toward Jack, closing the fifty yard distance between them more quickly than any man could. Jack told Sara to lie still and immediately turned and sprinted toward the water. If the robot had a laser or another weapon, Jack knew he didn't stand a chance. He was thirty yards from the water and the robot was halving the distance between them every five yards. The robot was but a mere five feet behind Jack when Jack dove into the water and swam as fast as he could. The robot stopped at the water's edge, evidently aware that it was not waterproof. It looked left and right, trying to determine a way to get to him.

After several minutes, it lost interest in Jack and turned toward Sara. Jack instinctively began to swim back to shore, but knew he would never reach the robot before it reached Sara, and there was most likely nothing he could do to stop it.

Just then two patrol cars and an unmarked vehicle drove through the driveway onto the grass, steering their cars directly toward the robot, while avoiding Sara. As one of the patrol cars was about to hit the robot, it leaped over the car, landed, pivoted, and ran back toward the patrol car.

Smith and Warfield jumped from their unmarked car and began firing round after round into the robot, which had no effect. The robot smashed its left arm through the driver's side window of one of the patrol cars, connecting with the patrolman's head, cracking his skull wide open, spewing blood and brain matter. The patrolman in the passenger seat jumped out of the car, swinging a shotgun over the rooftop and firing four shots point blank into the robot's head. The fourth shot jarred the head loose, creating a shower of sparks. The robot spun in place for several seconds, then fell to the ground, smoke protruding from the head and chest cavity.

EPILOGUE

Sara gave Jack a big hug before he helped her into the passenger seat of his car, having volunteered to pick her up from the hospital.

"Did we get North?" she asked.

"I'm afraid not. Not yet, anyway," Jack responded.

"What about the robots?"

"You should wait and hear it from Lou. It is truly a classic story of good versus evil. It was a close call, but they were destroyed, but not before sixteen people were killed. Unfortunately, one of them was Abir."

"I'm so sorry; I know you thought highly of him."

"I did. His family will be well taken care of."

"How did he get away with hiding a factory in Iraq, let alone funding it?"

"North is a very rich and clever man. He funded the operation by skimming funds from a number of operations and lied to Blackstone, relative to it being sanctioned."

"That bastard."

"Not to worry. I will find him and kill him if it's the last thing I do."

"And what about Scheinberg?"

"He most likely killed her."

"My God, and all for the power."

"Here we are—party time."

Jack and Sara held hands as they strolled up the Pendletons' driveway.

"You're my knight in shining armor, Mr. Landis."

"I hate to think what would have happened if the general hadn't helped me secure a jet home."

"That's right. We might have never had the opportunity to tell each other how brave and smart we are."

"Or stop artificial intelligence gone wild."

"Well, that too," Sara said, smiling.

"Now, we should get inside and join Lou's retirement party."

Inside the house, Smith was giving the DNI and Lou an update on the investigation. "In tracing the millions in Scheinberg's offshore account, we were able to determine the cash was laundered through the three hotels that were clients of her so-called florist shop, which was actually an executive escort service. My guess is we'll find North as a client, considering the allegation that he murdered Fulbright, or Shay, who turned out to be one of Scheinberg's employees."

"Did you ever find out if Scheinberg had a laptop?" asked Lou.

"Nope, not a clue."

"Speaking of clues, did your boss ever find out about us working together to uncover whodunit?"

"Yes, considering Bluescape helped lead us to North, it was easier to tell him. In fact, he agreed to meet with Hank to discuss the new technology. Where is Hank?" Smith asked, glancing around.

"He said he'd be here," Lou said. "Any new developments on North?"

"I'm afraid not. We found the boat anchored in the northeast corner of the lake, approximately half a mile from shore. There were chains with anchors and locks, not to mention a fair amount of North's blood. Given the tarp we found on the shoreline, we're pretty sure his intention was to kill Sara, wrap her in the tarp, chain her to the anchors, and throw her overboard to sink to the bottom of the lake."

"I thought he had surgery the day before and Jack buried a four-inch blade in his leg."

Smith nodded. "He is either tougher than we anticipated and swam to shore, or he brought more rounds of ammunition and shot himself and we've yet to find the body. We learned during the investigation that he was an avid swimmer."

"I vote for him rotting at the bottom of the lake."

"We all do. We continue to have an APB out on him and have federal, state, and municipal departments and agencies working with us."

"How about any ties to the Conover murder or Sara's brother's kidnapping?" the DNI asked.

"Afraid not. We can only speculate that North hired some goons to kill Frank, while the kidnapping is a real stretch to tag to North."

"Jack is not going to quit until he finds him."

"Let's hope so."

Lou and the DNI broke away from the detective.

"Are you sure you won't change your mind, Lou?" asked Clapper.

"Not a chance, James. The agency needs some new blood running the show," said Lou.

"I have to tell you that your decision to add Landis to the team ended up being the best choice. He single-handedly stopped what could have been a disaster. We are still trying to explain the robot situation to the Russians, while ISIS is claiming responsibility for destroying the robots."

"I can honestly say I won't miss it, and yes, Jack is a phenomenal young man. Do you plan to keep him on the team?" Lou asked.

"I have done everything short of begging him. Well, that's a lie—I *did* beg him."

"I trust he will come around. He was born to serve. I think Ms. Fahridi has his immediate attention for now."

"Imagine that."

"For what it's worth, I'm sorry for what happened."

"Again, I would have done the same," Lou acknowledged.

Just then the party chatter was interrupted by a honking horn in the driveway. Lou opened the front door and stepped out to see Hank standing next to the 1960 Dodge Dart, which was adorned with a giant red ribbon.

"Happy retirement," yelled Hank, beaming ear to ear.

As Lou smiled and waved, Kate snuck up behind him and whispered in his ear, "I hope to God this means he's done paying you back. We can't afford any more favors from Hank."

Please enjoy an excerpt from the next book in the series...

NORTH TO THE GRID

Richard North dragged himself onto the shore, exhausted after swimming a half mile with a four-inch-deep gash in his thigh. He loosened the tourniquet he had fashioned from a torn section of his T-shirt before jumping from the fishing boat into the lake. It looked like most of the bleeding had stopped. He then checked his groin and found that the stitches in his abdominal wall and scrotum from the minor surgery the day before to repair damage done by his prisoner's well-placed kick had held.

Sirens were wailing in the background as he hobbled through the dense woods, the foliage full at mid-summer. The police were no doubt en route to his estate across the lake. It had taken him thirty minutes to drive the boat to the designated spot, anchor it, and swim to shore. He had but precious minutes before the entire lakeshore would be swarming with police.

Where the hell had Landis come from? North wondered bitterly. He was supposed to be halfway around the world in Russia, working an operation. How did Landis know to look for him at his home and that he had Sara held captive? Had Landis arrived ten minutes later Sara would be dead at the bottom of the lake, and North would be making a clean getaway, ideally enjoying the national news that his robots had successfully reached Mosul and obliterated it. Instead, Sara was alive and he was injured and on the lam.

www.ingramcontent.com/pod-product-compliance
Lightning Source LLC
Chambersburg PA
CBHW071205210726
48293CB00002B/292